can't say goodbye

EDEN FINLEY

disclaimers

*This is a work of fiction.
The positions held by Kit at the Pentagon are used in a fictitious manner or don't even exist. Operations/missions and navy protocols are all made up and do not reflect the real US Navy's policies. And because I usually try to make my disclaimers humorous, Saxon James is the worst person in the world. But I love her anyway. Also, if it's in a disclaimer, it means it's true. It's like the internet.*

brady

ANYTIME MY BEST friend asks to go fishing, my answer is always yes. Because Felix Andrews doesn't mean on a boat. In the ocean. And he definitely isn't hoping to catch tuna. Nope. He's on the hunt for a SEAL of the navy variety.

Felix and I discovered Bottoms Up in Coronado our sophomore year and have been back on many occasions. It's the closest gay bar to the navy base … port? Whatever it's called. It's always packed with *seamen*, as Felix puts it.

Felix and I share an appreciation of bigger guys, but my obsession doesn't stop there. I like older guys. Someone who wants to look after me instead of the other way around.

Felix leads me out to the dance floor the second we enter the bar because he knows how to get attention, and in what he's wearing—midriff top, tight pants—there's no way he's not turning a few heads.

He puts on a show like he usually does, basically using my body as if it's a pole and he's being paid to dance up on it, but I'm not complaining because it has the desired effect.

Men cut in, dancing with him, dancing with me, dancing as a group … It's intoxicating being in the middle of a sweaty manwich.

On occasion, I've been taken home by more than one guy. I'm not sure if group sex can be called a kink, but if it is, it's the biggest kink I have. What's better than one dick but two?

Or, as my gaze catches on two guys at the bar, their long

muscular bodies facing the dance floor, military-grade haircuts, what's better than one *SEAL* but two?

One of them has lighter hair, the other a rich brown to go with his tanned olive skin. The dark-haired one meets my eyes, and his lips quirk. One looks like a typical military dude—huge and domineering—while the one smiling my way looks less scary, but they're both bulky and gorgeous.

The bigger one is all hard features, and that's the sexiest thing to me.

I break eye contact with them and go back to the guy I'm dancing with, a twink who's obviously here for the same reason we are. That's the only problem with Felix and me using each other as bait. I sometimes get the attention of others who are like him. It's not that I'm turned off by smaller guys, it's just that I have a type.

And the two guys at the bar are my type. With any hope, they're into three-ways.

I lean in and say in the guy's ear, "I need to get a drink," and leave him before he can offer to come with me. Within seconds, he's grinding up on someone else.

I go to the bar, and unlike Shenanigans—a college bar near campus—Bottoms Up doesn't make over twenty-ones wear a wrist-band to drink. This one uses good old-fashioned carding, and luckily for me, I'm six three, over two hundred pounds, and don't look like a college kid.

Still, when I get to the bar, strategically walking by the two guys I'm interested in so their attention is on me, I only order a Coke. If I do have the chance to hook up tonight, I want to be sober.

Felix and I have a system in place to make sure we're both safe when going home with strangers. Staying sober is one of our rules. So is letting each other know where we're hooking up and with whom.

As soon as the bartender hands me my drink and I pay, I turn, only to hit a wall of SEAL. It's the darker-haired one of the two. My drink spills all over his tight black shirt, and I would be mortified if it wasn't the move I was planning to do on my way back past them. It just so happened he approached me first.

"I'm so sorry," I say, trying to sound as sincere as I can.

The half smile he sent my way while I was on the dance floor is still in place. "I'm sure you are." Then? He reaches back and takes his shirt off, wiping down his wet abs with it.

I almost swallow my tongue.

A voice comes from behind me. "Ignore him. He wouldn't know the word 'subtle' if it hit him over the head."

I turn to find the other guy there, and I have no idea when he moved. If the haircuts, muscles, and dog tags hanging around the shirtless one's neck didn't tip me off about them being SEALs, their stealth would.

"I'm Kit. The show-off is Prescott."

"Brady," I croak and then clear my throat.

I was supposed to be approaching them or subtly moving closer and closer to them to get them to approach me. I love that they've made the first move, but they've thrown me off my game.

It's hard not to blurt out they should take me home and fuck me.

Kit takes a seat at the bar, facing outward like he was before. "Pres, go dry your shirt in the bathroom and put your abs away."

"I'm not complaining about the abs," I say. "At all."

Prescott laughs. "I'll be right back."

He heads toward the bathrooms at the back. I glance at Kit, silently questioning if we're supposed to be following him, but Kit chuckles and gets the bartender's attention.

"Another of whatever he ordered."

"It's Coke," I say.

"Ah. Let me guess. You either go to Franklin U or San Diego State."

"*FU* all the way." And yes, I meant to emphasize the FU part. It's the best thing about my school, really—the double entendres. "It's not just the name of the school but an invitation. In case you were wondering."

Kit throws his head back and laughs. "Forward, I'll give you that. But which one of us are you interested in?"

This is where it gets tricky. Sometimes it happens naturally, like on the dance floor sandwiched between two guys who offer to take me home. I've found there's no real way to ask to be spit roasted eloquently.

"What's your deal with him?" I ask.

"Roommates."

"Roommates as in actual roommates or roommates like in the fifties where *'they never married women and lived together in a one-bedroom apartment and shared a bed, but they were just roommates'*?"

"Somewhere in between?"

I grin. "Perfect answer."

"Why's that perfect?"

I step closer to him. Kit widens his legs so I can stand between them, and his hands land on my hips. "Because now I can ask for both of you without making it weird between you."

"Would you have cared if you made it weird?"

"I want a threesome, not to wreck someone's relationship."

A large presence appears, and Prescott is back. "Did I hear 'threesome'? Damn, Kit. You worked fast tonight."

"Surprisingly, I didn't have to work at all," Kit says. "Brady here might be even less subtle than you."

"I take it this isn't your first time picking someone up and taking them home, then?" I ask.

"It's our favorite thing to do while off duty," Prescott says.

I shrug. "Works for me. I'll go tell my friend I'm bailing on him."

Prescott sits while I go find Felix. He's at the other end of the bar ordering water, and as soon as I say I'm leaving, he wants *all* the details.

When I point out Kit and Prescott, he says, "May you have the spit roasting you truly deserve." Loudly. Luckily, the guys are too far away to hear it, but even if they did, I don't think I'd care. I'd hope they'd take it as a suggestion. But this is exactly why I love Felix. He's sex positive and doesn't judge me for who I am and what I'm into.

I'm not so sure I could say the same for many others.

I kiss the top of Felix's head and go back to Prescott and Kit with anticipation thrumming through me. I'm not going to get my hopes up though. Not yet.

I've been in situations before where couples have wanted to bring in a third only to get cold feet when it came to going through with it.

I get it, and it's understandable, but it's taught me not to count my chickens, so to speak.

"Ready to get out of here?" I ask them.

For their part, there's no hesitation as Prescott stands and wraps his arm around my shoulders. "Let's go."

Kit follows, and outside, the breeze cools my hot skin.

"Car?" I ask.

"Our place is close by," Prescott says.

No car means no license plate. "Hmm, okay. I'm gonna need to take photos of you, then."

They stop me and stand in front of me.

"Why?" Kit asks.

"In case I end up getting fished out of San Diego Bay. My friend back there will have a lead on where to find my killers. Oh, and the address of where we're going will help too. Thanks."

Prescott steps closer and reaches into my front pocket to pull my phone out. He's so close I can feel his breath on my cheek, and I shiver, goose bumps scattering all over my skin.

He holds up my phone. "As long as these photos don't end up on social media."

"They won't. Unless you kill me."

He laughs. "Of course. Get in here between us."

I blink up at him. "That sounds promising."

Kit shakes his head. "We're going to have our hands full with you, aren't we?"

"I hope so."

Prescott opens the camera from my lock screen and holds his arms out. "Smile."

I stick out my tongue instead.

"You do know if something did happen to you, that would be the photo splashed all over the news?" Kit points out. "Are you sure you want that?"

"Hmm, good point. Though, not at all reassuring. Take a couple more in case."

After Prescott's snapped a couple more pics, he hands the phone back to me. "Just so you know, if those photos do end up online, it could put our lives and careers on the line, so it would be smart of us not to hurt you in any way."

"In *any* way? What if I ask for it?" I bat my eyelashes one more time.

"Jesus H. Christ," Kit hisses in my ear.

"Mm, seems you've found a way to make Kit weak in the knees," Prescott says. "We're going to have so much fun with you."

"So, you said your apartment is close?"

"It's the apartments on Second Street."

"The SEAL apartments? I'm familiar." They're regular apartments, but everyone knows them as where a lot of navy guys live. I send Felix the text with the details and also tell him not to share the photo anywhere. Not that he would anyway because he's the only person who knows about my penchant for more than one man in my bed, and he isn't going to out me, but I add it so he knows how important it is this particular time.

Kit narrows his gaze. "How familiar are you with our building?"

"I haven't slept with any of your teammates, if that's why you're asking. I might have hooked up with a guy who lived there, but he wasn't a SEAL. It turns out it wasn't even his apartment. He was crashing with a friend who was a SEAL, and he pretended to be one too. He was kind of a dick, actually."

Prescott pulls me close again as we start walking. "Let's show you how real SEALs do it."

I say in a high-pitched and for some reason Southern accent, "All my dreams are coming true."

Prescott glances over at Kit. "I like him."

Kit's face pulls tight, as if he's gritting his teeth, and I know that look. It's the same look the last couple had when things started to get too real.

Prescott and Kit might be somewhere between roommates and something more, but one thing's for sure: Kit doesn't like sharing Prescott. The look is almost enough for me to call this off, but it's only sex. Kit can have Prescott all to himself tomorrow.

When we get to their building and they lead me inside, I stop just outside their door, my conscience telling me to at least make sure.

"I want to double-check that you two are cool with doing this?

Like, I want to come between you two, but I don't want to *come between you* … if you get what I mean."

Kit relaxes. A little. "It's sweet of you to check, but this isn't our first rodeo."

"Giddyup." Prescott smacks my ass.

Kit screws up his face. "Really, dude?"

"You're the one who mentioned rodeos. Which made me think of riding. Which made me think of—"

Kit holds up his hand. "We know what it made you think of."

The joking eases whatever tension I could sense before, and I'm so ready for this. I step through the door and prepare myself for one night of whatever goes, because as much as I'd love to come back here another time, it's safer if I don't.

No one can find out about this side of me. Not if I want the life my dads and brother expect of me. My brother's slated to be the next biggest thing in football, and eventually, I will be his agent.

Prescott's and Kit's careers aren't the only thing in jeopardy if the photo is leaked. I grew up in the public eye, even though my dads tried to shield my brother and me from it. They were the first out gay couple to be in the NFL together, so their whole careers were scandalous. Everything they've done since then has come under scrutiny. Becoming parents. Raising us boys. Me turning out to be gay. It's a whole mess that I don't want to add to.

So this has to remain my thing. I don't like that it has to be that way, but at the same time, it makes what I'm about to do even hotter. I shouldn't be here, letting these two grown-ass men have their way with me, but the forbidden element, the risk … it rushes through my veins and gives me a high.

"Drink first?" Kit asks me.

"No." I'm practically buzzing out of my skin. "I want you both so badly."

Kit's gray eyes darken as he steps toward me. He towers over me, his massive muscles bulging out of his tight shirtsleeves. And then he lets out the sexiest growl I've ever heard. "It's cute you think you're in charge here."

I shudder because it's the exact kind of thing that turns me on. I want to ask them to boss me around. I want them to make me beg.

Kit closes the small gap between us. "Do you have any limits?"

"Not that I'm aware of."

Kit steps back, and I already miss the warmth of his body pressed against me. "You have done this before, haven't you?"

I laugh. "I've done …" How to word this delicately? "… a lot of things, but if you're asking to whip out nipple clamps and chains, I'm less experienced with that. Not opposed to it, but it's hard to know if I have a limit with things I haven't done before."

The corner of his mouth turns up. "Wasn't meaning any of that, but good to know what I have in mind shouldn't even make you flinch. But if you are uncomfortable at all, tell us, and we'll stop."

I lick my lips. "What did you have in mind?"

"I swear I saw your friend's mouth say that you should have the spit roasting you deserve."

"You heard that?"

"Read his lips. Old trick the navy taught me. It was either spit roasting or stop boasting, but that doesn't work with the rest of the sentence."

I swallow hard. "I would really, really like that. I'm just a boy, standing in front of other boys, asking them to fill his holes."

Kit's gaze drops to my mouth, and then he runs his thumb over my bottom lip. "I can't stop staring at this hole." His finger dips inside my mouth, and I suck on it. "All I want is for these lips to be wrapped around my cock."

Prescott moves in behind me. "I guess that means I get to be the lucky one inside your ass." His hard cock digs into my back. "Are you okay with that?"

I let my head fall backward on his shoulder and wrap my arm around the back of his neck. "Definitely. But if one of you doesn't kiss me soon, I might change my mind."

There's a tug on my hip, my lower half getting pulled toward Kit.

"There you go thinking you're running this thing again," Kit says.

Prescott's laugh dances along my neck, and this … this is what I love about being with more than one guy at the same time. They surround me. They're all over me.

"Please kiss me," I beg.

"Brady's found your weakness." Prescott's lips hit my ear. "Kit's a sucker for manners."

"Good to know." I smirk.

"Don't give away all my secrets. Let him learn them on his own." Kit's mouth inches closer to mine. Slowly. Torturously. I'm not sure if he's doing it on purpose or if time has universally slowed down.

My lips part in anticipation. He's so close. My heart hammers, my cock aches, and I need to be put out of my misery.

But instead of giving me mercy, he keeps moving right by me, leaning over my shoulder and connecting his mouth to Prescott's.

I moan, which comes out more of a whine because I want that. Either mouth. Both.

"Stop being mean and give poor Brady what he wants," Prescott murmurs against Kit's lips.

"I think you should listen to Prescott." Wait, that was being bossy again, wasn't it? "You know, if you want to. Or whatever."

It must be what Kit was after because the next thing I know, he shifts and his mouth comes down on mine. It's warm and firm, and he pushes his tongue inside, taking immediate control. I melt between them, and when Prescott lowers his head and sucks on my neck, the sensation sends ripples of pleasure down my spine.

This is exactly what I needed, and I make a mental note to thank Felix for suggesting a night out.

My hands wander over Kit's wide shoulders, down his hard pecs and abs until I can lift the hem of his shirt, all the while trying to keep up with his forceful and dominating kiss.

Clothes move in a blur. Kit breaks from my mouth just long enough to get my shirt off. Prescott takes my pants off, and before I know it, they're naked too, their bare skin on mine, and I've never felt so alive.

Prescott's fingers wrap around my cock, and he rasps, "Bedroom."

They guide me, Prescott leading, giving me a sight of his round ass, while Kit pushes me toward a bedroom.

"Get on the bed," Kit orders.

I back away from him, preparing to lie down, but he shakes his head.

"Uh-uh. Hands and knees."

Turning my back to them, I make a show of crawling on the bed and stick my ass out.

"Damn," one of them whispers.

Nothing seems to happen for a long time, but I can feel their stares on me. I want to tell them to hurry up because I'm desperate, but I'm quickly learning that will only delay things.

Kit does things in his own time, and Prescott follows.

I force myself to take calming breaths before I get too worked up. By the time the bed dips and Kit moves on his knees until he's in front of me, I'm almost under control. Then his big fucking cock is right in my face, and all sense of calm is gone.

My breathing becomes stilted, my mouth waters, and all I want to do is lean forward and take that thing between my lips and suck until he comes down my throat.

His big hand grips my hair. "You want this?"

I nod.

Vaguely, I'm aware of Prescott moving around the room, but I can't tear my gaze away from Kit's cock. A drop of precum leaks from the tip.

"Clean that up with your tongue." Kit's command has me moving so fast I almost headbutt his dick.

Be cool, Brady.

This is everything I've fantasized about for as long as I can remember. I've had threesomes before, but this is a whole new level. I haven't had many situations where I've been the main source of attention.

Because of my physique, finding men bigger than me or more dominant is difficult. It's as if I put a silent wish into the universe for my ideal guys, and the universe delivered.

Kit's hand tightens in my hair. "Lick it."

I do as he says and lick the bead of precum. It's salty and heady, and I want more. "Let me suck you."

He releases me and says, "Do it."

At the same time I lower my head and take Kit's cock in my mouth, Prescott's hand runs down the middle of my back and comes to rest above my ass. He dribbles cold lube in my crack, and I groan around Kit's hard length.

I bob my head, trying to concentrate all my efforts on Kit, but Prescott teases my hole with his finger, pushing it in and out in rhythm with the blowjob. When I suck Kit into my mouth, Prescott's fingers deepen. I can't wait for it to be his dick.

I'm going to be filled from top to bottom. Literally.

Prescott loosens me up, expertly stretching and prepping me with very little sting. Soon enough, he's fingering my prostate, pushing three fingers in and out of me to the point I'm desperate for more.

If I didn't have a mouth full of cock, I'd be panting. Prescott distracts me too much, and I don't realize I've stopped sucking on Kit until he demands, "More."

I go back to focusing on my blowjob skills, but then Prescott says, "Ready?" and Kit pulls out of my mouth.

"No," I complain. I want both at once.

Kit grips my hair and gently pulls to get me to look up at him. "Just while you get used to him being inside you."

Prescott's cock lines up with my hole.

"Fuck. Condom?" I ask.

"He's covered," Kit says.

I frown.

"As in, he's wearing one. Not *it's cool, don't worry about it*."

"Okay." I trust them. Even though I have no reason to.

Prescott inches in slowly. The super slut inside me wants to say fuck it and push back, but while Prescott's cock isn't as big as Kit's, it's still a stretch as he takes his time.

I'm both impatient and hesitant, and I just want to get to the part where they're using me to get off.

"Brady, look at me," Kit says. He lowers himself so he's closer to my line of sight. "You got this."

"I do."

Either Prescott is shaking his head behind me, or Kit can tell that he's struggling to get fully inside me, but Kit leans forward and places a soft kiss on my lips.

"Focus on me, okay?" The gentleness contrasts with the domineering boss he's been thus far, but I'm not complaining. "Relax and breathe." He takes a deep breath, and I match it.

I keep my gaze locked on Kit's gray eyes until Prescott moves with ease, sliding inside my body and hitting my prostate with every thrust.

"Think you can handle not biting my dick off now?" Kit asks.

"Definitely. It would be a travesty for you to lose something that amazing."

Kit smiles. "I agree with Prescott. I like you."

I almost make a joke about them keeping me, but I don't want to risk them taking it the wrong way and throwing me out before I turn into some stage-five clinger. I know what this is, and I'm going to make the most of it.

And it's as amazing as I thought it would be, having one guy fill my hole while the other fills my mouth. Kit's velvety skin passes between my lips over and over again while Prescott's *don't hold back* rhythm pushes Kit to the back of my throat. I don't have control of anything. All I can do is stay as still as possible while they use me to get off.

My cock is needy. I'm desperate for it to be touched, but I'm too busy being turned inside out in every imaginable way to do anything about it.

The sounds of grunts and wet slurps fill the room. Moaning, heavy breathing, and even a whimper.

"He's so tight," Prescott says.

I want to say I have a name, but the argument doesn't come. My mouth is too full, and there's no way I'm stopping.

Except, well, when Kit pulls out of me.

Prescott continues to fuck me as I look up at Kit.

"I was right." His voice is gravelly, as if he's the one who's had a cock shoved down his throat this whole time. "Your mouth is fucking perfect."

"Then why'd you stop?" I ask.

"I think someone else needs me. Look at him." He nods at Prescott.

I turn my head to look over my shoulder. Prescott's brow is

scrunched, the look of determination and lust so hot as he pushes inside me over and over again.

Prescott whines. "Kit … I want … you. Fuck me. Before I come. I want you inside me."

Kit cups my jaw and lifts my chin toward him. "That okay with you?"

"A spit roasting and a train? Fuck, yes."

Yes, I love being the center of attention, but there's also something about being only a single element of someone else's pleasure that also gets me going. The idea of Kit fucking Prescott while he fucks me … I quiver and fear I might come from the mere thought of it.

Before Kit leaves me completely though, he leans down and kisses me, licking his way into my mouth.

Prescott slows his thrusts, but I'm so keyed up my whole ass tingles from every long, drawn-out brush over my prostate.

Kit slips off the bed and moves behind us, and I slump forward on my forearms. I'm given a welcome reprieve while Kit works Prescott open and murmurs words of encouragement for him to relax, but with each desperate whisper from Kit and every needy moan from Prescott, it doesn't take long for that urge to push back onto Prescott's dick to take over.

I'll admit to being a greedy whore in the bedroom. I want all the dicks. But this? Feeling Kit thrust inside Prescott, who then moves inside me? It tickles my natural instinct to take care of people—my real-life side—and the selfish need to be the center of attention in bed. Because even though Kit is fucking Prescott, he has both of us under his control. He's fucking me through Prescott, and I'm dying in the best possible way.

Sweat beads down my forehead. My ass squeezes around Prescott, driving him deeper and harder once he's adjusted to Kit's large cock.

Prescott chants, "Fuck, fuck, fuck, fuck, fuck," in a rhythm that only gets faster and more frantic.

He must be getting close because he reaches underneath me and wraps his hand around my cock. His curse words turn to pleas, but I can't tell if he's begging me to come or begging Kit to fuck him harder.

There's too much going on and not enough at the same time. I don't even have the voice to ask for more. Or less. Or everything.

"I'm going to come," Prescott warns, and it literally takes only two more strokes for me to fall over the edge before him. Only another two for Prescott to join me. Kit still pounds inside Prescott, and as much as I love the aftershocks, my ass becomes too sensitive, and I fall face forward into a pillow.

I manage to glance over my shoulder just as Kit's hand wraps around Prescott's throat and pulls him flush against his chest. Prescott looks like he's in the best pain there ever was, and in the next moment, Kit bites down on Prescott's shoulder. I either wasn't done, or I'm on a delayed reaction or something because my cock twitches.

I haven't even come down from the high yet but already know this is the best sex I've ever had. As tempting as it is to ask for a repeat another time, to suggest we trade numbers, the reminder that Kit and Prescott have something going on between them is evident by the satisfied smiles on their faces and the way they look at each other.

"I am spent," I say. "Let me catch my breath, and I'll be out of your way."

"If you do something for me, I'll even drop you back at campus," Prescott says.

"You don't have to—"

"I'm not doing it for free."

"What do you want in return? Should I be scared?" I roll onto my back.

Prescott leans over me. "Kiss us."

"Pfft, I'll do that for free. You don't need to drop me home for that."

"But he will," Kit says and moves beside me.

"We need to make sure you get home safely, or you might decide you don't want to come back," Prescott says.

"Wait … you guys want me to come back?"

"Of course. Kit didn't have a turn of your ass, and he and I share everything."

A quick look in Kit's direction tells me that might be true, but Kit doesn't seem happy about it.

"I'll leave my number, and if you both want me to come back, message me." I'll leave it up to Kit whether or not he wants to do this again.

"Done. Now, hurry up and kiss us." Prescott lowers himself on top of me, our lips coming together like magnets. His mouth is so different from Kit's. Prescott takes his time. He explores my mouth and drinks me in, but then Kit joins in. Three mouths, three tangled tongues. I get so lost in them I don't remember to breathe.

Despite them saying they want to do this again, I don't know if it'll actually happen, but fuck, I want it to.

CHAPTER TWO

I'M STILL awake when the door to our apartment clicks open. Prescott's back from dropping our latest hookup home, and like always, the temptation to ask him to sleep in my room, next to me, is almost overwhelming.

But I use all my years of training to keep my ass where the fuck it is and not even dare to move an inch. Because if I open those floodgates, there is no stopping the onslaught of emotion they're holding back.

Prescott and I don't do sleepovers. Not with anyone and not with each other.

Because we're on the same SEAL team, there are solid nonfraternization rules in place. Pres and I are the same rank, so that wouldn't be the issue, but the problem comes when being deployed together.

We've known the rules all along, but we broke them anyway. Repeatedly. We tell ourselves it's nothing because we only ever hook up when someone else is involved, and we're not a couple. We're best friends. Roommates.

And I fucking hate it.

Because Prescott is my world. He's my rock. Hell, he's the only family I have.

Telling him that would ruin everything. Our careers, my heart, and our friendship. So, I sit in painful silence, throw myself into the brief moments of passion we get, and try to hold myself together.

After tonight, I don't know how much longer I can do it. There was something about that Brady kid that was both unnerving and a breath of fresh air at the same time.

We've taken home our fair share of tipsy college students who want to "be wild" and have a threesome to have fond memories of a crazy time.

But Brady … Brady was different.

For one, he wasn't drinking. He couldn't and didn't want to blame his actions on alcohol. He was confident, sexy, liked my dominance and penchant for control, and didn't look at Prescott like he was the real reason he wanted to come home with me.

Prescott is gorgeous. He's part Native Hawaiian and has golden skin, stunning brown eyes, and a smile that could melt the pants off anyone on the planet.

I'm no slouch. I have the all-American light hair and pale gray eyes thing going for me, and I am a navy SEAL—that status is sometimes more important than looks—but next to Prescott? It's like I fell out of the ugly tree and hit every branch on the way down.

I think it's my hard features next to his softer ones.

Actually, a lot of people next to Prescott appear less fortunate-looking than usual. It's like how those car mirrors say objects are closer than they appear. Prescott should have his own label: objects close to me are better-looking than they appear.

Though, I will say Brady gave him a run for his money. He was hot while dancing with his twink friend, hot while swaying his hips as he sauntered past us, and so fucking hot when he was forward enough to ask me for a threesome.

He's well built. Smaller than us, but most people are. He's muscular and has stylish light brown hair and brown eyes. Hmm, maybe I have a thing for brown-eyed men.

The thing I think I liked about him most, though, was his respect for Prescott's and my relationship. Even if he had it wrong. We're not together, we'll never be together, but Brady asking if he would come between us in any way … I found myself focusing on him a hell of a lot more than I normally would in that situation.

Because whenever I have the chance to be with Prescott, all I want to do is make the most of it.

And as predicted, when Prescott doesn't come back into my room and I hear his bedroom door close, I wonder if Brady might be the guy I need. It's the first time in a long time that I enjoyed a third party for more than an excuse to get to Prescott.

I enjoyed *him*.

I continue to think about Brady the rest of the night, barely getting any sleep, hoping that he might be the perfect distraction to help get over my best friend. Because if I don't start doing it soon, I worry nothing else will help.

Other than moving out.

I set my alarm because I don't trust myself not to fall asleep and stay like that. I'm physically satisfied, but my mind's racing, and if I don't get in my morning workout, I'm an absolute pain in the ass for the rest of the day.

So when my phone goes off what feels like a short time later, I can be happy I at least got some sleep. I'm not so happy when I drag my ass out of my bedroom. My mouth is dry, I'm exhausted, and as much as I'd love to classify the bedroom acts as my workout, I have a physique I need to maintain. Sex isn't gonna cut it.

I'm putting on my shoes and socks when Prescott appears.

"Who's ready to go running?"

Why's he so loud? More importantly, why is he joining me? And excited about it?

"You never want to go for a morning workout," I say.

"It's the endorphins. Sex makes me happy. Happy people want to go running. Running makes you even more happy. Today is going to be an amazing day."

Today is going to be my usual form of torture: spending time with my amazing roommate while internally begging him to love me back.

He bounces around me, all ready to go. "Come on."

I go slower. Because fuck that energy.

"You don't seem as relaxed as I am. Did you not get enough last night?"

"I did. I just …" Couldn't sleep after it, have been contemplating my future, our future, at what point I might snap … "Didn't sleep well."

"I can't remember the last time I slept so well."

I finish tying my laces and stand. "I've never wanted to punch you harder."

"Lies. I know how to be really annoying."

"Well, that is true. Let's get this over with if you plan to talk the entire run. Try to keep up. Last one out locks up." I run for the door, but Prescott pulls me back.

We struggle and fight our way to the front of the apartment, and he edges me out at the last second. He laughs all the way down the steps, and it echoes up the stairwell.

I lock up and run after him, catching up in the parking lot, but instead of slowing to his speed, I slap him on the back of the head and keep running.

In moments like these, it's easy to let go of the growing resentment building inside me because we truly are the definition of best friends. But I know that as soon as we get home and the laughs stop, it'll be another memory weighing down my heart.

We run four miles to Silver Strand State Beach and then turn around to head back, but as I do that, Prescott grabs my forearm to stop me.

"Aww, can't keep up?" I taunt, breathing heavily.

His chest heaves. "What's the rush?"

He has a point. It's a gorgeous day; the sun is warm, but the breeze is keeping the air cool, and I've already learned that trying to outrun my feelings doesn't work.

We slow to a walk, but it takes less than a minute for the real reason he stopped me to take over.

"Brady gave us his number when I dropped him off."

Excitement flutters in my gut, but I know better than to get my hopes up. "Gave *you* his number."

"No. *Us.* I was thinking …" He bites his lip and glances out at the water.

"If you want to date Brady, I'm not going to stop you."

"Pfft. You know I don't date or do relationships. I was thinking of a repeat sometime. If you want it, that is."

We're on the same page about that, but … "You? You want a repeat with someone?"

"He was different than the others, right?" He shrugs. "Don't ask me why. I haven't figured that out yet."

"I know what you mean," I murmur.

He has a skip in his step. "So you're in? I thought I might have had to sell you more than that."

"Like you said, you don't date or do relationships. If anyone would need convincing, I thought it would be you."

"This is not dating. It's sex. And damn, I want to see him again."

Yeah, so do I.

CHAPTER THREE

brady

MY BROTHER HAS WAY MORE talent in his little finger than most of the guys on his team combined. I should be jealous—the public consensus seems to be that I am—but that's really not the case.

Growing up with famous football-playing dads, it was only inevitable that one of us followed in their footsteps. For me, I was happy Peyton loved football enough to take that bullet.

I belong exactly where I am: watching a game I love from the stands while my brother gets sweaty on the field below us. It's the last home game of his college career, and in a few months, he's going to get drafted. It's not an *if* for him. The only thing we're unsure of is what number pick he'll be. Peyton wants first, of course, but as his future agent, I would rather see him in the top ten or even settle for first round. Not only will that take the pressure off Peyton, but it might keep his giant ego in check.

I'm allowed to say that because he's my brother and I love him.

As much as I'd love for my wish to come true, our whole family will be shocked if he's not first. Peyton Miller, son of Marcus Talon, one of the greatest quarterbacks of all time? Yeah, every single team will want to snap him up.

I take in the Franklin U stadium for one of the last times and get a nostalgic pang in my gut. There isn't just a transition for Peyton coming up but for me too.

Come May, I'm going to graduate with my degree in sports management, and then I'll be saying goodbye to sunny California and taking an internship at King Sports, my uncle's firm in New York, while I get my law degree at NYLS.

Moving to New York is kind of daunting, even though I have a billion uncles there and my grandmother on Pop's side. I'm looking forward to New York and dreading it at the same time. I love it here in San Luco. The weather is amazing, no cold winters, but possibly the best thing about Southern California is Kit and Prescott.

Shocking the hell out of me, I not only heard from them after the first time we hooked up, but I've been back many, many times over the last several months. I'm under no delusion that I'm their only toy, especially while they're overseas saving the world, but when they're in Coronado, they make me feel like I'm the only one, and that's all I care about. We have no rules, we're not exclusive, and it's all a bit of fun.

Hot, sweaty fun.

But our time is running out now.

I check my phone for the hundredth time in the last couple of days. Kit and Prescott came home from a training mission a few nights ago and made me come so hard I almost blacked out, but then they dropped the bomb that they're only going to be in town for a week or two before deploying somewhere for months. Possibly longer. They couldn't tell me all the details, and they don't even know when they're leaving.

They most likely won't be back by the time I graduate.

It's driving me crazy that I haven't got a "*come fuck us*" text yet. Part of me worries they're already gone.

"Aren't future sports agents supposed to, I don't know, watch the game?" Felix asks beside me.

"Eh. Peyton's not even on the field."

"Look again," Levi says on my other side. To add to the ever-growing scandal that is the Talon-Millers, it turns out I'm not the only queer son in this family. Levi and my brother are into each other, but it's complicated for the same reason my situation is for me. Peyton and I are in the public eye—we have been our whole lives. We didn't choose this life, and it's unfair to drag other people into that environment if they're not one hundred percent ready for it.

When I look back at the field, I'm confused. "Wait. When did Fresno State score?"

Everything is all tied up, and Franklin has possession of the ball once again.

"While you had your head in your phone," Felix says.

Oops. Maybe I really do need to focus. If Franklin U takes out the win today, there's no way they won't make it to the semi-finals.

Down on the field, my brother throws a deep pass into the end zone, where his wide receiver is under it, waiting. Everyone in our section gets to their feet.

As the ball flies through the air, time slows, and as Bellows catches the ball, my phone goes off with an alert. The split second I look away, I miss the touchdown. I can't even be sorry about it though.

Kit: *Our place?*

"Fuck, yes," I yell.

Felix pops his head over my shoulder. "The touchdown or whatever you're looking at?"

I nudge him away from me but not before he sees the message.

"You have a three-way to get to, don't you?" Felix asks. "Really? Choosing sex over your own brother? You should be ashamed. *Ashamed.* It has been months of this poor attitude, young man."

"Whatever. If you had a sibling, you'd be exactly the same."

"True," Felix relents.

I turn to Levi. "Can you cover for me with Pey?"

"Hey, I told you I wouldn't spill your secret hookups to him, but I draw the line at lying to him about where you are."

I was hoping Levi was too drunk to remember walking in on me with Prescott and Kit after a party at our place the other night, but no such luck. We have a deal: he doesn't tell anyone about me, and I don't tell anyone about him and my brother. Friendship through friendly blackmailing is fun.

"You're going to have to tell your brother eventually," Felix adds.

"No, I won't. The guys are about to be deployed, so this is our last chance, and then we're over. If Pey asks, tell him I was here for the whole game, but once it was over, I left without explanation." When I drag my ass home in the early hours of the morning, I'll lie and say I met someone and had a random hookup. He won't question that.

Felix might have a point about telling my family—maybe not about Prescott and Kit specifically but about certain discoveries I've made thanks to them.

All throughout college, I felt like I was missing something when it came to dating. I'd meet guys, and they'd be great, but there's always been something about relationships that have felt like they were holding me back or trying to squash me in a box.

I had an inclination, a hunch about what and who I wanted, but it wasn't until I met Kit and Prescott that I realized being with more than one person isn't a kink. It's who I am.

I'm going to hate leaving the guys because they're the perfect arrangement for me. Sure, the thought has crossed my mind that I could really have something with either or both of them, but I also know that they have their own strong connection with each other. The last thing I'd want is to be a third wheel in a relationship. Not that they've ever made me feel that way before, but … that's sex. I wouldn't even know how to navigate a relationship with two people.

There are many reasons I'm keeping Prescott and Kit a secret. The media would be a frenzy of drama and negativity—something the Talon-Miller family does not need. Sinful Marcus Talon and Shane Miller raised sexual deviants. Cue all the conservatives clutching their pearls and making arguments as to why queer people shouldn't raise kids.

They can't see that growing up in a nurturing environment where we were not only encouraged to live our truths but were pushed to explore them meant that we were free to be who we are. The world is a lot gayer than people like to think.

Because of how I was raised, I know my family would be supportive of me being poly, but that doesn't mean they wouldn't have concerns. Mainly revolving around Peyton's and my careers.

And none of it matters anyway because tonight is probably going to be my last time with Kit and Prescott. I hate goodbyes, but if they're not going to make it back in time for graduation, all we have is now.

⚭ ⚭ ⚭

When the guys know I'm coming over to their apartment, they leave the door unlocked for me. I run up the stairs of their walk-up to the top, too excited to slow down as I enter without warning.

The shouting doesn't even register until it silences.

I pause inside the entryway. Footsteps sound, and both Kit and Prescott round the corner.

Kit immediately breaks into a comforting smile—something I've seen come out more and more as I've gotten to know him. His hard-ened features are easy to melt away unless I'm purposefully taunting him into keeping his stern persona in place. Prescott's slower to wipe the scowl off his beautiful face, but he eventually cracks a smile too. A small one.

I've been standing here for more than five seconds, and usually, we'd all be naked by now. Or on our way to being naked.

"Is … this a bad time?" I ask. "I heard yelling."

Prescott looks at Kit, but Kit's nonchalant as he says, "Roommate stuff. Get your sexy ass over here."

He doesn't have to tell me twice.

On my way, I shrug out of my jacket. Within seconds, I'm where I belong, sandwiched between two of the hottest men on the planet, and we're in our own bubble where the outside world doesn't exist.

Kit pulls me right to him, dropping his mouth to meet mine while he works open the buttons on my shirt. Prescott blankets my back with his strong chest and gets to work on undoing my jeans.

I moan around Kit's tongue as he kisses me hard. These guys don't do slow and sweet. At least, not while we're all horny and pawing at each other. Prescott is generally less intense, but after we've come our brains out, it's Kit who becomes the softer one. With each time we've hooked up, Kit has become less and less standoffish. At first, I thought it was because of his obvious hang-ups on Prescott, but being with him, seeing them together, I think it has more to do with Kit holding so much of himself back.

When my shirt drops to the floor, Kit pulls away and raises his arms over his head, pulling his T-shirt off in one quick swoop. His sweats go next.

Prescott sucks on my neck. I close my eyes and tilt my head to give him more access, but Kit steps into my space and grips my chin to tilt it upward.

"Open your eyes, Brady." His voice is raspy and so sexy.

When I do as he says, Kit's stormy gray gaze is on mine.

"Keep your eyes on me." He sinks to his knees.

My boxer briefs don't do anything to hide my hard cock, and I want nothing more than to move my hips closer so Kit's mouth brushes over it, but Prescott has me pinned in place.

"Are you not letting Brady go?" Kit asks.

Prescott thrusts against my ass, his hard cock pressed against me through the layers of material between us. He's still fully dressed, but he's only wearing sweatpants, and I can feel how hard he is.

Prescott's voice rumbles in my ear as he talks to Kit. "I'm thinking about how hot it would be if I held him back while you teased him. Licked him. Brought him so close to the edge and then backed off."

I bite my lip to stop the protest from escaping because I want that. I really, really want that, but I also want to come. There's a very good chance the second Kit's lips are wrapped around me, I will explode in his mouth.

"And I thought *I* was the mean one," Kit says with a smirk on his face.

It's true. In bed, Kit is the bossy one. Prescott is more playful. Outside of the bedroom, they're both laid-back and chill, though Kit seems to have more substance to him. Prescott is flirty and fun. There's some weird role-reversal shit going on with Prescott, and I can't help thinking it has something to do with what they were yelling about when I arrived. Now is not the time to ask about it though. I need to get off and don't want to ruin the mood.

"Look at the poor guy," Kit taunts. "He's already trembling, and we've barely touched him."

"I'm desperate," I croak. "I need you. Both of you."

Kit glances over my shoulder at Prescott. Prescott's arms tighten around me while Kit pulls my underwear down my legs to my ankles.

My cock is hard and leaking, and when Kit's mouth closes over the tip, my reflex is to push inside as far as he can take me, but Prescott is too strong at holding me back.

Kit does more than tease and lick. He draws his mouth up slowly across my tight skin. I reach behind me to cup the back of Prescott's neck and rest my head on his shoulder, but he doesn't let me.

"Nuh-uh. Kit wants you to watch him tease you."

The thing is, he might be trying to tease me, but I'm so pent-up that I'm already close to the edge. Watching him is only going to send me flying off it.

I shake my head. "I can't." The words come out stilted as I breathe heavily. "Not without … Oh fuck. I'm going to come already. Wait, wait, wait, I can't come so soon."

But it is too late, and as I fill Kit's mouth with my cum, a warm chuckle from Prescott hits my shoulder. Kit drinks me down, taking every last drop, but when I'm spent, he pulls off and joins in on Prescott's amusement.

Prescott releases me so I can pull up my boxer briefs.

"That was so not fair," I say.

Prescott pulls Kit up off the floor. "Nope. Not fair is Kit not sharing your release with me." He tugs on Kit's hand, pulling them together until their lips meet. They look so hot together when they kiss, two overly masc men trying to one-up each other and gain control.

When they finally pull apart, they both smile over at me.

"This isn't exactly the way I was hoping our last night would go." I pout.

They share a weird glance again, and Prescott looks pissed, but in the next second, Kit advances on me. "Our night is nowhere near over with."

Thank fuck.

prescott

OUT OF ALL THE young college guys Kit and I have brought home over the years, Brady is someone we've both gotten used to quickly. He fits with us. He's easygoing. Not jealous. He's fucking perfect.

But as much as I love having him here, Kit and I have issues we need to straighten out.

Best friends and roommates don't drop the bombshell that they're leaving without the expectation of it blowing up. Kit completely blindsided me.

Kit and I have been inseparable since we met during BUD/s training in our early twenties. We were both smart enough to have a few years of enlistment under our belt before we applied to BUD/s, but we still weren't prepared for what we had to endure. We were there for each other when one of us or both were ready to tap out of the rigorous tasks the navy gave us to prove we were fit enough to become SEALs.

After we graduated from the program, we were assigned to different SEAL teams, but we were both based here in Coronado, so we moved in together as roommates. Then came the awesome day I was assigned a new team. *His* team.

Somewhere along the way, lines blurred, starting with the night a hot little thing at Bottoms Up wanted to go home with two big, strong SEALs. It became a habit, picking up random guys, and it has worked for us for so long.

It's all top secret, and we have rules in place so the navy doesn't find out we're fraternizing, but it all doesn't matter now because the fucker is moving. To Virginia.

And if it weren't for Brady being here, I'd still be screaming about it.

Kit's going to be the next Sea, Air, and Land liaison at the Pentagon. Sure, it's an amazing opportunity, but this isn't an order. He volunteered for the position, and because no other SEAL wanted to step back from active duty to move to what is essentially a desk job, he had no competition. This type of position usually goes to guys past their peak, not thirty-year-old sailors at the top of their game.

The thing I hate most about what he's done is he didn't even ask me what I thought. Because he knew I'd shut it down before it was too late.

The thought of not seeing Kit every single day makes me want to cry. Or yell. So, I'm going to have to settle for fuck instead.

I remain where I am for now, watching as Kit slowly undresses while kissing Brady senseless. In these in-between moments where Brady is recovering, Kit is so gentle with him, and seeing them like that … it does things to my insides that has never happened with anyone else before.

Even though we've known for months that this will all end, my stupid brain has been thinking long-term and of ways we could continue what we have. Somehow. But the time has come to accept that it's not possible.

I try to tell myself that this is all surface-level shit because really, we don't know much about Brady, and when he is here, it's not like we talk about real stuff. But I'm realizing, too late, that maybe I feel more than surface stuff for them. Both of them. For different reasons. Trying for anything more would be a disaster though. Especially if it's going to be long-distance now.

Brady is ten years younger than us, but he doesn't look it. He's bulky and tall—not as tall or filled out as Kit or me but still larger than the average twenty-year-old. He says his family is big into football, and it's cute he thinks we didn't personally vet him after our first night together. But if he doesn't want us to know that his dads are the infamous Marcus Talon and Shane Miller, NFL legends, then we're not going to blow his cover.

Even if we're desperate for an autograph, we're not desperate enough to lose Brady.

Both Kit and Brady are naked now, still lazily kissing while hands explore. Brady grabs Kit's full, round ass and squeezes, drawing out a moan from my roommate.

Kit's eyes meet mine as he pulls back from Brady's mouth. "Are you joining us, or are you just going to watch all night?"

I force a smile for Brady's benefit because I don't want to drag him into our mess. "You know I like to watch."

Brady turns in Kit's arms, putting his back to him. Kit grips onto Brady's hips and grinds his hard cock against Brady's ass cheek.

"I need both of you tonight," Brady says, and I love how this college guy is somehow confident with his words and his actions but still manages to blush when we're with him.

He reaches for me, and like being tied to a string at the end of his fingertips, I go to him. As soon as I take his hand, Brady pulls me against him and kisses me hard. His arms go around my waist, holding me close, but Kit's hands are in more of a hurry to get me naked. His fingers tuck into the waistband of my sweats and push them down my legs. I don't break away from Brady as I step out of them, but when I go back to him and press against him, my hard cock against his exhausted one, he forces us apart and lifts my shirt.

"Take me to bed?" Brady pleads.

And this is the part I love most. Watching as Kit calls the shots. Giving Brady exactly what he didn't ask for but still giving him what he wants.

It's a power trip being part of that, and while it's usually Kit leading things with me following, tonight, I need something more.

I run my hand over Brady's light brown hair that's longer than either of ours thanks to military regulations and grip it at the roots. "I think out here is perfect for what I want to do with you."

"What's that?" he asks.

"Get on your knees for me."

Brady quivers the way I want him to, but before he can get down on the floor, I pull him closer to me and murmur in his ear.

"You're going to suck my cock while Kit preps your tight ass."

He whimpers this time, and it only urges me on.

"And when he's done, we're going to take turns using your hole to get off."

Brady grips my shoulders, his fingers biting into my skin, and I love how eager he is for it. His presence almost makes me forget that I'm mad at Kit.

Almost.

I pull Brady toward our couch in the living room while Kit goes to grab supplies. As I sit, I push Brady to his knees and widen my thighs. He leans forward, his wide shoulders nestling between my legs while he sticks his round, firm ass outward, just begging and ready for Kit to stretch him wide.

Brady dips his head and runs his tongue along the underside of my cock, drawing it out. Teasing.

I go back to gripping his hair tight. "Did I say you could tease me?"

The little shithead looks smug.

"Take all of me in your mouth," I order. There's a split second of hesitance in his eyes, but it disappears as soon as I stare down at him and say, "Please," in the cockiest way I can muster. He's probably confused because more often than not, I'm a brat alongside him. Sex is supposed to be fun and playful, which, come to think of it, is my motto for my entire life outside the navy, but tonight, I'm SEAL Prescott.

Because if I can't fuck this anger out, I'm worried I'm going to bottle it up and explode at the wrong time. And I'm not talking about orgasms. I need a clear head, especially with our team being shipped out soon.

Without Kit there next to me.

I shake off that thought and live in the now because if I get too in my head about Kit leaving, no matter how good the sex is, my dick won't be on board.

So instead, I focus on the sensation on my cock and watch Kit sinking to the floor behind Brady, getting ready to prep him.

Goddamn, the way Brady's deep brown eyes flutter when Kit presses a finger against his hole almost makes me come, but I rein it in. Because unlike Brady, who's already getting hard again, I generally only have one orgasm in me before I'm down for the count. I need at least a few hours in between.

Fucking twenty-year-olds.

Brady sucks me while his back arches deeper and deeper as Kit fingers him. I've been trying to avoid looking at Kit's face and focus on Brady, but when Brady hums around my cock, I can't help taking a glance at what Kit's doing to him.

Holy hell. Kit has his head buried between Brady's ass cheeks, eating him out, while Brady reaches behind him to hold Kit's head there. It might possibly be the hottest thing I've ever seen, but that's what it's always like with these two.

My hips buck off the couch, forcing my cock farther into Brady's mouth while I continue to watch Kit feast on Brady like he's his last meal. Technically, it is.

Which I hate.

The both of them turn me on something fierce, but it's not just the sex. It's something else. Something I can't name or place. I don't want any of it to end.

I can understand why Brady has to walk away. He's graduating college, and he'll move across the country before the team gets back. Saying goodbye to him will suck, but it makes sense.

Kit leaving doesn't make sense to me.

At all.

He's my best friend, and we're closer than brothers.

Brady brings me back to the moment by practically choking on my dick. When I pull out of him, he glances up at me through glassy eyes, and I wipe a tear away with my thumb.

"You think you're ready for us?" I ask.

He swallows hard, his Adam's apple bouncing. I lean forward and wrap my hand around his throat, not tight, just gripping hard enough to feel him swallow as I press my lips to his. He drinks me down, sucking on my tongue like it was my cock, and I pull back, smiling.

"Kit can have his turn first. You think you can take him while you suck me off?" I know he can do it. It's his favorite thing. Brady loves being filled every which way 'til Sunday.

Brady's voice is raw. "I can … do it."

"Remember to watch the teeth," I say and settle back against the couch. There have been some close calls in the last few months that adds an element of risk when doing this.

Will I come, or will my dick be bitten off? Hard to say. It's like extreme sports for sex.

The long, warm slurps as he works me over drive me crazy. Almost as crazy as watching Kit slide his condom-covered cock inside Brady's ass.

There's a brief moment where Brady's mouth stops moving while he adjusts to Kit's size, but his tongue never stops lapping at my dick. It rewards him with a drop of precum, and he's quick to capture it. When Kit thrusts inside harder, Brady pulls off my cock completely but doesn't leave me high and dry. His hand replaces his mouth while he rests his head on my thigh. His breath is warm on the inside of my leg, and I run my hand through his hair more softly now. Not because he needs the break but because I don't want to let him go.

We haven't known Brady long, and Kit and I have a complicated history that the navy would hate if they ever found out, but everything is just … ending.

And I don't like it.

Brady's breath increases with every thrust, his hand tightening around my shaft. His grip is firm, almost to the point of too firm, but it's okay because it helps bring me back from coming before I even get inside him.

Kit blankets Brady's body, leaning over him and kissing the middle of Brady's shoulder blades while he thrusts hard inside his body.

Instinctively, I reach for Kit, cupping the back of his head. When he glances up at me in surprise, I hate myself because I'm supposed to be mad at him. But I can't deny that my best friend has a hold over me. It's always been there between us, this short tether intertwining our lives. We've been in each other's orbit for almost ten years, and this is how it ends.

That anger whittles away to sadness, so I push forward and seal my mouth over Kit's and kiss him like it'll be the last time.

Everything we're doing will be our last time, so I want to make it worth it.

"I want you to pull out when you come and come all over his back so I can lick it off him," I say.

Kit's eyes roll back in his head, and Brady moans. I have them both right where I want them.

"Do it," I say to Kit.

His movements turn erratic, and I know he has to be close. In the next second, he quickly pulls out, whips off the condom, and jerks himself until he paints Brady's back with cum.

Brady's hand on me slows while he breathes deeply, and for a second, I think Brady's come again too, but when I crook my finger under his chin and lift his face toward mine, the lust and want in his eyes is as strong as ever. The desperation is a turn-on.

"You ready for me now?"

"Yes." He nods. "I need it."

I place a gentle kiss on his nose and tap his shoulder to rise up on his knees to let me off the chair.

Brady lays his forehead on the couch cushion while I move behind him, and Kit gets out of my way. I'm dying to get inside Brady, but Kit's cum on his back is too hard to resist. I run my finger through it and lift it to my mouth.

Kit reaches for the strip of condoms lying on the floor and breaks one off, opening it and rolling it down my cock while I lower my head and lap at his salty release on Brady's skin.

I slip two fingers inside Brady's used hole, and even though Kit just fucked him, it grips me tight.

"I need inside you," I murmur against his back.

"Now," Brady pleads.

I straighten up and grip my cock, guiding it to his hole. It's difficult not to slam inside him. He's ready for it. He wants it. But I know if I go hard and fast immediately, I'm going to come.

So instead of doing that, I enter him as slowly as I possibly can. He makes cute sounds of protest, which only gives me more incentive to go slower.

"Kit," Brady whines for help.

"Like he's going to get me to move faster," I say and push in a little deeper.

It's still not enough for Brady. "No, but if I ask him nicely, he might suck my dick while you tease me."

"That's true," I say.

Kit acts tough, and he has this power-top attitude about him, but he's a sucker for politeness. It turns him into a big teddy bear.

Brady lifts his head and pleads with Kit. "Please. Or I'm going to have to take things into my own hands."

Kit looks to me for direction, which is weird for us because he's usually the one in charge, but as if sensing I need this, he's giving me this control. It's a moment that I want to savor, but Brady becomes too impatient and pushes back, filling himself with my aching dick.

I relent. "I think I've been cruel enough."

Kit scoffs. "Amateur." Yet he positions himself on his back on the floor, his naked SEAL form on full display for me to admire while he ducks his head under Brady. I can't see what he's doing from here, but by the noise that leaves Brady's mouth—a sob-like cry of relief—I can imagine.

I let Kit have a good taste of Brady's delicious cock before I move. Kit stills so that every time I move inside Brady, Brady thrusts inside his mouth.

I want Brady to beat me across the finish line. I want to wring him out before I start pounding into him so I can get off, but my body flushes with heat, and my orgasm builds. Then builds some more.

It's unstoppable at this point. Inevitable. Impending …

I can't. Hold … out.

Brady's shudder, followed by his ass tightening around my cock, sends me over the edge, and my body floats while my brain tells me to keep going. I need to keep fucking Brady until I'm sure he's come too. Kit makes a choking noise, and Brady slumps, and only then do I let myself come to a stop. Every last, slow thrust inside Brady makes me shiver.

And when I finally pull out of him, the three of us fall into a pile of twisted limbs on the floor.

"I'll get up and go home as soon as I catch my breath," Brady says, but by the sound of his wispy voice, I can only assume that will be never.

I don't want him to leave. As much as I'm desperate to yell at Kit some more, what the three of us have is rare. It started as fun, and that's all it has been. But staring at the end of us … living it … I'm not ready yet.

"Stay," I blurt.

Kit lifts his head, his gray eyes meeting mine. "Huh?"

"He should stay with us tonight."

It's Brady's turn to look at me. "I … I haven't done that before."

"What, you can have our dicks inside you, but you draw the line at sharing a bed with us?"

Brady laughs. "Hey, I'm good with it if you are. I just figured you guys didn't do sleepovers. Every time we've hooked up—"

I reach for his hand, which is right by mine. "It's our last night. You said it yourself."

"I'll stay."

Kit helps Brady off the floor and then looks at me.

"We'll take Kit's bed," I say. "It's bigger."

And as we each clean ourselves up and move to Kit's room, still naked, I can't help the pang of longing that hits my chest when we're curled up together with Brady between Kit and me.

It's a heartbreakingly perfect moment that will never happen again.

So I hold on tighter and breathe them in to try to remember this for as long as I can.

CHAPTER FIVE

I CAN'T SLEEP. Despite the amazing sex, it wasn't enough to wear me out. Physically, I'm exhausted, but I'm all jumbled up inside.

I stare at the ceiling while Brady is curled into my side, with Prescott spooning him from behind.

This move to Virginia is the right one. The job will be good for my career. Distance from Prescott will be good for my heart.

It's not my fault I went and fell in love with him. It's his fault for being *him*.

I knew he'd be pissed when I broke the news to him—hence doing it after I sent Brady a text to come to our place—but I expected him to be over it by the time we'd come our brains out. Maybe it was the wrong time to bring it up, but I knew he wouldn't make a scene in front of Brady.

Prescott covered his anger well, but taking control the way he did was a clear-cut message to me. He can't control what I do, so he was controlling something he could. I'm not sure if Brady noticed the switch in Prescott, but I did.

Brady's too important to both of us to drag him into our mess, and tonight is supposed to be about him. Prescott is deploying, I'm leaving, and come May, Brady will be graduating and moving to New York.

I slip out of bed, careful not to wake either of them, put on some underwear, and go to the kitchen for a glass of water. It does nothing to wet my dry mouth.

Instead of going back to bed, where I'm going to continue to stare at the ceiling, I move out on our balcony that overlooks the complex's pool. Not that I can see it because it's the middle of the night, but the view into pitch-black darkness is more fitting to my mood than staring at the dated popcorn ceiling above my bed.

I'm doing the right thing.

I am.

But I must not have been as quiet as I hoped because Brady appears, wearing a pair of my sweats with his light brown hair disheveled from sleep. I love that he's comfortable enough to wear my clothes and make himself at home, even though we haven't done the sleepover thing before. He has napped in between rounds, hung out till all hours of the morning, but he's always gone before sunrise.

Back when Prescott and I were his age, we always knew we wanted to be SEALs, but we spent so much time trying to make that happen that it wasn't until later that we began working ourselves out. We both knew we were gay, that we were sailors and military for life. But it was like that was our entire personalities. To be Brady's age and know who he is, what he wants, and what he doesn't want, it's admirable.

It's something I noticed about him the first night Prescott and I picked him up from Bottoms Up. Brady's young but confident in his own skin. He's not shy about asking for what he needs, but he also knows his place. For someone so young, he's so mature when it comes to this sex stuff.

And while my emotional attachment to Brady isn't as deep as it is for Prescott, there's no denying it would be easy to fall for Brady too. Here I was worried that Prescott might develop real feelings for Brady and ice me out or that Brady would become clingy and turn both Prescott and me off, and then I'm the one to go and screw everything up by wanting things I can't have.

"Sorry, did I wake you?" I ask.

"I got cold." Brady takes the seat next to me.

"Cold? Aren't you originally from Chicago?"

"Well, when you have two bodies glued to you working like furnaces, you notice when one is missing."

"Ah."

"Want to talk about whatever's going on between you and Prescott? Because I don't buy the roommate drama for a second."

That's another thing I noticed about Brady right away. He's a perceptive fucker. I was hoping we were more subtle earlier, but I guess not.

"He's mad at me."

"What did you do?"

"I ..." I don't want to say that I'm running away, even though that's exactly what I'm doing, so I go with facts. Only the facts. "An opportunity came up for me to work directly with the Pentagon. Which means moving. To Virginia."

"You're leaving him?"

"I'm not leaving *him*. We're not together. We're roommates who have fun with hot young things we pick up in bars." I take another sip of water, hating myself for reducing Brady to that.

He's so much more than that, but it's all been unspoken.

"Yeah, I'm gonna have to call bullshit on that one," Brady says. "Also, share. I'm thirsty after these two hot *old* dudes fucked me until I almost passed out."

"We are not old."

"Mmhmm. I don't think anyone whose age starts with a three is allowed to say that."

"I'm twenty-nine, you fucker."

Brady drinks the rest of my water, and I swear it's only half to distract me from his mean, mean words. "Oops."

"I'll get you some more." I go to stand, but he grabs my wrist.

"I'm good."

"You might be, but I'm not. You drank all my water."

I love the cheeky expression he gives me while I go get us some more. It's moments like these I'm going to miss most about him. I mean, I'll miss the sex too, but in the quiet post-orgasm bliss, I see the real Brady. The guy who makes me and Prescott come back for more.

He isn't a naive college kid, and I really, really like that.

I also don't like it because he never holds back what he's thinking, and when I get back to the table with another glass of water each, he lays into me right away.

"So, yeah. Bullshit."

"What's bullshit?"

"That you aren't together. I know you guys told me you don't hook up without a third there, but I don't believe that. I never did."

"It's true," I say. "Mainly because the only time we're allowed to hook up is when we're not on duty. At work, we don't even touch—not even in a friendly manner in case people figure us out."

"I thought it was okay for gay dudes in the military now?"

"It is, but there are strong fraternization rules. Didn't we explain this all to you once before?"

"It's hard to remember what you guys tell me when I'm desperate to get into your pants. If you need me to retain information, you need to tell me after I've blown my load."

"That would've been helpful to know a couple of months ago. Not the night before we—" I cut myself off from saying *break up* because it's not like we're together. We have the same deal with Brady as we do with each other. We can only cross lines temporarily before boundaries need to be put in place.

"Part ways?" Brady says, finishing my sentence I'd already forgotten about.

"Exactly."

"This job you took. Why is Prescott so mad if you're not anything more than friends? Still calling bullshit, by the way. Even if you guys don't see it or say it, I've always thought you were a couple. And if you're not, you should be one." Something like sadness flits through his gaze, and whether he knows what he's talking about or not, one thing is clear: if Prescott and I were a couple, we'd still want Brady too.

"The position I'm taking wasn't an ordered transfer."

Brady smiles. "Ah. And he's pissed off because you're *not* a couple, and you're voluntarily moving away from him. Got it."

"You're such a smartass," I mutter.

"Why did you apply for the transfer when you're clearly in love with Prescott?" His tone is teasing, but I tense because he hit the nail on the head. His face falls. "Oh. You applied for it *because* you're in love with him."

"Shh. Don't say that around him."

"Why not? You two belong together." Again, with the small look of sadness.

"It's not that easy. And maybe one day you will understand, but you're—"

"If you say I'm only twenty and don't know what I'm talking about, I'm going to lose my shit at you. Just warning you now."

"Good to know." And then I shut my mouth because that's exactly what I was going to say.

We fall silent after that, and for all of Brady's complaining that he's cold, he doesn't make a move to go back inside. Or put on a shirt.

"Damn it," he says eventually.

"What?"

"I just realized with you leaving … this really is over. I was kind of hoping I could fly out here and still visit you guys whenever I got the chance. And when you were actually here. The whole SEAL team thing really ruins spontaneity for you guys, huh?"

"It really, really does."

"Damn, this sucks."

"You told him, then." Prescott's voice startles both of us, and I can't help worrying about how long he's been standing at the open doorway. He's only in his underwear like I am, and his bulging muscles are tight as his arms are folded against his wide, golden-skinned chest.

"He did, and any hope of catching up with you guys again in the future has been dashed," Brady says.

"I heard."

I try to recall every single sentence Brady has said in the last couple of minutes that Prescott could have heard. "What else did you hear?"

I make the mistake of tilting my head toward him, and Prescott's soulful brown eyes are locked on mine.

"That Brady wants to see us again but can't."

Here we go. I didn't think he'd make a scene in front of Brady, but apparently, I was wrong.

"It made me think," Prescott continues. "Why can't we see each other again? All three of us."

Impulsive Prescott strikes again. This is the guy I'm used to. The act now, think later type of guy who has gotten us into some serious trouble in the past on missions. I swear it's ninety-five percent luck we haven't been KIA. "I can give you three reasons. Coronado, Arlington, New York."

"Obviously it won't be able to happen often, and it's not like we'll be exclusive while we're apart, but think about it. I could apply for leave, you won't be on active duty anymore, and Brady … he gets summers off. School breaks between semesters? We could totally manage once a year where we all get together."

Brady's face lights up, and it's clear he's in.

My heart lurches, wanting to say no. Wanting to protect myself. But who knows? Maybe some time away, even if it's only six months … maybe that will be enough for me to emotionally distance myself from Prescott.

Then I don't have to lose out on either of them completely.

"We should do it," I say.

Brady jumps up. "Good. Now that's settled, take me back to bed."

"You can't be ready to go again already," Prescott says.

Brady looks over his shoulder at me. "What were you saying about you guys not being old?" Then he turns back to Prescott and whines. "It's been *hours*. And if you really can't get it up again, I'll let you blow me. I'm a generous man like that."

I laugh as I stand and follow them inside. "I've worked out why Brady likes having two men in his bed."

Brady faces me. "Apart from it being hot as fuck?"

"Apart from that. It's so they have a chance to keep up with you, isn't it?"

His smile doesn't reach his eyes, but there's still hunger burning in his light brown gaze. "You've worked out all my secrets. Now, what are you going to do with me?"

"We're going to shut you up the best way we know how."

"Yes," he hisses and runs back to the bedroom.

Prescott steps in front of me. "Did you mean it? That we can still … you know … this isn't goodbye?"

I pull him in for a hug. A hug that fills me with both regret and resentment, though neither aimed at Pres. I hate what our friendship has become because I have no control over my feelings for him. Having to break it all down, I know I need to leave to get some space.

"You'll always be my best friend," I say. "Distance won't change that. And the once-a-year thing sounds great."

He nods. "Once a year. Only on leave."

I hope that's enough to bury the longing that stabs at my heart.

CHAPTER SIX

WHEN PEOPLE ASK me what military life is like, they're often disappointed when I say it's a lot of waiting around. And for the last few months, stationed in the Yellow Sea, that's all it has been.

It's times like these where I hate my job. Okay, no, I still love it, but Brady graduates in a few days, and I'm doing nothing. I could be there to see him one last time before he leaves for New York.

Instead, I'm stuck here, doing what I've been doing for months on end.

One good thing to come of it is that I've dealt with my anger over Kit leaving. If dealing with it means burying it deep and pretending he never existed. But while I miss him like crazy, I didn't realize how much I would miss Brady on this deployment. I've gone over it and over it in my head and have come to the conclusion that I can't get him out of my mind because I knew the last time was the end of what we had. Sure, we've agreed to meet up occasionally, but it's changed between all three of us. If I'd been deployed knowing both of them would be in the San Diego area when I got back, it wouldn't be as hard. Maybe.

Shanahan, the newbie on the team who I may or may not hold a tiny bit of undeserved resentment toward for replacing my best friend, approaches me while I'm having downtime on my bunk after a workout.

"Did you hear?" he asks. He's all bright eyes and puppylike, and it's hard to hate him, but I growl anyway.

"Hear what?"

"We're going home early."

I sit up and hit my head on the top bunk. "We're what?"

He shrugs. "They didn't say why."

"They never do."

"But who cares why? We're going home." He dances out of the room, and as much as I try to suppress it, I laugh.

We're going home. I might be able to make it to Brady's graduation.

I stand. I need to get to the communications room so I can contact Kit. Maybe he'll be able to make it too.

Another fun fact about military life is that when they tell you you're going home, it's not an immediate pack your things and go, which is why it takes me way too long to get back Stateside that I worry I'm actually going to miss the graduation after all.

After what feels like an eternity of boats, planes, and layovers, I finally arrive back in California. And if I don't go home and change, I might be able to make it with only seconds to spare.

After getting back to port, I immediately head home and jump in my car, racing the clock to get to Franklin U. And of course, traffic and parking is a bitch because Brady isn't the only one graduating today.

I'm still in my camo uniform, and I probably have that sweaty scent that you only get from traveling for days straight, but I'm here. About a mile from campus.

Guess I'm not done sweating.

I am, however, late. Damn it.

I make it to the football stadium, where the commencement speech is underway, and there's a sea of purple graduation gowns taking up half of the damn field. The guests are positioned behind them, a packed house by the look of it, and some leftovers are standing at the back. I spot Kit almost immediately, his tall frame standing toward the very back with his arms folded, sunglasses covering his face, and his resting bitch face in place. He always looks so serious and stoic, and one of my favorite things used to be making him lose his composure.

Damn, he looks amazing. My heart gives a nostalgic little twinge at seeing him again. And when he spots me, he gives me exactly what I want—that smile I love dragging out of him. He lifts his hand to wave, and I jog over to him.

He immediately pulls me into a hug, and if we weren't in such a public place, I'd be tempted to kiss the fuck out of him because this time apart has done nothing but make me miss him on that level.

When we were living together, he was always there. We trained together, deployed together, went out together. Going from that to nothing has been so hard.

"You actually made it," he murmurs. "You stink, but you made it."

"I did. They told us days ago we get to go home early, and then—"

"Then they screwed you around. Why am I not surprised?"

"Is that why you took the liaison job? Sick of all the disorganization that is the navy?"

"The sad part is it's actually very organized. They just like to make things complicated. And no. I took the job to advance my experience and career."

He says that, but all it will do is advance him to desk jobs. How is that advancement?

Okay, so yeah, all that not actually dealing with my resentment is bubbling to the surface, so I change topics. "Brady seen you yet?"

"Don't think so. I snuck in the back—"

"Like you always like to do."

Kit snorts. "I thought maybe these six months without me might have made you mature a little, but I can see it's gone backward."

"Yep. What are you gonna do about it?"

He turns his head, but I can't see his eyes through his blacker-than-black glasses. "I could shut you up."

His tone is more flirty than threatening, but that can't be right. Our previous arrangement had rules. No showing affection, no flirting. It was how it had to be because we were worried about getting sloppy at work and accidentally being too comfortable with public affection.

Does being in separate parts of the navy now negate all those old rules? If I leaned in and went for a kiss, would he be up for it?

His lips quirk, but then he turns his attention back to the stage.

Names have begun being read out as graduates take to their walk to get their diplomas.

"Is it weird I'm proud of Brady even though I had nothing to do with his success in college?" I ask.

"Not at all. I'm proud of him too," Kit says with affection in his tone.

When Peyton Miller's name is called out—Brady's brother—the entire crowd goes wild. Yet, when Brady's name is called out, it's only a group of people who stand and cheer. Sure, it's a big group of people, but not every single person in the damn stadium.

"Do you think that's why Brady never told us who he was?" I ask. "The reaction to his brother compared to him?" In the group of people cheering, I spot the NFL legends that are Brady's fathers.

"Probably, but question. If all of those people over there are here for Brady, how are we going to lure him away from them?"

"Ooh, I could create a diversion while you kidnap him."

"Or we could text him and give him the heads-up." Kit takes out his phone and types away.

"Sure. Be efficient and boring. You don't even know how I was planning to create a diversion. I'm in uniform. I could be all, 'There's a threat to National Security, and you all need to get out of here,' and then you could swoop in and—"

His phone dings, and he chuckles at Brady's response.

I glance over his shoulder and read: *You really think I didn't see Prescott's entrance? My man in uniform radar went off. Stay where you are, and I'll sneak away when this is done. Good thing about graduating with my brother is the attention can be split between us.*

"Seriously, you need a shower." Kit shoves me away from him.

"I know. It was either go home and shower and miss this completely or be here for Brady."

Kit gives me one of his warm smiles. "It's cute you care about him."

More than I should, I think. "He's different. Don't ask me why."

"I think it's his confidence. Being with us wasn't a matter of doing wild shit in college. He was there because he liked us."

"Well, everyone likes me, so you must have been the problem with the others we've hooked up with."

"Tell me, was it your humble side everyone liked so much?"

"That and my dick."

"Of course."

The ceremony comes to an end with the traditional cap throwing, and almost immediately, the graduates disperse to find their family and friends in the crowd. There's so much purple everywhere I lose sight of Brady within a couple of seconds, but then he appears, weaving his way between groups of people while stripping out of his gown.

He's damn near glowing under the California sun. When he reaches us, he holds his arms wide and hugs us both but then steps back. A lot. There's a good six feet between us.

"I can't believe you're here. Both of you. It's good to see you."

"If you're wondering what that bad smell is, it's Prescott," Kit says.

"Hey, I literally had to run here from the airport."

"How long are you here for?"

"I just got home, so it should be another year to eighteen months before I'm shipped out again," I say.

"I leave tomorrow," Kit says. "When Prescott texted and said he might be able to make it back in time to surprise you, I knew I had to make it. Even if I couldn't get any time off."

Brady turns back toward the crowd, looking in the direction of his family. "So, like, everyone in my huge extended family came out for this. I need to spend some time with them."

"We understand," Kit says.

I fold my arms. "I told you we should have kidnapped him."

"I guess that also means you know who my family is now." He stares down at his feet.

Kit and I look at each other. Time to let the cat out of the bag.

"Brady, we've always known," I say. "You don't think we looked you up after the first time we took you home?"

He doesn't lift his head, just continues to stare at his feet. "Oh. Let me guess, you want an autograph?"

"Nope. Have no desire to walk up to your dad and say, 'Hey, I'm a big fan. So big I fucked your baby boy.' I like my face, thank you very much."

Brady finally looks up. It's obvious he has an issue with his family, but I have no idea what it is.

"We're not going to ask you to do anything you're uncomfortable with. You should know that by now," Kit says. "And if you have to spend the night with your family—"

"No, no. Don't get me wrong. There is no way you two are getting out of making me come later, but I need to have dinner with my family first. Is that okay?"

"We'll be at our apartment," I say. "Come over whenever you can get away."

"Leave the door unlocked for me." He bounces away, running to the group of people who cheered for him and his brother. None of them are paying attention to us, and I'm surprised and impressed by how stealthily Brady slips back into the group in his robe as if he was there all along.

"I'm happy you made it back in time," Kit says.

"Yeah. Me too."

The only problem is we've barely said hello again, and I'm not ready to say goodbye.

brady

LAW SCHOOL IS KICKING my ass, and so is my internship. Spring break can't come fast enough. It's been nine months since the last time I saw Kit and Prescott when they showed up at my graduation, and even though they've tried to set another meetup since, I've been juggling working at King Sports and studying. Law school is not as easy as an undergrad in sports management. Who knew?

The one time I might have been able to meet them somewhere for one night—suggesting somewhere in the middle of nowhere America halfway between the two coasts—Prescott couldn't leave Coronado because his team or squad or whatever they're called were on four-hour alert, which meant they had to be ready to deploy if needed within four hours.

I've spent most of my last nine months in a classroom or following my uncle around the country scouting summer camps and colleges for upcoming hotshot athletes. At one point, we were in LA, and I was tempted to try to sneak away for a few hours to see Prescott, but I figured it would be weird with just the two of us.

Well, not weird weird, but a bit weird. It's not like all three of us have to be together at the same time, but I dunno, I thought it might be awkward. That and I really didn't have the time to make it to San Diego anyway.

I was convinced this *on leave* deal Prescott and Kit made wasn't going to work, but then the planets aligned, or the sex gods took mercy on us, and we've planned one whole week together. As soon as this new player signs his deal with us, I am out of here.

In three hours, I'm going to be on a plane heading for a small island off the coast of Tampa in Florida, where I'm going to come as many times as I can until the point where I'm going to pass out or die of dehydration.

I don't plan to leave the hotel room if the guys let me. I'm sure a tiny little island in the Gulf of Mexico will have food delivery options.

Hmm, maybe not. But I'm sure if I begged, Kit or Prescott would go fetch sustenance for me.

Fuck, *Kit and Prescott*. It feels like forever since I've seen them.

As much as I wanted to stay more than one night with them at graduation, I couldn't really swing it. Not with my family wanting to spend every waking moment with Peyton and me.

While everyone was celebrating our graduation, drinking and having a family party at our house, I snuck away for a couple of hours. Had an amazing, sweaty, cum-filled time and then came back to my bed in the early hours of the morning. Everyone thought I'd gone to sleep early.

Too much excitement about my future. Definitely not so wrung out from two dicks filling me up.

I can't wait for it to happen again.

Nine months with barely any contact has been hard. With Kit and Prescott being SEALs, their social media is limited. Their personal accounts are anything but *personal*. Their full names, Guy Kitchener and Jimmy Prescott, is the most I've ever learned from them. They can't share much on their profiles because of security issues, so the only times we've been in contact is via group text message.

They've asked how my life is going and things like that, but it's always a one-sided conversation with them because other than SEALing—totally a word they use all time and not a term I made up that annoys them to no end—they don't have much personal lives. It's a reflex to be vague about my life when they have to be about theirs.

I'm nervous to see them again. I worry about our dynamic being suddenly different or them not liking me now that I've lost a little muscle mass. I was never at their level of physique, but I used to hit the gym with my brother and his teammates. I was once a center in football. I've been bulky nearly all my life, but I barely have time to breathe, let alone work out, so I'm not as big as I was in college.

Prescott and Kit are SEALs, for fuck's sake. They were bigger than me before. Now …

The thought of them throwing me around fills my mind, and a shiver runs down my spine. My suit pants tighten because my cock is already on vacation and imagining what the guys are going to do to me. It's highly unprofessional while negotiating signing a new client.

A new pain-in-the-ass client too. This guy Uncle Damon has chosen to represent is pissing me off. He thinks he's going to be the next biggest queer quarterback in the NFL. Better than *Peyton Miller* even. Even though he's going in undrafted and hasn't even been on a team for the last twelve months. It's like he saw my brother and said, "Hey, I played college football. I could do better than that guy."

Fucker. My brother kicked ass his rookie season with Arizona, taking the team further than they have been in a long time. Sure, they were knocked out early in the playoffs, but they *made* the playoffs.

Torey Nelson is saying how he could've taken Arizona all the way, and I'm silently gritting my teeth.

Uncle Damon can tell I'm getting agitated, too, because he smiles at me and then says to Torey, "Sorry, did I introduce you to my intern? Brady Talon, this is Torey Nelson."

Suddenly, the guy's façade drops. The chair he's been swinging on falls forward, the front legs hitting the floor with a loud thud. "T-Talon?"

Damon's smile widens. "We're a family-run agency. Peyton Miller is one of my clients, and if we're going to sign you, you will be part of this team. This family. Which means I would advise you not to compare yourself to anyone else on my roster."

"Or maybe anyone who is competing at the NFL level when you're not," I say, and when Uncle Damon glares at me, I add, "yet."

As if realizing this isn't a done deal and he's risking losing the representation *he sought out*, not the other way around, Torey turns from cocky and arrogant to ass-kisser. Of course. Not that I should judge him. If we hadn't grown up in the family we did, we might not know how to act around prospective agents.

We've always been told that being confident is a good thing, but there's a fine line between that and unattractive cockiness.

When I decided I wanted to be a sports agent, I knew I was going to have to learn to deal with an athlete's ego. I thought it would be easy, having grown up with Peyton Miller as a brother. Turns out when you don't love the person you're representing, it's really hard not to tell them to cut the shit. At least with Peyton, I can tell him that and he won't fire me.

Uncle Damon has this amazing touch with all of his clients. He's patient but can be stern when he needs to be. I need to learn that tact. I'm trying to swallow down my annoyance and remain professional, but I don't know if I'm pulling it off.

"Of course," Torey says. "I'm a team player. I promise. Ask any of my coaches and teammates."

"There's nothing wrong with healthy competition," Uncle Damon says, "but it's when it becomes toxic, you'll get a reputation for something you don't want to be known as: a sore winner or loser."

"Yes, sir."

I try not to laugh at the sudden flip in attitude.

"You might want to learn some humility." Uncle Damon stands. "We'll leave the meeting here for now. If you're still interested in representation, we'll be happy to sign you with King Sports, but it depends on what kind of agent you're looking for. We're hands-on, and we will call you out on poor behavior. Someone else might be more willing to kiss your ass and let you get away with the shitty attitude, but they'll also be the first to drop you at the sign of a scandal."

Torey swallows hard. "I want a supportive agent. I want someone who will fight for my rights as a queer athlete, and that's why I came to you first. The things you've done for the queer community—"

Uncle Damon sits back down at the negotiating table. "Those things were only achieved because of the standards I put on my players. Image is everything, and unfortunately, in this business, everything can be taken out of context or twisted. Some agents believe any publicity is good publicity, but I've had clients almost lose their places on teams because of poor decisions. If you are interested, we can get you signed and send you a PR coach to train you on how to conduct yourself in interviews, with press, and also other players. You're allowed to hate anyone internally, but we'll train you to be nice to them anyway."

Even though he's talking about sports and specifically what he expects from his players, I can't help applying it to the industry as a whole.

My uncle has had his own time in the spotlight over the years because of what he's done for out athletes, who he has signed, and other articles because of his achievements in both his professional and personal life. The public has followed him from his career-ending sports injury to becoming an agent, and then his love story and how he met his partner, whom he refers to as his husband even though they're not legally married.

He's done so much for LGBTQ athletes, but I still worry about what would happen if it got out about me. The gay thing is more widely accepted than it once was, and being from a predominantly queer family, it's not being gay that I'm worried about. It's that I had to go and take it a step further and be polyamorous.

There's such a stigma when it comes to polyamory and open relationships. People see it as cheating and throw judgment.

It's why I haven't told anyone about Kit and Prescott outside of my best friend and Peyton's now live-in partner, Levi. I'm reluctant to say anything about Kit and Prescott because … it almost feels like I have to come out? And after having no nerves over doing that the first time, it's a completely different experience to worry about not being accepted.

Not that I think my family wouldn't accept me, but … they're at least going to ask questions, and the answers aren't something I'm ready to give yet. Hell, I barely know how to explain how I feel about it all.

I think because society has screamed about soul mates and finding *the one* and admonishing infidelity, being with more than one person is seen as wrong, so my brain believes I'm doing something I shouldn't.

Is there such a thing as internalized polyphobia? Maybe I have that.

"Brady?" My uncle's voice pulls me out of yet another internal debate.

When I glance up, both he and Torey are standing.

Oops.

I stand and hold out my hand for Torey to shake. "It was really nice to meet you, and we look forward to representing you."

I'm given a tight smile in return, and after Torey leaves, my uncle just looks at me.

"Were you paying attention at all?"

"Of course I was. You said you'd train him not to be a douche."

"But he walked out without signing anything. Said he wanted to 'think about it.' We're not representing him."

Oh. I cover my blunder with all the confidence my last name could bring. "Yet. But it'll happen. He'll sign with his tail between his legs."

Damon grips my shoulder, and his green eyes hold a brand of cheek I'm used to only seeing from his partner, Uncle Maddox. "So glad you're on board."

My gaze narrows. "On board?"

"If he does sign, Torey Nelson will be your first-ever client. It will be good practice for when you take over your brother's account from me."

I blink. Then blink again. "Isn't it too soon for my own client? I've still got two years of law school left."

"I'll give you a more senior agent to oversee all dealings, but the best way to learn is with a hands-on approach."

"Can I take back what I said? Maybe not sign *him*?"

"Nope. Now, go have a fun spring break."

If only he knew he's telling his nephew to go have fun being fucked repeatedly by two men who are ten years older.

I mock salute him and make my exit. My suitcase is stashed under my desk at my cubicle, so I grab it and head for the elevators. A nervous twitch starts as soon as the doors close.

Because it's really happening. I'm going to see Kit and Prescott again.

Actually, to be sure, I take out my phone and make sure there's no last-minute change of plans. I've been anticipating this for so long that I haven't allowed myself to get excited because anything could have screwed it up. From messages where one of them is getting married to a rogue out-of-season hurricane taking out our destination, I've thought of them all.

Which is going to suck because that doubt isn't going to go away until I am physically in their presence. The one night at graduation wasn't enough, and them turning up for me unexpectedly made me fantasize about every unrealistic expectation since then.

How dare they not randomly come to New York and surprise me even though they don't know where I live, whether or not I'd be in town, or if I'm seeing anyone. Why does spontaneity need to be all logical?

On the way to the airport, I try to tune out the nerves by putting on my headphones and listening to music.

I've gotten so used to traveling these past twelve months that I move through check-in and airport security with ease. I've learned to sleep on planes, so from the minute we take off until we land, I nap. It's good because it makes the flight quick, but instead of waking up refreshed, when I land in Florida, I'm bone-tired, and my gut hurts from all the what-ifs.

What if they hate the way I look now?

What if one of them doesn't turn up?

I've dated guys in the last year. And by date, I mean go out a couple of times, have sex, and just feel … like it's not enough. I even tried an app for couples to find a third, but all the couples on there didn't live up to Kit and Prescott.

There's a pull I have toward them, an inability to forget how it feels to be with them. Yeah, it's all based around sex, but there's a level of comfort with them too.

As if sensing that I'm close, I get a text message from Kit.

Room 5A in the terrace wing when you get here. Door's unlocked.

At least I know Kit is there. That fills me with some relief. And more nerves. Fuck, I'm a wreck. Maybe I should've tried to settle it with alcohol on the flight or, I dunno, asked someone for an Ambien. Though I'd probably still be asleep on the plane if I did that.

The taxi pulls up to the beach resort, and I take a deep breath. It's not the most fancy of hotels, but it looks nice from the outside, and from what the guys tell me, it's gay-friendly, which is a bonus. No one should blink at the sight of three men hanging out in what is obviously a couple's retreat.

I think.

It's thoughts like this that give me anxiety over who I am. What I want.

Then I remind myself that what I have with Prescott and Kit hasn't changed. It won't get out because there's technically nothing to get out. It's always only been sex, and as much as I want more with Kit and Prescott—to explore this connection with them—I can never have it. Even if the triad thing didn't have such a big stigma, they're both in special forces and need to keep a low profile. They wouldn't have that with me. Not with who my parents and brother are.

So I'll do what I have always done when it comes to my SEALs: remind myself that they're a guilty pleasure I'm going to let myself have. On the down low. Whenever we can all manage it.

The small, two-story resort is easy to navigate, and as I reach our door, I need to steel myself. But then murmurs come from inside, and I have to laugh.

"That sounded like footsteps," one of them whispers. "Think it was him?"

"Fucking hope so." That's definitely Prescott. "Being naked while waiting for him and without being able to touch you is torture."

Naked?

Like, right now?

I practically knock the door off its hinges I enter so fast.

And there they are. My guys. *Not naked.*

Prescott smiles. "I knew that would get him moving."

"I hate both of you." I pout, but silently, I'm thankful because he made me ignore my insecurities and push through. And now that I'm in their presence, all that doubt, that dread, that anxiety floats away and is replaced with insatiable need.

"We'll make it up to you," Prescott says and holds out his arms for a hug.

I don't hesitate to run into them and wrap my hands around his back and bury my head in his shoulder.

Then Kit is behind me, and I'm where I belong. Where I've wanted to belong since we first met.

With them.

CHAPTER EIGHT

THANK fuck Brady's finally here.

Prescott has only been here for half an hour, and things between us are … stale. I've been trying to keep up with Prescott's carefree nonchalance, but I'm not as good at it as he is.

Over the last year, Prescott and I have barely managed to stay in touch. The most we interacted in person or via text all had to do with meeting up with Brady at graduation and organizing this trip.

We've both been busy, obviously, but it's so much more than that. I've been too chickenshit to reach out because as much as time away has helped me deal with my feelings for Prescott, they're still there.

Going to Brady's graduation was a test to see if I'd gotten over the hold Prescott has on me, and I failed miserably. I missed Prescott even more than I anticipated. Hell, I missed Brady too. It was great to see them, but I went back to Virginia even more torn up than I was before.

"Question," Brady says. "Why *aren't* we naked? Isn't that the best way to start a vacation?"

Prescott pulls out of his arms. "Patience, little one."

Brady hangs his head, and I hold him from behind even tighter. "Is that your way of insulting how I look now? Because I'm all skinny, and my muscles have deflated, and—"

Skinny? He's far from it.

"Hey, whoa." Prescott cups Brady's cheek. "What are you talking about? You're still hot as fuck. When I first saw you, I thought you worked hard to lose all that bulk."

"Not at all. I did nothing to lose it … which I guess is why I did. Apparently, when you work out every day with a football team during college and then stop, it's the equivalent of popping your muscles with a pin like a balloon." He gestures a bomb going off with his hands and even adds in sound effects.

"You're fucking gorgeous," I murmur into the back of his hair. "Muscles or no muscles."

"Agreed," Prescott says. "Actually, I might even like this itty-bitty-sized Brady."

Brady folds his arms. "I am not itty bitty. Now, about that naked thing …"

It seems other than some new self-image insecurities, Brady's still the bright-eyed brat that he always was.

"I figured you'd want to shower after the plane ride, maybe have something to eat and settle in," I say.

Brady turns between us so he faces me now, and the permanent gleam in his deep brown eyes shines brighter. "Well, I am hungry for something." He reaches for the fly on my jeans, and behind him, Prescott laughs and grips the top of Brady's shoulders.

"You're still a horndog." Prescott steers him away and into the main bedroom with the giant king bed and a bathroom big enough for the three of us to fit comfortably. It was one of the reasons I chose this place. I looked through countless reviews to find somewhere that could accommodate us.

"Shower," Prescott says, and then I hear the bathroom door close.

He comes out of the room, shaking his head. "Are you ready for this week?"

There's more forced nonchalance on my part. "Between the two of us, I'm sure we can handle him."

Prescott smiles, and it reminds me of the smiles he used to send me. Those knowing ones he gives when he thinks I'm full of shit. Which I'm not. At least in this instance. Because Brady, I can handle. Give him attention, affection, and orgasms, and he's happy. It's Prescott who I'm worried about.

From best friends to … this: a weird energy that feels like running into an old coworker.

"Should we feed him first or give him an orgasm to keep him quiet while we eat afterward?" Prescott asks.

I rub my chin. "I have a better idea, but we're going to need some rope."

Prescott raises his eyebrows as if to say, *"Go on."*

"Or did you bring a belt? We can improvise." I take my belt off, but Prescott is only in sweats.

He grins. "I have no idea what you want to do, but I'm in." He disappears into the bedroom, and while he's gone, I pull out the food I cooked when I first got here and checked in.

My flight was the first to land, and I had hours to kill. Cooking helped me get over my nerves and pass the time. I take it out of the fridge and pop it in the microwave to heat it back up.

Prescott gasps when he returns from the bedroom with his belt. "Is that your famous lemon butter salmon with sweet corn fritters on the side?"

"I figured you might be missing my cooking now that you live alone."

"I've banned myself from cooking because I set the kitchen on fire one night."

I'm not surprised. "How are you surviving?"

"I'm wasting away. Feed me, Kit. Please." He puts his belt on the counter and lifts his shirt. His abs are tight, and fuck him for doing that.

"Speaking of wasting away …" I glance toward the bedroom. "Do you think Brady's okay?"

"Because he lost some weight? What, is he too small for you now?"

"You know that's not it. I'm worried about him pushing too hard. Law school and interning? Not even having a chance to work out in big, corporate New York? It's not … him. I don't think he's taking care of himself. I bet he skips meals."

"You're overthinking this," Prescott says, using his reassuring tone and everything. I almost believe him. "He still looks healthy."

"He can't keep that pace though."

Prescott lets out a sigh that sounds like a laugh. "Typical Kit. Always wanting to take care of everyone." He moves closer to the kitchen counter. "Tell me, have you found someone to take care of you yet?"

Our eyes lock, and the air is sucked out of the room so fast my head spins.

Time apart hasn't changed a thing. I'm still helplessly in love with him.

The microwave beeps, but I ignore it.

There are more pressing matters, and I can't help myself. I round the counter and press against him.

When he first arrived, we shared a friendly hug, but after that, I made sure not to touch him in any affectionate way to try to keep our friendship separate from what we do with Brady. This whole trip is supposed to be about carefree fun and sex, and I've been failing at it since minute one.

Prescott sinks into my arms. "I've missed these big hands on me."

"I've missed your mouth more," I rasp. "You going to give it to me?"

There's a brief moment of panic where I think he isn't, but then he leans in. I can already taste him just from the anticipation of his familiar mouth on mine. He moves closer. Less than an inch to go. And then? The fucker pauses. I've never wanted to punch him harder.

A desperate whimper leaves me without permission because I don't beg. I don't *whimper*.

Prescott still doesn't give me what I want and looks over my shoulder. "I think Brady could sense us getting started without him."

I listen and realize the shower's not running anymore. "Think we should put on a show for him for when he gets back out here?"

Sure. *For Brady*. Honestly, any excuse to have Prescott's mouth on me.

As if hitting the right nerve, pushing past the awkwardness between us, Prescott closes the gap and finally presses his lips to mine. That's one thing we have in common: we'll do anything to tease Brady and bring out his bratty side.

But there's no predicting how much Prescott's mouth on mine would bring me to my knees. I knew it would be difficult and that all those suppressed feelings might surface, but I am not prepared for it to take over.

I moan into his mouth, and he grips my hips in his large hands.

Prescott makes my heart race and my skin break out in goose bumps. My body yearns for his. He makes my gut flutter, my dick ache, and my brain ask useless questions like *"Why can't we have this forever?"*

And for a stupid moment, I believe it could happen. That Prescott could one day love me the way I love him. But he's not the only one in this fantasy. I picture a time in the future, after Brady gets dating and messing around out of his system, where he'll be ready to settle down with us. It's like imagining winning the lottery and envisioning how to spend every dollar. That tiny chance of it happening gives you hope, but time after time, reality hits you in the gut.

Brady's footsteps sound, and then Prescott and I both get what we want: Brady whining.

"I'd almost forgotten how hot you two are together."

I smile against Prescott's lips.

"I get the sense I'm intruding." Brady's voice sounds so unsure that Prescott and I move at the same time. We break apart and approach Brady, who's standing there in only a bath towel, his hair still wet from the shower.

Prescott and I have done this threesome thing more than Brady has—presumably—and we've learned that if one feels left out, it can ruin the experience for all of us.

"You're never intruding," I whisper into the back of Brady's neck and press against him from behind.

"Never," Prescott agrees and closes in on Brady's front.

"Promise?" Brady asks, and I want to kiss him senseless.

Jealousy doesn't belong in these types of situations. It's a natural emotion, and it's bound to happen, but the important part is showing that person how important they are to us. To me.

Brady might know how deeply I feel for Prescott, but there's one thing he doesn't know. He's so much more than an excuse to get to Prescott. It started that way. They all did. Every guy we brought home from Bottoms Up served one purpose—to get me closer to Prescott. Until *him.*

Brady brings out my nurturing side. Prescott says I have it with everyone, but I don't. It's reserved for him, Brady, and it used to be for my rotating SEAL team at any given moment. Brady's the only one who accepts it freely though. Hell, sometimes I think he craves it more than I do.

With Prescott and me, we're always fighting for control because we thrive on it. He's not the type of guy who'd ask to be held or taken care of, and I'd never want to change him. Brady makes me soft. The vulnerability and trust he puts in us when it comes to sex is so special and rare. And when the three of us are together, something magical happens. It's something deeper disguised as sexual chemistry. I'm certain of it. I don't know exactly what *it* is other than something I'd love to explore.

One day.

In an alternate reality because it can't happen in this one.

"Let us show you how much we want to take care of you," I say and then meet Prescott's gaze.

Prescott agrees. "Yeah. Let us show you how much we love teasing. *You* specifically. Together."

I nod. "It's like a team-building exercise."

Brady throws his head back and reaches behind him to grip my neck. "I don't care what you call it. I need it."

"You might regret that," Prescott warns.

I turn and grab Prescott's belt as well as my own from the kitchen counter, and when Brady tries to complain at my absence, Prescott takes Brady's chin in his forefinger and thumb and moves it so Brady can see.

His brown eyes, which are a shade lighter than Prescott's, burn with need, and when he takes in our makeshift restraints, that need only shines brighter.

"Go sit at the table," I order, and Prescott directs him to the closest chair.

Just before he pushes him down, Prescott whips off Brady's towel.

I pass Prescott one of the belts, and then we mirror each other, kneeling next to Brady.

Brady's cock is already hard and leaking, and as much as I want to lean over and taste him, he's going to have something to eat before he gets the sweet reward of relief.

Prescott follows my lead as I wrap my belt around Brady's ankle and calf, securing them tightly to the leg of the chair.

I stand, and Brady reaches for my shirt, but I grip his wrist and order him to drop it.

I tap my chin. "We need to restrain his arms too."

Brady groans, but I can't tell if it's in frustration or want.

Prescott disappears and comes back with the top sheet off our bed. He doesn't waste time spinning it to make a long, thick rope that we can wrap around Brady's torso and arms and tie at the back so he can't undo it.

And the thing I love most about that is Brady doesn't even struggle as we do it. I reward his trust with a scorching kiss while Prescott finishes knotting the sheet.

When I pull away, Brady tries to follow, but our restraints work great for something we came up with on the fly.

Brady is so sexy tied to the chair, and he'll be even sexier in a moment. Sure, he'll complain, but if he has a mouthful of food, he's not going to be able to talk much.

I go back to the kitchen to get utensils and bring the plate of food to the table, and I put it in front of him. "Now, let me feed you."

He slumps. "All of that for some food? I'd rather eat something else." Because he can't move his hands, he stares at my cock, which is trying to escape my pants.

"Food first. For every bite you take, Prescott and I will take off one item of clothing."

"Ooh, strip dinner. That could be a fun game." With Brady suddenly on board, I cut him a bite-sized piece of salmon with a bit of corn fritter.

"Damn," Brady says as he swallows his first bite. "That's actually really good."

"You sound surprised that a SEAL can cook."

Meanwhile, Prescott sits at the table and shoves a whole fritter in his mouth. "You say that like you're not the only SEAL I know who *can* cook."

"I guess I'm losing my shirt first?" I ask him as he continues to stuff his face.

"Can't talk. Eating." Prescott steals the fork I'm feeding Brady with the second I put it down so I can get out of my shirt.

As soon as he takes a huge bite, I steal it back. "Get your own."

"Why does he get to be fed and I have to fend for myself?"

"I don't see you tied to a chair," I argue.

Brady grins over at Prescott with that bratty smile I've missed so much.

Prescott stands and mumbles all the way to the kitchen. "Brady gets to have all the fun."

"Oh, so we're playing that game, are we? Looks like I have two needy men on my hands." My cock gets even harder if that's possible.

Prescott winks at me as he gets a fork from the drawer. "I know how much you love that."

And he's right. I fucking do. "Help me take care of Brady first. Then you'll get to have your own fun."

"Deal, but in the interest of speeding things up." Prescott approaches the table, puts his fork down on the plate, and then steps back.

The fucker gets completely naked, taking away the whole reward system for Brady.

Brady shifts in his chair. "Yay. Prescott's in a nice mood."

"Nice to *you*," I say.

"That sounds like a you problem."

"Not necessarily." Prescott climbs *onto* the dining table and rests back on his ankles with his knees spread wide. His thick cock points upward and right toward Brady. "He doesn't get dessert until he eats all his dinner." Prescott wraps his large fingers around his shaft and strokes himself slowly.

"This isn't fair," Brady complains.

"That sounds like a you problem," I mimic. I lift the fork with some more food on it and move it toward his mouth.

He takes it and then talks around his food. "Fuck both of you."

We laugh at him.

"That's the point," Prescott says. "Eat up so you can … eat up." He wipes a drop of precum off the tip of his cock, but instead of letting Brady have a taste, he licks it off his thumb himself.

"Okay, shove the food in my mouth, and hurry up." Brady's desperate. Right where we want him.

"It's cute you think you get any say in what pace we go," I say.

He whines. "I want you both so bad. It's been too long. I want … I need. Please."

When I feed him another forkful of food, he practically swallows it whole. I let him get away with it because at least he's eating something of nutritional value. And despite Prescott's reassurances, I can't be sure Brady is looking after himself properly.

He does still look amazing, despite the sudden weight loss in a short nine months and the tired-looking eyes he had when he first came in. Though, there's no sign of that fatigue now.

All that's in his gaze at the moment is determination and need. His laser focus is on Prescott fucking his hand just out of his reach.

When he's almost eaten two pieces of salmon and a whole fritter, he shakes his head. "If I eat any more, I'll go into a food coma and won't be able to move to get my fuckening on."

I put the fork down on the plate. "What makes you think you're allowed to move now? We're going to come to you."

Prescott releases himself and shoves the plate of food out of the way. Then he inches forward on his knees, settling in front of Brady. There's too big a gap and height difference for Prescott to feed Brady his cock, but Prescott is excellent at improvising.

"I'm going to jerk myself off and come all over your face. Unless you can catch it in your mouth."

Brady opens immediately, and the view is positively sinful. I can only take so much before I want to get in on the action. I shift my chair to the side so it's perpendicular to Brady's and run a hand up his thigh while working open my pants with the other.

Brady's quads are tense, and with the way his cock looks like it's trying to lift him off the seat, I'd guess his glutes are too. He's leaking everywhere.

I want to duck my head and suck on the red tip, but there's not enough room to maneuver between him and the table, so I give him the next best thing.

Gripping his cock with one hand, I stroke myself with the other. He's slick from precum, and I spread it over his tight, velvety skin. I spit in the hand that's working myself over for ease.

We're all so keyed up. Prescott is panting and jerking faster and faster. Brady looks like he's trying with all his energy to focus on Prescott and not on what my hand's doing. He trembles but keeps his mouth open, ready for Prescott's release.

And when it happens, the pleasure building in my balls, the heat in my gut … the look on Brady's face as Prescott comes all over his cheek, his chin, and he does manage to get some in his mouth … it's all too much.

My hands frantically work at getting Brady and me to the finishing line faster, and all it takes for me to let go is the warmth filling my hand when Brady lets out a curse and stiffens.

The room fills with the scent of cum and the sound of three heavy breaths. I release Brady and myself and sink back into my seat while I try to regain composure.

Prescott's the first to move, climbing down off the dining table and releasing Brady from his restraints.

As soon as he's free, Brady jumps up. "That was fun. When's the next round?"

Prescott turns to me. "We might have to take it in shifts to keep Brady satisfied."

I might be boneless. I might be spent. But that's not going to hold me back. "Challenge accepted."

CHAPTER NINE

I WATCH the water from my lounger on the terrace, cool wind whipping by, coffee in hand, the smell of salt and beach in the air. Kit really embodies a seal. Only this time, I'm not talking about the naval kind. At the ass crack of dawn, I heard him slip out of bed, and I knew exactly where he was going. I like sleep, and if I don't have to be on duty at a certain time, everyone knows they'll find me in bed, so I let him go and rolled over to cuddle Brady.

And two hours later, Kit's still swimming. I can see him from where I am, his strong arms coming out of the water to propel him forward. He swims out about half a mile and then comes back and repeats it. I didn't know it was possible to do laps in the Gulf of Mexico, but he's made it a thing.

I'm tempted to go out there and join him now that I've had a chance to wake up properly. I could sneak up on him and pretend to be a shark. But I still have coffee left, and as much as pretend drowning Kit sounds fun, I don't want to be sucked into his orbit again.

Him leaving hurt, and while there's a small part of me that hopes he'll be back on the West Coast in another year, I haven't had the guts to ask him. The average time serving in his position is two years before most SEALs ask to be reinstated to active duty because sitting behind a desk isn't the reason we joined the military, let alone endured BUD/s training. But from what little he said yesterday when

I first arrived, Kit seems happy where he is. I don't get it. I will never get it. I just need to accept that.

I was completely ready to cancel coming out here, and while things are kind of strained between us, Brady is holding us together. Plus, I have to admit, being around both Brady and Kit is like putting on a worn-in pair of combat boots. It's familiar and warm.

Movement comes from the corner of my eye, and I turn to find Brady behind me, stretching and yawning in the entryway. He's shirtless, only wearing his bright rainbow boxer briefs that hug his package in the right way. They're tight and show off every ridge.

"Morning." I reach for his waistband and pull him toward me by his underwear. When he's close enough, I pull him down on my lap.

Brady doesn't hesitate to lie back and use me like his own personal lounger, and I love that he has no hesitance when it comes to Kit and me.

"How'd you sleep?" I ask.

"The best I have in a long time." He snuggles in and rests his head on my chest. "Where's Kit?"

"Out there." I point with my free hand while I sip my coffee with the other.

"Ooh, is that coffee? For me? You shouldn't have." Brady takes my cup, and I let him. Doesn't mean I won't give him shit about it though.

"You do know Kit's the nurturing one, right? Steal a SEAL's coffee, you'll wake up at the bottom of the ocean tomorrow."

He's not intimidated even a little bit. "Any other SEAL maybe, but you'd never do that to me. Neither would Kit."

True, but I kiss the top of his head and mutter, "Smartass."

He settles in my arms, and it's a comfort I didn't even know I'd miss. Affection between the three of us has always been given freely, but there's something different about casually touching between rounds and doing it while hanging out.

It makes me want to be closer to him. Not just physically.

"Tell me, how are you really coping with law school?" I ask.

"Next question."

"No. Answer me. I remember being your age—"

"A billion years ago."

"Nine, fuck you very much. But my point is, being a SEAL was my dream for so long, but when I got it, it was fucking hard. Kit got me through it. We got each other through it, and in the end, it was worth it. Is being a sports agent worth it to you?"

I can't see his smile, but I can sense it.

"It will be. In the end. It's just shit because it's a lot of work. Like you, I've had this dream forever. It helps that my family ..." He tapers off like he always does when it comes to them.

"What's the story with them? Why are you so uptight whenever they're mentioned? Are they secretly assholes and that whole public persona is an act? Did they hit you as a child? Do you need Kit and I to pay them a visit?" I'm mostly joking. Although if he were to say yes, I'd be on the next plane to wherever they are and beat them to a pulp no matter who they are.

But Brady cracks up laughing. "Jesus, no. My dads are great, my brother is—"

"Only the most successful rookie in the NFL right now."

Brady groans. "No, you *can't* be a fan. *This* is why I don't talk about them and why I try to dissociate from them as much as I can."

I grin. "Is that why you're Brady T on all your socials?"

"Yep. Do you know how hard it is to have the last name Talon? I love my dads to death. I would do anything for them. But being their son is hard. It's next to impossible to know who's in my life for me and who's in it to get to them. Or my brother. And finding out at graduation that you and Kit had known the whole time who they were—"

"Come here," I say.

He hesitates.

"Brady. Come here." I'm sterner this time, and he immediately sits up to put the coffee cup on the side table, but when he lies back down, he turns so his front is pressed against mine.

We're face-to-face, and he's so close I want to kiss him instead of reassure him, but at the same time, I know what it's like to be over-shadowed by family.

My family is supportive of me and my choice to join the navy, but my siblings are what I'd call out of my league. I'm a lowly sailor wanting to serve my country. One brother is a doctor in the Doctors

Without Borders program, my other brother is a lawyer, and my sister is some high-up manager in corporate business. They moved from Hawaii to the mainland for college and never looked back. They're on six-figure salaries and live in penthouses. I live in an apartment the size of a shoebox that I'm struggling to make rent on now that Kit has moved out. I'm waiting for a one-bedroom to open up in the building so I can move into it.

It doesn't matter how supportive my family is when it feels too hard to measure up. I love my life, and I'm not ashamed of it, and my parents never make me feel like I'm the disappointing child, but on paper, I look like I don't measure up to my siblings. So I get where Brady is coming from.

"Your brother has got nothing on you," I say.

"Do you mean it?"

"Kit and I don't like football that much anyway." A tiny lie but well worth it.

Brady smiles, and I'll never get over how much I love putting that look on his face, but this is usually Kit's job, so I do what I do best. Deflect with comedy.

"Besides, your brother's taken, isn't he?"

Brady pushes up and slaps my chest with a thump. "Asshole."

"I'm kidding. I'm kidding. I'm not interested in your brother. Or your dads, for that matter."

"Why? They're closer to your age than I am."

I jab him in the ribs. "You little shit. It's only nine years. *Nine.*"

"Serves you right. Don't piss me off, Pres. You have no idea what I could do."

"You're so cute when you try to be threatening."

He crosses his arms and pouts.

"That whole innocent pretend-upset look might work on Kit but not on me. Sorry." But it does work. A little bit. "Okay, you gave me something real. What if I do the same?"

"It better be worth it," he warns.

I sit up and wrap my arms around his waist. His pout slowly dissolves as I move in closer. "I've missed you."

"Y-you have?" His brown eyes meet mine.

"More than I thought I would."

"Why? Can't you find another toy to play with in Coronado?"

"You're so much more to me than that. You're fun. You're hot as fuck. You're hilarious, and I love watching the way you have Kit wrapped around your little finger. I know this only on leave thing isn't ideal, but I'd like to think that outside of that, we're at least friends."

He averts his gaze now, looking guilty.

"What is it?" I ask. "What's wrong?"

"A few months ago, I was back in California for a few days for work, and I thought about contacting you to catch up—if you were even home—but then I thought that might be weird? A-are you saying if that happens again, I can come see you? And if I did, would it be like …" He waves a finger between us. "This? Or friends?"

That's a heavy question for which I don't have an answer. If he had contacted me during this past year, I wouldn't have hesitated to catch up with him if my schedule allowed it. But without Kit? Maybe it would have been awkward. "We never discussed that possibility last year, so maybe we should have that conversation with Kit."

Then again, Kit and Brady are only six hours apart. If anyone is going to meet up while we're not together, it would be those two. Would I feel left out if that happened? I can't really tell. I don't think I would, but I wouldn't know until I was in that position.

The truth is, outside of these meetups that I hope will continue, we haven't promised anything to each other. We're free to do whatever we want. And if I think about it deeply enough, no, I wouldn't mind if Kit and Brady found comfort in each other while we're apart.

It's only the thoughts of them being together and deciding they don't need me that fill me with insecurities. Which is stupid because I've never been an insecure guy before.

But Kit means the world to me, and Brady is … Brady. The thought of never seeing one of them again hurts more than I can bear. Even though we've been apart, there's always been that promise of seeing each other again. Having both of them shut me out completely? I don't think I could survive it.

I'm so lost in my thoughts of what-ifs that I don't see Kit until he's upon us.

"You two look cozy." He's dripping wet from head to toe, his rippling muscles on full display, and it makes my mouth water.

"You look wet," Brady says.

"I'm about to go get all this salt water off me in the shower if either or both of you care to join me."

Brady, of course, doesn't hesitate, and as I watch them go inside together, I try to picture it happening in the future without the option to follow them.

Damn it. This vacation wasn't supposed to be about deep thoughts and contemplations. It's all fun. Only fun. Nothing has changed, and there's no real future between the three of us.

Maybe I need to let whatever happens happen, and we can go from there.

It's not like I can be heartbroken from a hookup arrangement.

Right?

∞ ∞ ∞

Why is it that a weeklong training mission feels like a month, but a week on leave flies by in a blink?

We all need to get up to pack and head for the airport, but it's so warm in bed with both of them. We've spent the last seven days fucking Brady every which way we could think of, and he's come so many times I've started worrying for his health. Losing that much bodily fluid can't be safe, can it?

Me, on the other hand, I'm going to need a vacation from my vacation. I thought BUD/s training was hard. It's got nothing on the sexual stamina of Brady Talon. Okay, so maybe that's being overly dramatic, but I can't help it.

I'm dead tired, and if I could, I'd lie here for the next week and not move. It's a gut-warming emotion I don't get to experience often, but I'm … happy.

The warm and fuzzies disappear, though, when Kit reminds us, "We're going to miss our flights."

"I don't see a problem with that," Brady says and then grinds back against me.

I grip his hip hard. "We don't have time for that because someone promised we'd pack last night after he had his fill."

"And I'm still not full," Brady says.

"Will you ever be?" I murmur into the back of his neck.

"Of you two? Never."

And even though I thought it would be impossible to get hard again, Brady manages to get me there with just his words. Okay, and his hand reaching behind him to stroke me also helps.

I kiss his shoulder and thrust into his fist.

The bed shifts, and Kit stands. "You take care of him while I pack for all of us because I have no idea how this place managed to get so trashed."

I do: Brady. He's a mess. I find it funny, but that might have more to do with the way it makes Kit cringe.

Kit grabs a condom and lube on the nightstand and passes them to me.

"Are you sure?" I ask.

He nods. "I don't think I'll be able to get it up again until our next meet anyway. I'm spent."

Next meet. He wants this to happen again, and I already can't wait for it.

We haven't had the conversation yet about what's going to happen during this year—whether or not we're comfortable with meeting up separately—and I know time is running out to ask about it, but I haven't had the balls to bring it up. And Brady hasn't mentioned it again.

Brady whines, grinding against me some more. "Hurry up. Ugh, next year, I'm making us all get a blood panel done so we don't have to waste time with condoms. I need it, and I need it now."

The thought of going bare with both of them … fuck, I want that. The navy regularly tests us, but we've never really spoken to Brady about his history, and now's not the time to do it. So instead, I roll the condom down my shaft, cover it in lube, and say, "Next year," before I push inside him slowly.

By some miracle, I'm hard, but I don't know how long that'll last. All I need to do is last long enough for Brady to get off. I'm basically ruling out any chance of me coming again. I've lost count at how many orgasms I'm up to over the week, but it's been more than I ever thought possible in such a short window of time.

Even though he's still stretched, the lube is only on my dick, so it's tight when I slide in deeper. He squeezes around me and shudders.

"I'm suddenly regretting volunteering to pack," Kit rumbles from somewhere behind us.

"Does it really matter if we all miss our flights?" I ask, my voice breathless and heavy.

"Well, you might be charged with desertion if you're late to report back to port."

"Don't remind me."

Brady reaches behind him and pushes my ass so I sink inside him further. "Less talking, more fucking."

I slam inside, losing myself in him, and the frantic sounds of Kit throwing things in bags are drowned out by Brady's needy moans. Our bodies come together over and over again. I'm desperate for it to last, but at the same time, he needs to come soon because as much as I'd love to stay inside him all day, Kit's right. I can't miss my flight. I run my hand down his chest and wrap my fingers around his hard cock.

"Brady," I croak, the impatient tone giving him warning.

"I'm close."

"What do you need?" I whisper.

"I need … need …" He's even closer than I thought. He needs that extra push.

"Kit?" I ask. "You need Kit?"

"Yes," he hisses. "Please."

"I'm on it." Kit climbs back onto the bed in front of Brady. He bats my hand away and swallows Brady's dick.

I slow my thrusts because I know with every single one, Brady will move inside Kit's mouth, but then Kit and I lock eyes, and he gives me an almost imperceptible nod, but I get it. We still have that nonverbal communication from when we were on the same SEAL team.

Working together, I let loose on Brady's ass while Kit takes all of it. And watching him, watching Brady's cock slip between Kit's lips, it feels like Kit's mouth is wrapped around my own dick.

Where I didn't think it was possible, when Brady tenses, his ass tightening around me while he fills Kit's mouth, it's all over for me too. The sight of Brady's cum slipping down Kit's chin is what does it. It hits suddenly but softly. Instead of a rush, it's a slow burn. Warmth and satisfaction wash over me until I slump and roll onto my back.

My dick slips from Brady's ass, but he doesn't move. Kit's the only one who still has any energy.

He stands from the bed and goes back to packing, throwing clothes at us in the process. "Get dressed."

In unison, both Brady and I let out a long whine and then laugh.

I go to the bathroom and take care of the condom, wash my face, brush my teeth, and then reluctantly head back into the bedroom to throw my clothes on.

Brady hasn't moved from his spot.

I poke his back with my big toe. "Did I kill you?"

"Yep. Can't. Move. And unlike you, it doesn't matter if I miss my flight."

"But do you really want to be here on your own?" I ask.

That gets him moving. He sits up. "No. One week wasn't enough."

I glance between Kit and Brady and agree. "One week will never be enough."

The mood takes a dive really fast. I get the sense Brady won't bring up what we spoke about, so I take it upon myself to do it.

"Hey, Kit? Brady and I were talking about possibly meeting up outside of … this arrangement."

Kit's gaze flits between the both of us. "Just the two of you?"

I run my words back over in my head and realize the mistake. "No. Well, maybe. But we mean—"

"Any of us," Brady says. "Over the summer, I was in LA, but I wasn't sure what Prescott would think if I turned up at his apartment unannounced. Or how you'd feel if I saw him without you."

"And you two are only six hours apart," I add. "We didn't discuss what the rules would be if we found ourselves in the same town." I know Kit had been to Coronado, but both times, I was on a training mission so didn't get to see him.

It doesn't seem to be as easy a decision as it was for Brady and me, and I get the impression Kit's holding something back.

Eventually, he agrees. "If that's what you both want."

"Is it what you want?" I ask.

"I didn't actually think about it until now. I mean, when I was sent to Coronado, I thought I'd see you, but I didn't think it would have been like …" He points in a triangle to each of us. "This. But if you two want to do that, then I guess it's okay. It might be a little weird because our deal up until now has always been about the three of us, but I think as long as we all communicate about it, it'll be fine. And if any of us are uncomfortable with it, we speak up."

"Deal." Brady jumps up and goes over to Kit to kiss him.

Kit's the one to pull back. He slaps Brady's ass. "Get dressed already, and stop trying to delay us."

"If you want me to go faster, spanking me isn't the way to do it."

The little shithead bends over, picking up the clothes on the bed with a dramatic bend in his back so his ass sticks out, but Kit has willpower of steel. He doesn't take the bait.

"Fine." Brady straightens but then pauses. "Wait. These are navy sweats. Where are my clothes?"

Kit rubs the back of his neck. "They could be in Prescott's stuff for all I know. I just threw everything in the closest bag."

"Mine now." Brady goes commando and pulls on my sweats. "I'm military, bitches."

"That's cute," I say. Though he does look amazing in my clothes. It's like he's branded in *us*. By us.

The way Kit's eyes darken with lust, I'd say he finds Brady way more than cute. He has such a soft spot when it comes to Brady, and it's hot as fuck watching him check the time on his phone, sigh, and step forward to kiss the tip of Brady's nose. Like he doesn't have the time to give that little bit of affection but does it anyway.

I love seeing that softer side of him, and I long for him to direct it my way. This week has been amazing, but there's not just physical distance between Kit and me anymore. There's a wall between us that's been there since he left California.

I want to tear it down, but I'm too scared to see what's on the other side of it: the real reason he left. Why things are normal between us but different at the same time. It's like we're playing our roles the way we think they should be played.

"Let's get out of here," Kit says.

Here comes the hard part.

I'm walking away with not only the knowledge I'm not going to see either of them for a long time but also with the regret that all week, I haven't had the guts to call Kit on his distant crap.

But if I do it, he might take away any opportunity for this to happen again, and I'd rather have him like this than not at all.

While I'm getting dressed, Kit does one last check around the hotel room to make sure we have everything, but when we go to walk out the door, he stops and blocks our path.

His gaze flicks between Brady and me, and then his big arms swallow us both whole. "I know we were happy about getting flights leaving at relatively the same time because it means we could go to the airport together, but I'm now realizing the downfall of that plan."

I hold on to him, taking every inch of affection he's willing to give me. "What's that?"

"We're not going to have the goodbye I want."

Brady pulls back. "You literally just had the chance to take my ass."

Kit cradles the back of Brady's head. "That's not what I had in mind. This isn't about … that."

"What's it about?" I ask.

"It's about this." His grip around us tightens. "Us. The world is still trying to fully accept two men kissing in public. Three? Forget about it. I know we don't have the time, and—"

"I don't care about the time," Brady whispers. "I'd take a later flight, stay longer, call in sick to work, and put off my law degree if it meant I got five more minutes with each of you."

"I can't say goodbye." I shake my head. "I'm not ready. This week was …"

"I want more of this week. Which is why we should get it out of our system now so that when we get to the airport, we can act like it's not goodbye but see you soon. I need to trick my brain into thinking this will happen again." Kit's gray eyes plead with me to reassure him.

"This has to happen again," I say. Because this can't be it between us. It just can't.

Do I really think this arrangement is sustainable? No.

Do I want it to be? Hell yes.

"We'll make it happen," I say more confidently this time.

The pleading in Kit's eyes melts into relief, and then he gives me that softness I've been craving all week. He tilts his head and leans in, touching his lips with mine gently. We're risking being late, and he's kissing me.

"I believe you," Kit says.

"So do I." Brady wraps his arm around my back. We're all physically connected, breathing as one.

I want to see them again, no doubt. For a day, a week, a month. The only problem with that is each time we make it happen, this has to happen as well.

The goodbyes.

What goes up must come down.

All hellos morph into goodbyes.

THE CALENDAR HAS NEVER MOVED SO

SLOWLY. It's only a couple of weeks later, when I'm having sleepy and sexy thoughts of Prescott and Kit in bed, that my phone vibrates with Prescott's name on the screen. I get excited thinking he's calling to arrange our next meetup already until I answer it.

Before I can even say hello, a slurred voice fills my ear. "You ruined me for all other college dudes!"

I grin. "I'm failing to see the problem here."

"The problem is I'm not getting laaaaaid."

Again, not a problem for me. While we know we're not exclusive, I'm not going to lie and say I like the idea of Pres or Kit with someone else.

"I probably should have warned you of the side effects of sleeping with me. Might cause lack of interest in others. No one will ever compare. Once you have me, you're hooked."

"You're definitely my drug of choice."

"But I'm much healthier. Sex is good for you."

"Not if you're not getting it." There's a loud bang.

"What was that?"

"I couldn't get my front door open, so I threw my shoe at it."

I laugh. "How drunk are you?"

"Drunk enough to try to open my door with my shoe. What does that tell you?"

"It tells me that this once-a-year thing isn't enough. Or that maybe Kit stopped you from doing stupid shit when he lived with you."

There's a softer thump this time. "I think it's both."

"Did you make it inside your place, or are you slumped against your door?"

"I'm in. Apparently, keys work better than shoes."

"Who would've thought that?"

"Right?" Prescott lets out a loud breath. "I hate that you and Kit are on the other side of the country."

I debate whether I should admit how much I hate it too.

"I get it," he slurs some more. "Well, not so much Kit, but with you it makes sense. Even if you could've done your grad program in California. I understand the interning for your uncle thing. Kit's thing doesn't make sense. I hate it. And maybe I didn't realize how much until Florida."

"I know. I hate it too."

"Have you managed to meet up with Kit at all yet?"

"Nope. He's always busy."

"So you have talked, then."

"Texted."

Prescott goes silent.

"Did you pass out?" I ask.

"No, I'm here. On my couch. Drunk. Horny."

I groan. "My favorite kind of Prescott."

"You know what my favorite kind of Brady is?"

"Naked?"

"Well, yeah, that helps, but you know what I was thinking?"

"You're drunk. Will any of your thoughts make sense?"

"While I was out there tonight, meeting guys and trying to find someone to hook up with, not one of them said anything real."

I roll over in bed, facing the empty spot beside me. "What do you mean? From memory, the night we met, I asked for a threesome, we fucked, and then I went home."

"Yeah, but it was different. You were so ... so ..."

"Hot?"

"Nooo."

"I wasn't hot?"

He grunts, and I can totally see him pulling a frustrated expression where a line appears in his forehead. "You know what I mean. It was different with you."

I want to believe that so much, but there's one obvious factor he's not considering. "Could it be that you miss Kit? I know I wasn't the first guy you two took home. Maybe dumb college guys back then were more appealing because going home with one of them meant you got to be with him too."

"Ergh. Don't even go there."

"Why not?"

"Because he left. It's whatever. I'm dealing with it."

"Sure sounds like it," I say. I've always made it a point not to get in between Prescott and Kit's relationship, but Prescott sounds so heartbroken. I don't even know if he's aware of it. His dismissive "whatever" is very telling. He doesn't want to show how much it hurts.

"Enough about me. Talk to me about you. How's work and school and—"

"Exhausting, but I appreciate you asking." I yawn and finally look at the time. "Fuck, it's 3:00 a.m."

"Oh shit. Time difference. Sorry, I forgot."

"Kind of easy to when you're that trashed."

"I'll let you go."

"I want to keep talking, but I need to be up in two hours to get into the office and catch up on admin work before classes."

"Can … uh …" Prescott hesitates.

"Can what?"

"Can I call you again? But sober?"

Will being in contact with Prescott make missing him and Kit better or worse? I'm not sure. But I do know I like hearing from him, and after we end this call, I'm going to go back to sleep with a huge smile on my face.

"Please call me again."

"I will."

∞ ∞ ∞

Time after that night does seem to move quicker, and I can only thank Prescott's and my phone calls for it. Months and months of sporadic phone calls is getting me through. But the truth is, the longer that passes, the more times Kit's too busy to meet up or joins one of the phone calls only to cut it short, I get the impression Kit's pulling away from us.

I understand Kit's connection to Prescott is deep and that he moved to Virginia because he's in love with Pres, but I feel like Kit's punishing me, too, by trying to avoid Prescott.

Prescott called a couple of nights ago to say that Kit was going to be in Coronado this week sometime. He asked me if I could get a day or two to fly back and see them, but it's impossible because work is kicking my ass.

I'm currently in Philly with Uncle Damon at a photoshoot for Kelley Afton, the latest rising MLB star to break down that closet door, who looks like he's about to puke.

"I'm nervous." Sure, he can stand on that pitcher's mound and look cool, calm, and collected. He can strike out the best hitters in the league and not break a sweat, but a simple photoshoot is too much for him.

In his defense, all he's wearing is baseball pants, cleats, and a baseball cap. Plus, I don't think it's the actual photoshoot that he's worried about but the aftermath that's coming.

Though, it shouldn't be a surprise to many when this news comes out. While King Sports has a diverse range of clients, it's known for being the agency queer athletes want to sign with, and that's because my uncle has spent his entire career advocating for people who identify as LGBTQIA in this industry. Not only athletes but others like me—the ones who work behind the scenes. The majority of people who work here are queer because they know it's a safe space for them. King Sports is the ultimate agency for queer people in sports.

"It's a nerve-racking situation," I say.

Uncle Damon turns to me and cocks an eyebrow because I'm supposed to be silent while I'm here. I'm his shadow. I'm learning how he does things.

I shrug. "I know you said to be quiet and be invisible, but I'm just empathizing with the guy. Taking this step is a big deal because it's so hard to know how people are going to react. It's a statistical fact that when an athlete comes out, ticket sales to their games and social media follows drop, while attention in the media increases."

"Fuck, really?" Kelley asks. "Maybe I shouldn't do this. I shouldn't, should I? I'm making a huge mistake."

Uncle Damon hangs his head. "And this is why you were supposed to pretend to be invisible."

"I'm not finished yet," I say and step closer to Kelley. "But everything I just said? It's temporary. Because once your story is told, it's done, and after everyone has talked about it, had their say, they move on. You killed it your rookie season, and now is the time to do it—while you have time off and aren't in the spotlight where the media can rip into your playing. Then, in a few months when everything has settled down, instead of being the nervous wreck you are, you'll be free. No more worrying about when the right time is. No more fear over who will find out. This is it. You do this, you get through it any way you can—I've heard hiding in a cabin without TV or internet access is a great way to hide for a while—and then when all the news blows over, that's when you can relax and enjoy your life. Because everyone in the queer community deserves that."

Kelley's shoulders sag in relief, color returns to his cheeks, and he manages a smile before turning to my uncle. "If I do have to go hide in the woods, can I at least take your intern with me to talk me down from future panic attacks?"

"We're ready for you," someone calls out on set, and Kelley sucks in a deep breath.

He mutters under his breath, "I can do this, I can do this," and then puts on a confident mask and struts into the studio as if he wasn't about to walk out two minutes ago.

"That was impressive," Uncle Damon says to me. "A little too panic-inducing for me, but you might make a great agent yet."

"Might? Only might?"

Uncle Damon laughs. "Hey, you're still green, and I haven't been able to teach you everything I know yet."

"How long until you let me run on my own?"

"How long until you finish that law degree?"

Ugh. Another year and a half.

Uncle Damon's hand lands on my shoulder. "I know it might feel like I'm holding you back sometimes, but I'm actually not. If anything, you've got more responsibility than any of the other interns."

I snort. "Yeah, you actually let me talk to the athletes."

He scowls. "No, I tell you to be invisible like everyone else, but you don't listen to me."

"I would never go against your word, Uncle Damon. You're my favorite fake uncle out of all my fake uncles."

Uncle Damon turns back to focus on Kelley on set. "So much like your fathers," he says under his breath.

I grin at him even if I'm not sure he can see it. Being compared to my famous dads in this instance doesn't get to me like it used to. Growing up and playing football with my brother, we absolutely hated when we'd be compared to the great Marcus Talon and Shane Miller. But being told my attitude is exactly like them, I'll wear that like a badge of honor because even though they're embarrassing, they're two of the best people on the planet.

Uncle Damon represented them both when they were in the NFL, and they were some of his first-ever clients, so they were really close. They still are. I refer to Damon as my uncle because we were raised that way.

We watch while Kelley's put through different poses, but while an assistant comes out to oil his chest more, my phone dings in my pocket.

"You better not be thinking about taking that phone out here," Uncle Damon says.

"What if it's Torey? He might need his agent." And yeah, I'm still stuck with the entitled football player after scoring him a spot on Chicago's training squad. I'm sure it had everything to do with his talent and nothing to do with my dad winning a billion Super Bowl championships for the team back in the day.

Uncle Damon had said that I can't send all my football players to Chicago as easy as that, and one day my clout with the team won't carry my career, but I think he's just pissed that I succeeded with my first-ever client without trying very hard.

Uncle Damon stares at me. "Is it Torey?"

I take out my phone, and there in my notifications is a photo of Prescott and Kit shirtless and smiling at the camera with the text message underneath it saying, *What should we get up to while you're not here? Have time for a video call?*

Fuck. It's been a little over six months since we met up in Florida, but it feels like three years. I'm ready to see them again. In person. This is so not fair.

As quickly as I can, I hide the screen from my uncle, but I'm not fast enough. He at least sees the pic because he says, "Who are the guys in the photo?"

Here would be a good time to come up with a lie, but all I can think to say as I put my phone back in my pocket is, "Porn alert. My favorite couple posted a new video."

Because telling your uncle you watch porn isn't as embarrassing as saying, "The guys who love to rail me any chance they get."

Which in the past six months has been zero times. I've been begging them for the past three, at least, but their schedules never aligned, and the one time we might have been able to manage it, I had exams.

Prescott suggested Kit and I catch up to, in his words, "Scratch Brady's itch," but apparently, people who work for the Pentagon can't just disappear to have a fuckfest.

Kit was apologetic and called National Security stupid.

I had to agree. How dare the government want to protect us all.

But now they're together, and I'm not there. Does it hurt? A little, but only because of FOMO, not because I'm jealous. And a part of me is even happy that if I'm not getting it from them, at least they can be together.

"That's an overshare," Uncle Damon says. "I don't need to know what you're into. To me, you're still six years old and running around with Peyton and daydreaming about being in the NFL together."

"Ah, six-year-old me had no idea how much he'd grow up to

resent football." My phone tries to burn a hole in my leg. I want to reply. I want to video call. But I can't. Not here.

"Do you really resent it?" Uncle Damon asks. "Would you rather not represent football players?"

"No, I love football, you know I do, but I resented the pressure of living in my dads' shadows. I like being behind the scenes. I like being invisible."

"Except when I ask you to be?" Uncle Damon asks, and I laugh.

"Something like that."

"I'm going to hit the restroom. Don't burn down anything while I'm gone." He walks away, but I call after him.

"I haven't set a fire since I was six. You have to realize I'm grown-up now."

He shakes his head but keeps walking, and the minute he's out of sight, I pull out my phone and text:

I hate you guys. I'm at work and can't video call. Please, please, please send me photos though. Make them hot.

And for the rest of the day, every time my phone vibrates, I don't dare take it out of my pocket.

I'll save that for when I'm home.

CHAPTER ELEVEN

HE'S ALL OVER ME. His hands, his mouth. I'm lost somewhere in a world between euphoria and heartache. Because this is the first time Prescott and I have ever been with each other. Alone.

It's better and worse than I ever thought it would be.

He's on his back, splayed out for me while I move inside him, and even though he's got his phone in his hand, taking photos of my cock inside his tight hole, I don't care. Because for some reason, and completely unexpectedly, I'm excited to include Brady in on this.

It's hard to believe Prescott and I had never fooled around solo before, but it makes sense. Before, we had to find loopholes to fuck because of our positions at work, but now that's not a factor. We don't have that restriction anymore.

All Prescott has to do is breathe in my vicinity, and I drown in my feelings for him. No matter how long goes by between seeing Prescott, no matter how many first dates I have in Virginia without wanting a second, nothing can break this hold he has over me. Except for maybe Brady. I thought if this ever happened—if I had the opening to be with Prescott and only Prescott, the only thing I'd be able to focus on is him, but Brady's at the forefront of my mind.

I might have made the excuse to call him so I'd have a reason to pounce on Prescott, but when he said he was unavailable, I was genuinely disappointed. Just like the one time he tried to catch up with me and I was too busy with work.

Thinking about what Brady would be doing if he was here with us right now, I've never been so tuned to someone else while being with Prescott—not even when they're in the same room, kissing me.

Brady's thousands of miles away, and yet to me, he's right here with us.

"We should go into the porn industry," Prescott pants.

"You should, maybe." I slow down to admire his body. "People would go nuts for these abs." I trail my fingers over his delicious skin and down to his prominent V.

"You mean, they'd *nut* over these abs."

I laugh. "That too."

"If I'd known mentioning porn would slow you down, I would've kept my mouth shut." He writhes beneath me.

"Just a sec. Give me the phone."

He passes it over to me with the camera app open, and I hold it above me with my head back. I blindly hit the button, the fake shutter sound clicks, and then I look at it.

"Okay, you're right. This is pretty fucking hot." I show him.

At the angle I took it, it's a photo straight down my hard muscles with Prescott under me, the mushroom head of my cock lined up with his hole.

"It's good to have backup careers." He hits a few buttons. "Okay, I think we've given enough spank bank material for Brady. I need you to finish me off."

With pleasure.

And even though I'm getting every single thing I've ever wanted —the very thing I thought would complete me—there's something missing.

No, not something.

Someone.

I miss the fuck out of Brady.

⊗ ⊗ ⊗

"We have to make another time to catch up with Brady." I pour us protein shakes while Prescott recovers. He's moved from the bed to the couch, but that's all he's managed so far. Well, that and going through and analyzing every photo we took.

"That's all you have to say?" Prescott turns from his spot. "Not, wow, this is amazing art and we should blow it up and hang it for everyone to see? Look at this one. It was before we'd even got really started, but it's hot as fuck." He holds up his phone, and I can see from here that it's one he took of me on my knees, looking up at him while running my tongue along his cock.

I put the blender in the sink. "You just want to have a photo where your dick takes up an entire wall."

"You know me so well."

Well, I used to. I have no idea what Prescott has been up to these last two years since. I mean, I see what he's doing at work, thanks to my job, but his private life has been that—private. I almost don't want to ask him because I'm scared of the answer, but I miss him.

I miss our friendship. And I figure after what we just did, I have some kind of right to ask.

I take our shakes over and sit next to him. "What have you been doing during your downtime?"

"A little of this. A little of that."

"Is this and that a hot fellow sailor and a hot, young college student from the Franklin U campus?"

He waves me off. "Nah. College students are so needy. Were they always that needy?"

"Brady's needy," I point out. I happen to love it about him because I like feeling wanted and useful.

"Not like these guys. Brady's needy because he likes the attention of who he's with to be on him. He couldn't give a fuck if no one else saw him with us. He actually likes that we're a secret. One guy I tried to take home from Bottoms Up wanted to show me off to his friends first and kept delaying getting out of there. It's like he wanted everyone to know he was with a SEAL."

"Oh no, everyone wants me," I wail.

He shoves me, and I barely manage to keep my drink in its glass.

"You know what I'm talking about, and I think, in a way, so does Brady."

"Yeah, I do." I tell people I'm navy but leave out the SEAL part. "But how so with Brady?"

"Well, you know how he was super sketchy about talking about his family when we met and how disappointed he was when he found out at his graduation that we knew exactly who he was?"

I nod.

"I spoke to him in Florida about it, and he doesn't like people knowing who he is because he'll always be an NFL legend's son. Or brother. Peyton is one of the biggest players right now—the next GOAT. We think we have it bad for being a SEAL. Brady's family is *famous*. Which is why he's different than other college-aged guys. Because while they want attention from everyone to show off, Brady wants attention for being himself. Not who his family is."

Damn, if that doesn't make me want to fly to wherever Brady is and give him a hug. "You got all of that from one conversation about his family?"

Prescott breaks eye contact with me and glances away. It's something he does when he thinks he's in trouble or knows he's done something wrong.

"What is it?" I ask. "What are you hiding?"

"Well … it hasn't been one conversation. Brady and I … talk."

"You talk?"

"On the phone. It started a couple of months ago after another failed attempt at taking someone home. I drunkenly called him and said he'd ruined for me all other college boys."

I try not to let the sting show. "To be fair, you are getting older, and college guys are getting younger."

"That doesn't make sense. They're not getting younger, but I *am* getting older, and young guys don't do it for me anymore. I think I'm … Growing up? Ergh. Kill me now."

"You're only about fifteen years too late, but I'm so glad you finally hit adulthood."

"I'm proud of me too."

Silence falls, and as I guzzle down my shake, I can't help thinking about Prescott, Brady, and their phone calls.

Both our phones sound at the same time, and while that could've been work related when we lived together and were on the same SEAL team, it can only be one person now.

We smile at each other and both say, "Brady."

Prescott's phone is beside him, so he grabs it, and we share his screen. As suspected, it's our group chat, and seeing that Brady texted both of us, it eases the doubt that tried to take root over their friendship outside of our arrangement.

He opens the message, and there's a video attached with the caption: *Look what you made me do at work! I'd planned not to look and I failed.*

And when Prescott presses Play, we're rewarded with a quick ten-second clip of Brady's hand jerking his amazing cock in what looks like a bathroom stall. If it were me, I would've stopped recording before the money shot to be a big ol' tease, but Brady's too nice to tease, and when cum explodes all over his hand and some on the bathroom stall wall, my cock tries to get back up again but can't. Prescott's is still down for the count too, even though he lets out a groan of want and licks his lips as he watches the video again.

"Question," I say. "Why did you think I'd be mad that you and Brady have been talking? Not gonna lie, it … well, no, it doesn't sting, but I guess …" *I miss talking to you too. Yeah, don't say that.* "You and I just had sex without Brady. You guys are allowed to talk—"

Prescott puts his phone on the coffee table and turns to me. "I dunno. Since you moved across the country, it's not like you were returning my phone calls, so I stopped calling. And with Brady, we can talk like we used to when we lived together."

I wish I could tell him why I stopped taking his calls—I thought that space, this new position, and three thousand miles would make the longing hurt less—but I can't do that without putting it all out there, and what the hell good would that do? It's the same internal fight every single time. The same problems. They're not going away with distance.

"I miss living with you, if that's any consolation."

"When are you going to return to active duty already? Come hoooome."

I rub my jaw. "I, uh, I've actually been offered a promotion."

"I don't care if you come back with a higher rank than me and you get to boss me around."

"It's a civilian leader in charge of training operations at the Pentagon."

"Whoa, wait. Civilian? You're leaving the navy altogether? Why? How is that a promotion?"

"Because it's a lot more money. And I like Virginia."

Prescott mock gasps. "You bite your tongue. No West Coast boy is allowed to like the East Coast. I'm offended on behalf of all your people."

Hey, if he's joking, at least he's not yelling at me for wanting to stay where I am.

"It's a good opportunity for me," I say.

He grits his teeth. "Then I'm happy for you."

"Yeah, you're really selling that. Look, I miss you too, but it's not like we're … It's not … you know …" My throat goes dry.

"It's not like we're what? Friends anymore? Yeah, you've made that clear." Prescott stands, but I grab hold of his forearm.

"That's not it. I miss you, I do. I miss hanging out with you, talking to you whenever I want, being with you and shooting the shit. I've missed all of that more than I've missed the sex."

He huffs and slumps back down onto the couch. "My dick is offended."

"What if I make it up to him with another blowjob?"

"Damn it," he whines. "I want to say yes, but little Pres isn't cooperating."

"Next time, then."

He turns to me, his deep brown gaze cutting through me. "Which will be when exactly? You have to head back to port soon, don't you?"

"In about an hour. Then it's straight back to Virginia. I don't know when I'll be back here on official business, but are you able to apply for some leave coming up? I'm thinking that maybe because Brady missed out this time, we could go surprise him in New York when—"

"Yes," Prescott says immediately. "But it has to be soon. We don't know when our next deployment is, but rumors are it'll be in the next two months."

"I've heard … similar."

"Let me guess, from top secret Pentagon people, so you can't tell me even though it has everything to do with me."

I touch my nose.

"I hate the military sometimes. It sucks that the higher-ups know our fate, but they don't warn us or brief us until the very last minute. It's like they make plans for our lives without so much as acknowledging we're human beings. We're just a number to them."

"How dare they protect national security by not telling every single solider their plans!"

He gives me the stink eye, and I laugh.

"I do get what you're saying, but it's a developing situation, and we might not even be needed yet."

"You forget you're not part of that *we* anymore. Or you won't be when you start your new job." He shakes his head. "I still can't believe you're leaving the military. I might complain about it, but I can't see myself doing anything else. Ever. We were supposed to be career, man."

"Sometimes dreams change."

"What's your *dream* now?" It's hard to miss the sarcasm in his emphasis of the word *dream*. "To find a man and settle down and …" Prescott screws up his face. "Have a real relationship for once?"

He mocks the idea, but it's exactly what I want. "Is it so much to ask that I want to find someone who wants to be with me and share their life with me?" *Who won't let me move across the country because they can't stand to live without me?* "I want someone to love me so much they couldn't walk away if they tried."

"Why do you need to leave the navy for that?"

"You know how hard it is to keep people interested when you up and go for months at a time. You're always away on training ops or real ops, you can't talk about it with your partners, and it's an all-round lonely life. The only people you have is your team, and I don't even have that anymore." I hold up my hand to stop him from cutting me off and saying I could have it back if I asked for my old post. "I'm ready to leave the navy, Pres. I'm ready to grow up."

Prescott looks as heartbroken as I feel whenever I'm with him.

CHAPTER TWELVE

IT'S ONLY a short two weeks later, in the middle of Kit and me trying to work out when we can surprise Brady, that there's a group text from him:

I know this is last-minute and most likely not plausible, but I've been sent on assignment to babysit an athlete who wants to hide from the media for a while after coming out, so I'm in the Catskills, at a semi-private resort, and I would really, really love it if you could join me here. Even if it's only for a couple of nights. One night. I can't stop thinking about those photos you sent me, and I need to see you both again.

Kit is the first to respond. *You're in a cabin in the woods with a queer athlete? Sounds to me like you could have your own fun.*

I grin at the text, but only because I know Kit's not being dismissive. He's asking flat out if Brady is involved with this other guy.

Brady replies: *He's a client. My uncle might love me, but he's not above firing me.*

And then it's followed by a stream of taunting messages from him.

Even if this guy is hot.

Bulky for a baseball player.

Accidentally walked in on him in the shower, and let me just say baseball pants, as tight as they are, still hide how sexy his ass is.

Oh, did I mention I also have a fellow intern here too? He's your all-American type of blond-haired ex-athlete. Also gay. Two guys. Neither of who I can fuck unless I want to be fired. What's a boy to do?

My phone starts ringing, and unsurprisingly, it's Kit.

"Can you swing it?" he asks as soon as I answer.

"I probably can. Hold up."

I pull the phone away from my ear and open the text chain and type: *How long are you there for?*

He answers immediately. *Two weeks.*

I put the phone back to my ear. "I should be able to get a couple of days off next week. Everyone knows deployment is coming sometime in a couple of months, so I'd have to figure out what days might be approved, seeing as everyone wants to go see their families and shit."

"We should do it," Kit says.

"And this has everything to do with Brady and nothing at all to do with the two guys he's being forced to spend two weeks holed up in a cabin with?"

"Hey, we might not have rules for when we're apart, but we were trying to plan to go see him, and if two guys are going to make him come, it should be us. For his job's sake. Plus, we'd be better at it than some stupid athletes. We're SEALs."

"Correction, I'm a SEAL. You're ex-navy."

"Not yet, I'm not. My answer is yes. I don't care how we figure it out, we're going to New York."

Turns out, Kit might have a possessive streak I didn't know about. He's dominant, yes. Likes to call the shots. But possessive? Not over anyone I've seen. It makes sense in a way because he loves to feel needed. And right now, Brady needs us.

∞ ∞ ∞

"Why is it so freezing?" I complain as soon as the airport sliding glass doors open and spit us out onto the sidewalk.

"Because we're in Albany in November? It's not even snowing. You've endured training and missions in colder weather than this."

"Not recently," I grumble.

Kit wraps his arm around my shoulders. "Think of how warm all three of us will be later."

I can't wait to have Brady in our arms again. It's been seven months since we last saw him in person, and even though I loved every second of my meetup with Kit, having Brady there only would've amplified it.

We order a ride share and make our way to the pickup area, and Kit laughs at me while I jump up and down from the cold. I can see my breath when I exhale, so I'm not being as dramatic as Kit thinks I am.

The place Brady booked is a cabin over an hour away, and we'd contemplated renting a car, but the way Brady explained it is there's nowhere really to go anyway. The whole point of the trip is for his client to be in the middle of nowhere, which is why they've booked summer cabins this close to winter. Because no one else is stupid enough to be here in November.

Except us.

"Brady's lucky he's hot, that's all I'm saying," I say as our ride arrives.

Kit throws our bags in the trunk. "And funny."

I open the passenger door. "And fun."

As we list off all the things we like about Brady, it hits even harder than before. Fuck, I've missed him. And Kit.

I saw Kit last month, but it's not enough.

On the drive, I can't help myself. I reach over and put my hand on top of his. The driver either doesn't notice, doesn't care, or is too scared to be a homophobic dick to two guys who could easily kick his scrawny ass.

It might not be snowing yet, but it looks like the sky isn't going to hold out for long.

By the time we pull into the resort entrance, outside is dark, and light flurries float to the ground.

Brady's already checked in for us and gave us a cabin number, so we bypass the lobby and reception desk and walk down the narrow path, following the arrows to our cabin.

"Still cold?" Kit asks.

I shiver. Yes, I'm still fucking cold. "There better be a fire. And a million blankets."

"I'll build you a fire, and it looks like our own personal blanket is up ahead." Kit nods to a shadowy figure standing on the porch of one of the cabins.

The flurries are getting heavier now, and as the shadow moves, Brady steps into the light from the posts lining the walkway.

At the sight of him, an emotion I can't place overwhelms me, and for some reason, I want to run to him and break down and cry at the same time. I don't understand it, and I don't have the time to decipher it because I was only allowed three days away. Three nights. That's all we get.

Brady runs toward us, his gaze flicking between Kit and me.

Kit points to me. "He needs it more than me. He's freezing."

Brady jumps into my arms as I drop my bag to the wet ground, but instead of kissing me senseless, he leans over and pulls Kit toward us, pressing his warm lips against Kit's cold ones.

Brady has his legs wrapped around my waist, my hands are supporting his ass, and as I watch him and Kit make out, the coldness seeps from my bones and is replaced with a fire that only burns when I'm with them.

I lean in and suck on Brady's neck.

He pulls away from Kit, murmuring, "I need your mouth too."

I lift my head, and he kisses me. Instead of it feeling like he hasn't kissed me in years, it's like he's kissing me as if he'll never get to do it again. He throws himself into everything, doesn't give up, and he's so damn passionate.

The way he kisses, the way he fucks, all the way down to his chosen profession and his family. He might not like talking about his family, but it's obvious they mean a lot to him. Brady knows what's important. He makes us a priority in his life, which lets me know that he cares about us way more than he should. Way more than we agreed on.

But that's okay because I'm starting to suspect I feel the exact same way.

"Where's your client?" Kit asks, making Brady break the kiss.

I've never hated Kit more.

"He's with the other intern Thad. I told them I was going to go to reception to ask for firewood."

"How long does that give you? Five minutes?" I trace my lips over his cheek and down his neck. "That doesn't give me nearly enough time to do what I want to do to you."

Brady shivers. "Nah, I told Kelley I needed a break from Thad, and I told Thad I needed a break from work and then said to both of them I was going to get the firewood. I have until at least dinner."

"You're a genius," Kit says.

"No, I'm horny, and I've missed you guys, so take me to bed already."

He doesn't need to ask us twice.

brady

PRESCOTT'S certainly not complaining about being cold now.

We're a naked pile of intertwined limbs, sweat, and cum. The only sounds to fill the room are our heavy breaths and the crackling fireplace that I lit before the guys got here.

I could stay like this forever. In their arms. Happy.

"Didn't you say something about having to be back for dinner?" Kit asks.

No. I don't want to think about that. I want to bask in this. In this moment.

I asked them to be here for me, and they came. I thought it was a long shot. I didn't think it was possible. When I asked them, I was fully prepared for them to say they can't get away. I would've understood. But this … this means so much to me. And now that I've got the need to blow my load out of my system, I don't want to leave. I want to stay here, wrapped up in them. I want to know what they've been up to, how their work is going—whatever they're allowed to tell me.

I haven't only missed their warm bodies. I've missed them. I've missed the teasing and the way they take care of me.

"Brady?" Kit nudges me.

"Calm your balls," I complain. "My brain is only now coming back online. You short-circuited it."

"You're welcome," Prescott says. "But speaking of dinner, what is there to eat around here?"

"There's a restaurant on-site or a convenience store in the lobby with some basics. If I can, I'll sneak you some food from the cabin I'm staying in. We came with a fully stocked fridge for the big and tough baseball player who's freaking out over ruining his career after his rookie season."

"Sounds like hard work," Prescott says.

It's not really, just exhausting. I start to slowly make my way out of bed. I find my boxer briefs and put them on. I should shower, but Kelley and Thad are probably wondering where I am. "That's the thing. It's not hard work, which is why Uncle Damon put two interns on the job, but Kelley is … sensitive. He's had a couple of harsh comments online, so it's basically our job to get him to stop dwelling on it, but it's kind of hard when Thad holds resentment over Kelley because he's in the big leagues when Thad couldn't even make the minors after college and now he's in his backup career." I sigh just thinking about walking back into that cabin and dealing with both their broody moods. "Ooh, idea. What if we chop off one of my hands and put it on their doorstep and pretend I'm being held for ransom? That could buy us all the time we need while you guys are here."

Kit and Prescott look at each other, and Kit mumbles, "And he says this Kelley guy is dramatic."

"Fine. It doesn't actually have to be my hand. We could find a dummy hand and pretend it's mine."

Kit stands and rounds the bed, standing naked in front of me. His muscles are tight, his abs still insanely defined even though he's been at a desk job for two years now. "How about this …" Uh-oh. He's using his adult tone. "You go do what you have to do, and then when the other two are asleep, you can come down here and join us."

"I feel guilty inviting you here and then not being with you."

Prescott joins in now, all his golden-brown skin on display. How do they think I'm supposed to walk out of here when they look so glorious naked?

Prescott's hand lands on my shoulder. "You'll be with us when you can."

"Okay, on a scale of one to illegal, how bad would it be if I put sleeping pills in their dinners?"

When they both only blink at me, I hold up my hands.

"Okay, okay, bad idea. I guess I'll see you when I can get away, then, since you won't let me drug people."

"How dare we keep you out of prison!" Kit cries.

"I was going to make them go to sleep early, not poison them. Geez. Calm down." I throw back on my layers, but apparently, there's not enough of them for Prescott.

"How are you not cold?"

I shove my foot into my shoe. "Grew up in Chicago, remember? Also, I'm going into my second winter in New York. I'm reacclimated to the cold."

"Next meetup is somewhere like Florida again," Prescott says.

I love that there's no question in his tone. There is going to be a next time.

I shouldn't have it in my head that one of them is going to end it because that anxiety of it being possibly the last time always plays in the back of my mind and puts a dark cloud over the fondest of memories of us being together.

"Sounds good. And when I get back later tonight and you two oldies are ready to get it up again, I'm thinking we should update our photo albums."

Both their brows scrunch in confusion.

"I need more photos of you guys in compromising positions. The ones you sent from your meetup last month have already worn out my spank bank quota. They're still hot, for sure, but I need more."

Prescott looks at Kit. "Maybe the sleeping pills aren't a bad idea."

"Woohoo, two against one. I win." I stand upright and kiss them both on the lips softly. "I'll be back soon."

Kit's voice follows after me. "I don't actually have to tell you not to drug them, do I? Prescott was joking!"

"I know *I shouldn't*. Does that count?"

Kit looks genuinely worried while Prescott tries to cover a smirk.

"Fine. No drugging. That'll give you guys more time to recover anyway." I leave with a spring in my step as I make my way back to one of the cabins at the back of the property. It's a two-bedroom. Kelley has the master, while I share twin beds in a room with Thad.

Ugh. Thad.

Thad's a recent graduate from Olmstead University in New York and occupier of the neighboring cubicle to mine back in the office. He's six feet of tattooed, bitter ex-baseball player, and I don't even know if he wants this job. Others would kill for his position, but in his defense, his number one dream was making it to the majors, and it's only been a couple of months that he's had to deal with that loss.

I grab firewood from the box outside our cabin so it looks like I actually did something while I've been gone and head inside. "I'm back."

Thad enters from the kitchen area and mouths, "Help me."

I drop the firewood and rush into the kitchen to find Kelley pacing back and forth. "What's going on?" I ask.

"Have you seen everything that's being said online about me?"

I glare at Thad. "How did he get access to the internet? We took his phone."

"You didn't take his," Kelley says and points to Thad.

"You also asked if you could use it to look up a recipe, not go on social media!" Thad yells.

I pinch the bridge of my nose. "Thad, why don't you get started on dinner, and Kelley, you're coming with me."

"Where?" Kelley asks.

"For a walk. The cold air might shock your system and get you to come back from the brink of a panic attack."

Babysitting therapist mode activated. All the tension that Kit and Prescott fucked out of me is back.

Kelley's so out of it he doesn't even grab his coat to go outside.

I chase after him with a coat, scarf, and beanie. "Jesus, Kel, wait up."

He slows, and I hand him his things. Once he's wrapped up and no longer risking hypothermia, we stroll in the opposite direction of Kit and Prescott's cabin. I don't think I'll be able to concentrate on this conversation we need to have if I'm thinking about them.

I need to compartmentalize.

"Calmed down a bit yet?"

"No. Straight people never have to put up with this, and it sucks."

"I beg to differ." I take out my phone and open the cesspool that is social media and read. *"Liam Johnson needs some glasses if he can't even hit a ball pitched by Ben Michaels who throws like a girl. They're both pussie*s." I find another. *"Henry Williams is a piece of shit.* Ooh, this one doesn't even say why. Go, Henry."

"That first one was insulting their games not who they have in their beds. And the second one is right. Henry Williams is a piece of shit."

I grin. "Is your handle atBigCock6969?"

"No. It's just a common fact," he mutters. "The difference between what those guys have said about them and what's being said about me is that's smack talk. They're actually attacking me for who I am—for my identity."

"Actually, my point here was supposed to be that even without the queer element, toxic masculinity is still prevalent in sports. Humans can be trash, and we need to think of the internet like a landfill. It's where all trash go to express their unwanted opinions. Sure, if you go digging around, you might find something nice, but wading through the dumpster fire to get there isn't worth it. Which is why Damon put an internet ban on you."

Kelley deflates. I think I'm getting through to him. Maybe.

"I spent my entire time in the minors being good and holding back who I was so I would be accepted. Now I have my dream of playing major league baseball, and I want to share that high with someone. But it's shrouded in hateful comments."

"You have to remember there's a lot of support out there too," I say. "It's easy to focus on the negative because the trauma of it sticks in your mind, but there are people who are on your side. The league, your whole management team, your teammates. Fuck the haters. Fuck the trash."

Kelley finally manages a bright smile. "I'd rather not fuck them, but I get what you're saying. You're really good at this, you know."

"What?"

"Reassuring me. You did it at the photoshoot, and now here, and … I think I want to ask Damon for you to take over as my main contact at King Sports."

"Y-you … you want me to be your agent?"

He nods. "I know you're only an intern, so your uncle might not let it happen—"

"I have another client. A football player. I'm in charge of his account, but I have to get any decisions signed off by a senior agent."

"Then it's settled. I want you to work for me."

Prescott and Kit visiting, adding a new client to my roster … This might be the best damn work trip ever.

CHAPTER FOURTEEN

BRADY DOESN'T KNOW IT, but we heard everything he said to Kelley Afton. Prescott and I went to find food when we saw Brady storming out of his cabin after someone.

I'm not gonna lie, I was both impressed and taken aback at how in control he was. It also made me realize that outside of what he does for a living, who his family is, Prescott and I don't really know the ins and outs of Brady's real life.

Which is why, when he finally makes his escape and finds Prescott and me on the porch of the cabin overlooking a small lake, instead of taking him inside and back to bed, we invite him to sit with us.

He glances between Pres, who's got about ten blankets piled on top of him, and me, who has no blankets, and he climbs into my lap.

"Hey, why'd he get your body warmth?" Prescott complains.

"He looks like he needs it more than you do with how you're buried under a pile of blankets. Why is Kit torturing you anyway?"

I smile. "I'm making him breathe in the fresh cold air. It's so beautiful and peaceful out here." The moon is high, and it's close to complete silence. The air is so crisp it stings my lungs. In a good way.

Brady settles in my arms. "Definitely more peaceful out here than back in my cabin, that's for sure. I'm getting the impression my uncle sent Thad out here with me as punishment instead of help."

"Why would he punish you?" I ask.

"Maybe not punish. More like sent Thad as a babysitter, but it's totally the other way around. They keep sniping at each other, and I'm in the middle."

"I thought you liked being in the middle?" Prescott waggles his eyebrows.

"Of you two, yeah."

That fills me with more warmth than the heat his body's radiating.

"What made you want to become a sports agent?" I ask. "Was it always the plan?"

Brady laughs. "Fuck no. I love football. I loved playing as a kid and back in high school, but I remember the exact moment I decided to give it up." He stares out at the water and licks his lips. "You know who our dads are, and they wanted us to be like them. From the minute we were born, all they ever talked about was us playing in the NFL together like they did. So, we trained. A lot. But it wasn't that easy. Our coaches always compared us to our dads, and this one day, I was over it. Coach had literally said out loud in front of the entire team that maybe Peyton didn't have Talon DNA after all because there's no way a Talon could play that sloppy."

"What the fuck?" Prescott exclaims.

"Our dads never told anyone who was the bio dad of which child, and growing up, everyone assumed I was a Talon because it's my last name, but as we grew into teens, it became obvious."

I hum. "I remember seeing an article where your brother and dad were photographed next to each other. They almost looked like twins."

"Ugh. Never let my dad hear that, or he'd gloat about how he can pass for being in his twenties again."

"Hey, maybe your brother looks fifty? You don't know what I meant."

"You're sweet for trying to cover." Brady kisses me. "But anyway, the fact Coach brought DNA into it, belittling how hard Peyton and I had worked to get where we were, it'd taken all of my strength not to punch our coach in the face. Pey was the one who held me back. I hated the comparisons. Peyton took them easier than I did, but that day, I saw how truly worn down he was. It was the moment I realized that if we both pursued football, the chances are we'd be drafted to different teams, and we wouldn't have each other to get through those situations together anymore. I vowed to have his back like he had mine. I figured being his agent was the best way to do it."

"Wow," Prescott whispers.

Brady turns his head toward him. "What?"

"Nothing. Don't get me wrong when I say this because I admire my siblings and what they've achieved, but … Well, I guess I'm so different from them that making a big sacrifice like that out of love wouldn't even occur to me."

"It's not a sacrifice. I really love it. Even when my clients are divas or anxiety-ridden. Actually … they're the only two clients I have so far. Fuck, all athletes are going to be that demanding, aren't they?"

"Well, you know your brother. He's your base level."

"Ergh. They're all going to be over-the-top monsters. Maybe I'm not cut out for this job after all."

I can't tell if he's joking or not, but either way, that can't be true. I witnessed how good he is tonight. It might have been the sexiest I've ever found him. Brady's confidence in himself is what has had me coming back for more. Well, that and the way he gives up control. With his client, he was the one in charge. So knowing he gives that all up for us is so sexy. A total bottom with a toppy attitude.

"I'm sure whatever you wanted to do, you'd excel at," I say.

"Except cleaning," Prescott says. "Don't become a housekeeper or maid. Your definition of tidy is … not."

"Agreed," I say. "Do anything except that."

"Excuse me, but I was on vacation in Florida, okay? You don't have to be tidy when you're on vacation. Besides, you guys picked up after me anyway, so why clean when I could sunbake?"

"Life motto, right there," Prescott says. "Something we should all live by. Like, always. Mainly the sunbaking part because that would mean we'd be in a climate where it was possible to sunbake without getting hypothermia."

Brady leans in close to my ear, his breath ghosting over my skin. "I thought SEALs were supposed to be tough?"

I laugh.

"Heard that," Prescott mumbles.

"I'd offer to take you inside and warm you up, but I get the feeling Kit's holding us both hostage out here." He'd be right about that. "My guess is he's so old he can't get it up again yet and is stalling."

Little shit.

I poke his ribs. "I'm so sorry for being interested in your life outside of us."

Brady pulls back so he can stare down at me. "Is that what this is?"

"That, and it really is a beautiful night."

Brady wraps his arms around me, snuggling into me. "It really is. If it weren't for Prescott possibly dying, I could stay out here with you all night."

"All night?" Prescott squeaks.

"Should we at least go inside and sit in front of the fire?" Brady asks.

I pat his cheek. "Fine. Lounging in front of the fireplace sounds nice too."

"Thank fuck." Prescott stands and runs inside so fast he drops blankets on the way.

"And you say I'm the messy one." Brady picks them up as he moves inside.

With one last look out at the still lake and frozen night air, I follow Brady and Prescott to make the most of this short time we have together.

Prescott's on the couch in front of the fire, with Brady lying down and using Prescott's lap as a pillow. Prescott's running a hand through Brady's hair gently, and they look so … domestic.

We've reached the level of comfort between us where affection is given freely, and for a brief moment, I imagine a future where this could be ours permanently.

Brady lifts his head. "I saved you a spot."

I eye the couch's length where Brady's feet are sticking off the end. "Doesn't look like you did."

Next thing, his legs go up in the air, and I wedge my big body underneath him.

We're all still bulked up with warm clothing, but it won't take long in here for us to thaw out.

"Okay, so I told you something about my real life, now you two have to tell me why you became SEALs."

Prescott's answer is easy. "Adrenaline junkie. Wanted to serve my country."

Mine is less so. "I didn't have the best upbringing, and when I came out, I didn't really have anywhere to go. I had no one. The military made the most sense for me."

"Yet, he's throwing that all away now," Prescott says.

Brady sits up. "What?"

"I got a promotion. Of sorts."

He looks back at Prescott. "Did you know?"

"He told me when he was in Cali."

"An opportunity came up, and I thought …" My gaze flicks between the two of them while I contemplate how much I should put on the line here. "I thought being a civilian with a normal civilian job, there'd be more chances for us to … for all three of us …"

I did it for you. Both of you.

For the first time since I told Prescott that I was quitting the navy, he doesn't stare at me with disapproval.

His warm brown eyes are soft. "You could've told me that."

"You were a little too busy yelling at me."

"Tell me more about your shitty childhood," Brady says through a yawn. "And then after all this talking, take me to bed. I still need those pics."

Please, he looks completely wrecked.

"You want the story of the poor kid who grew up in the sticks in a conservative family who got kicked out for being gay, so he joined the military? That's pretty much all there is to it."

He closes his eyes. "Tell me a happy memory. You have to have at least one."

As I think back and start in on the story of maybe my favorite childhood memory—one that doesn't include my parents but a summer I basically spent at my best friend's house—Brady drifts in and out of consciousness.

"And he calls us old," Prescott murmurs when Brady falls asleep.

"We'll let him rest. I get the feeling his job is kicking his ass. Plus, he's probably needing to catch up on law school stuff too. We're here for a couple of days."

"We should at least get him into bed."

"That's my line," Brady mutters, but he's still out of it.

"Trust him to hear that while he's asleep," Prescott says.

"I'll carry him." I slip out from underneath Brady's legs and then put my arm underneath his neck and the other under his knees.

I carry him bridal style through the cabin to the bedroom and lay him down.

He briefly opens his eyes, sits up, and says, "I'm awake, I'm awake. Let's do this."

But Prescott and I shake our heads and help Brady out of his outer layers and shoes and socks. We do the same for ourselves, set an alarm, and then slip into bed with him.

"You like taking care of him," Prescott says.

"I like taking care of both of you. I guess it's because I never had anyone caring for me growing up. I don't want anyone else to ever feel that way."

Prescott sighs. "It sucks I'm about to deploy again. I want more time."

"We'll have time when you get back. We'll make sure of it. A weekend here, one night there, a week when we can manage it."

Prescott's lips are in a tight line.

"I don't want us to stop," I admit.

"Neither do I. If I'm back before summer, we should go see Brady in New York. Otherwise, we should plan for something while he's on break. A longer visit this time."

How does forever sound?

Before I can ask that question aloud, I can already hear the answer: impossible.

"Just make sure to come home to us," I say instead.

"You know I will."

CHAPTER FIFTEEN

THE FIRST THING I do as soon as my team gets back Stateside is call Kit.

Six months of barely any contact made this deployment feel extra long. Actually, it ended up not even being six months. It was five months, two weeks, and one day. Not that I was counting.

The whole time, I was itching to come back home. To talk to Kit, to Brady. They were all I thought about.

Which is why, the second I could get leave, I took it. It's only for two nights, and flying all the way to New York for them might be a waste of precious time, but I need to see them. Both of them.

Maybe I should've tried to organize a proper weeklong vacation with the guys, but I'm impatient, and we can organize a long trip later in the summer. The only time we've been able to arrange a visit that long was in Florida over a year ago. The Catskills was an amazing few days—minus the cold—but it wasn't long enough.

It's never long enough.

Now that Kit's a civilian, he's in a position where he's able to drop work quicker than ever before. I hope Brady is able to do the same.

When I land, Kit's beaten me to it, and he waits for me outside my gate.

"What took you so long?" he asks as I practically tackle him into a hug. He stays upright though. If I'd done that to Brady, he'd probably fall.

"Oh, I don't know. Maybe that your flight was one hour and mine was five?" We make our way toward the exit. "You still got Brady's address after sending him that care package after Florida?" I had to laugh when I heard about that.

Kit sent a "Congratulations surviving your first year of law school, but if you're going to keep up the pace you're going, you're going to need this" and filled a box full of protein bars and other nutritious snacks. Brady called me to complain about Kit expecting him to eat kale chips. It was cute in the way he screamed, *"Kale chips, Prescott! This is unacceptable."*

"Unless he's moved." Kit stops walking. "Do you think he's moved? He hasn't said anything, but you talk to him more than I do. He was staying with an uncle, wasn't he?"

"Cousin, but it's his uncle's house."

"Well, hopefully, his family still lives there and can tell us where he is if he's moved out."

We're both buzzing with excited energy as the car drops us off, and Kit shoves me as we walk up to the expensive brownstone. "You're practically vibrating."

"It's Brady. And you. And I've been at sea for six months."

Deployment is often lonely, but the last two have been especially hard. I love my job, I love being a SEAL, and I would never want to give it up, but I can't help noticing that the shine it used to have hasn't been as bright since Kit left.

I've been telling myself it's because we went through BUD/s together. We had each other's backs for years. He wasn't only a teammate but my kindred spirit.

I thought I'd be over it by now, but I'm not.

And then there's Brady, who not only lives in my head rent-free but has wormed his way into my thoughts as often as Kit.

Kit and Brady are the only two men who have the power to destroy me, but I can't walk away.

Proof of that comes when Kit rings the doorbell, and the sound of the door opening makes butterflies and anticipation bubble up inside me. Only the person who answers isn't Brady.

It's a young guy, college-age probably, with dark hair and brown eyes. He's tall and lanky and looks nothing like Brady. Though he's told us if he refers to cousins and uncles, they most likely aren't related by blood. I can't think of the cousin's name Brady lives with. It's Seven. Or Three? It was a number. I just can't remember which one.

"Is Brady here?" Kit asks.

The kid frowns. "He, uh, usually comes home late on Friday nights. Was he expecting you?"

Kit and I look at each other.

"We're friends from Cali," I say. "We wanted to surprise him while we were in town."

"What are your names? I'll message him and—"

"Mind if you only tell him that he's needed at home? Are we okay to wait for him in his room?" I ask.

Again, with the frowning. "I don't know either of you, so I'm not just going to let you inside my house."

I take out my phone and open my photos app to find a pic of the three of us together—that's safe for other people's viewing. "We're not stalkers or anything."

"That sounds exactly like something a stalker would say, and if you really knew Brady at all, you'd know who his brother is and that this isn't the first time randoms have shown up here hoping to catch sight of a Talon or Miller."

Finally, I get to a photo that's not of us naked. It was taken in the Catskills the night after we got there. It's the three of us on that back porch, on another moonlit night. Brady's in between us and looks so fucking happy.

I hand him my phone. "See? We know him."

"You could've met him on the street and asked for a selfie." And then he does the worst possible thing he could do. He swipes.

"You might not want to—"

But it's too late. He cringes as he sees his cousin doing things—naked, sweaty, sexy things—and quickly hands back the phone. "Okay, you know him. Come in and make yourself at home while I go bleach my eyes."

"I tried to warn you," I say as I step past him. "And to be fair, you broke a cardinal rule. You never swipe when you're looking at someone else's photos."

"Lesson learned." Brady's cousin closes the door behind us.

Kit adds, "And if you can't guess, we're kind of on the down low, so—"

"I'm going to pretend that I never saw anything. In fact, I'm going to message Brady, tell him he has a package waiting at home for him, and then I'm going to go to the library to study and try not think about what he's doing at home with …" He waves his hand in our general direction. "All of that."

"We'd appreciate that. We're so far on the down low his own brother doesn't know about us."

That makes whatever-his-number-is pull back in surprise. "Really?" Then an evil smile takes root across his face. "I'm always the last to know everything in this family. I finally have one up on everyone."

"But … you can't tell anyone," I point out.

"I don't even care about that. Okay, I'm getting out of your hair. Maybe I'll even find a friend who got summer housing to crash with tonight so you can … catch up. Yes. Let's go with that phrase. I am picturing drinks and board games and nothing else."

After he picks up a laptop bag, he waves and tells us to help ourselves to the fridge. He's gone a minute later.

I cock my head at Kit. "Should we be worried that it was so easy for him to trust us here alone? He basically said Brady has had stalkers."

"Technically, he's seen us both naked—"

"And balls-deep inside his cousin. How does he know that isn't where our obsession began and now we follow Brady all over the country? Or how does he know we're not blackmailing him with those photos? Maybe we should look at getting Brady a better security system."

"Better … than his cousin? What, you want to volunteer to be his bodyguard? Besides, the superfans would be after his brother, not Brady."

That's true. But—

Kit steps toward me. "Look at you, worrying. It's so cute. That's usually my job."

"Shut up," I grumble.

"I still worry about him too, but Brady's a big boy and can take care of himself."

"You've always liked it when he makes you feel needed though," I point out.

"I do. I like it when I feel needed, period. When we lived together, I liked that you needed me."

I step closer to him and lower my voice. "Don't you get it? I still need you. I will always need you, Kit."

"Then why the distance? Not physical, but … whenever we're together, it's like old times, but when we're apart, we barely speak."

I avert my gaze because I don't want to say that him deciding to move across the country hurt me. It broke me.

"Because I've been mad at you." I've never had the guts to tell him this before, and now that it's flying out of me, I can't stop it.

"For leaving? For quitting the navy?"

"For wanting to get away from me."

My admission hangs heavy in the air. I haven't wanted to admit it to myself, let alone out loud, but Kit leaving was the wake-up call I needed. My anger that followed, even though I've tried to deny it, is because I've wanted something deeper with Kit for way too long.

Kit's mouth opens, but nothing comes out. He can't even deny that he left because of me. I don't understand it.

"Why did you agree to meeting up once a year if you left to get away from me?" I ask.

He still doesn't talk. I don't even know if he can at this point. He stares at me, his pale eyes searching for an answer I'm not sure he has.

And now that I've made myself that tiny bit vulnerable, the walls are closing in, and it's all becoming too real. So I do what I normally do—deflect. With anything. With humor, with sex, whatever I can.

"Should we snoop around Brady's place?"

"Don't do that," Kit says.

"Do what?"

"Change the topic because the conversation is getting real."

"What conversation? You weren't saying anything!" I don't like silence. It makes my skin crawl.

"Because I don't know what to say."

"You could start with telling me why you took the job at the Pentagon to begin with. And not the *it was a great opportunity* bullshit either."

He hesitates, like he knows the answer will tear me apart. "I can't lie."

"So it was because of me?"

Kit winces and then all at once lets out, "It's because I realized I didn't know how to live without you, and for *roommates*, that's not a good thing."

When hope blooms in my gut, that maybe this is more, he clarifies.

"Codependent best friends is so overdone. I needed to leave to become my own person."

And while I can't fault him for that, I am disappointed that the distance between us now hasn't given him the same clarity it's given me.

We stand in silence, inside Brady's New York home, at a stalemate. I can't deny we were breaking all kinds of rules when we lived together. And that it would have to have stopped eventually. I just thought it would happen mutually.

One of us had to take that step, and it happened to be Kit.

He breaks the awkward eye contact first. He puts his hands in his pockets and glances around the open-plan living room and up the stairs to the right. "I am interested to see how Brady lives."

Now he's the one deflecting, but I'm not an asshole like he is, and I'm not going to call him on it.

"You want to go to his room and see if he has clothes all over his floor here too, don't you?"

"Of course I do. I don't believe anyone can be a slob like that twenty-four seven. He wasn't even staying in our cabin in the Catskills, and he still managed to get everything *everywhere*. He can't be like that all the time, can he?"

"Only one way to find out …" I nod toward the staircase.

Kit hesitates and bites his lip. It's so sexy when he does it. It's his only physical tell when he's not sure about something. He's always so confident.

I reach for his hand. "Come on. I'll lead you."

At that moment, the door opens and Brady steps through. "Pey?" He calls out and stalls when he sees us. His eyes widen. He glances around as if asking himself if he stepped into the right house, but all he says is, "Am I dreaming? When Four texted that I had someone waiting at home for me, I thought Peyton and his boyfriend came home from their vacation early."

I knew his cousin had a number for a name.

Kit smiles. "We wanted to surprise you."

Brady looks dumbfounded. "How … How did you know where I live?"

"You don't remember my care package I sent? I kept that information in my back pocket for if I ever needed it, and it turns out we did."

"Oh, right. The kale chips. How could I forget. Still mad at you for that, by the way." Finally, the shock wears off, and he approaches us with his arms wide. "I can't believe you're both here."

The second the three of us are wrapped around each other, it's relief and happiness. It's sunshine after a rainstorm. It's clarity in my heart and calmness of my mind.

I'm beginning to realize that *zing*, that powerful and overwhelming feeling of serenity and peace only happens when we're all together.

The only time I've felt this alive in the last two years has been with them. Not out at sea like it used to be. That thought also makes my heart sink. Because after we've gotten our fill this weekend, we'll all go home again.

Every time I see Kit and Brady, the harder it is to be apart.

Suddenly, instead of enjoying both of them, instead of reveling in being wrapped in their arms, I'm drowning in anticipated loneliness.

CHAPTER SIXTEEN

DAMN, it's surreal having Kit and Prescott in my house. They're *here*. In New York.

I pull back. "How long are you here for?"

"Only the weekend," Kit says.

"Unfortunately," Prescott adds. "We wanted to try to organize something longer, but this was a last-minute thing. We took what we could get."

I hold on to Pres a little bit tighter. How military spouses do this is beyond me. I got used to talking to Prescott frequently when we've been apart, but the last six months has been barely any communication due to him being away.

"I missed you," I say.

I've missed both of them, but it weirdly hits the hardest when they're right in front of me.

"Let's take this upstairs," Kit says, and fuck yes—oh, shit, no, wait. It's a mess up there.

"Hold that thought," I say. "I need to … do something first. Stay here. I'll be right back."

As I turn on my heel and run upstairs, I hear Kit say, "Note to us: Brady's not good with surprises."

"That just means we have to surprise him more," Prescott says.

The idea of them coming back to me, over and over … I almost can't take it. I want them so badly, but I'm scared of the mess they'll leave when one of us has the guts to finally end this.

I shut myself in my room and hurry to tidy up. Kit hates mess to the point he's weird about it.

The knock on my door makes me jump.

"Is everything okay in there?" Kit asks.

"Uh-huh. I'm …" Cleaning my room? Could I sound more like a five-year-old? "I'm …" I go with the first thing that pops into my head. "I'm breaking up with someone!" I facepalm because I'm not even seeing anyone. I don't date. It's hard to when my heart belongs elsewhere.

"You're what?" The door handle jiggles, and I rush over to make sure it's locked, which it is.

"Oh, I'm seeing this guy, but it's no big deal. I was going to break up with him anyway." Mainly because he's imaginary.

"You don't need to do that," Prescott says. "We know the score."

"Uh, yeah. But I mean, this guy. He doesn't. Give me five minutes to send him a text. I have to get the wording right."

There's more knocking—no, more like banging—on the door now. "Brady Francis Talon. Open this door now," Kit says, and I know I'm in trouble.

You know people are serious when they make up a middle name for you.

I open the door a crack. "Francis?"

Kit shrugs. "I didn't know your middle name, so I went with his." He points to Prescott.

"Your name is James Francis Prescott? You almost sound as snooty as my cousin, Noah Huntington the Fourth." Am I stalling? Why yes, yes I am.

"Can you let us in?" Kit says, his tone soft and soothing.

"Umm, no. Very important breakup going on in here."

Prescott catches on before Kit does. His lips twitch. "You're cleaning your room, aren't you?"

"No? My room is always immaculate. Why do you ask?"

Prescott turns to Kit. "Think you can handle a little mess?"

"For you two? I could endure torture training."

Prescott leans against the door jamb. "Fun fact: while the rest of us went through *real* torture training, they locked Kit away in a room that looked like a hoarder lived there. He almost rang the bell that day and tapped out of the whole program."

Kit shoves him. "Liar." Then he turns his gray eyes on me. "What's the truth? Because if you really are breaking up with someone because of us, we're going to need to discuss that."

They're going to say that we're not serious enough for that kind of drastic move, but the truth is, if I was seeing someone, I wouldn't hesitate to end things just for one weekend with Kit and Prescott.

That's the kind of power they hold over me.

I've thought about maybe trying some more poly apps and going out with people who know I'm involved with other people and are cool with it, but even though I've only seen Prescott and Kit twice since graduation, I haven't wanted anyone else. The thought is there, just not enough desire to go through with it.

I open the door wider.

Prescott laughs. "Told you he was a slob all the time."

"I tried to tidy—"

Kit steps forward and hugs me. "I don't care that you're messy."

"Not what you said five minutes ago." Prescott picks up a pair of dirty underwear off the armchair in the corner of my room and drops them on the floor so he can take a seat.

"He's trying. That's the main thing," Kit says.

"Why do I feel like you're about to pat me on the head and call me a good boy like I'm a dog?" I ask.

Kit's hands slide down to my ass and squeeze. "Not so much like a dog, but I do want you to be a good boy."

I shudder, and my cock hardens even more. Before Kit, the whole praise kink didn't do anything for me, but with him? I love it. I also love that Prescott goes between joining me in acting bratty and being stern like Kit. And by stern, I mean taking turns fucking me so hard I can feel them both for days.

I don't even know how this dynamic even started, but like most things with Kit and Prescott, it evolved that way, and I went along for the ride. Maybe it's that I haven't ever been with anyone like them.

Being the size I am—taller than most, more muscular even if I've slimmed down a lot since college—people assume I'm the one to take charge.

I'm not. I have to hold my shit together and be "on" so much at work, for my clients, for my family, that when I'm getting off, all I really crave is to let go.

I chose a career where I'd have to look after others because I did plenty of it growing up with Peyton. I was the one who'd help him study so he could keep his grades up. I was the one who switched shirts with him the night he got high at Levi's graduation party so our dads couldn't smell the weed on him. His future has needed protecting since I can remember, and I chose to do it. Taking this career path, I'm going to have a million Peytons to look after, some with an attitude like Torey and others who are sweet but filled with anxiety like Kelley. I'm the one who will need to be there for them. Which is why, when I get *me* time, I want to be the one taken care of.

Kit and Prescott are my vacation from the real-life pressures that I'd hoped would go away when I quit football in high school, but they never really did. They're just different pressures now.

"What's it going to be?" Kit rumbles in my ear. "Are you going to be a good boy for us?"

I glance up at him through my lashes. "Only if I don't have to clean my room."

Kit laughs. "I don't give a fuck what your room looks like, only that you're naked in it."

"I'm on it." I struggle out of my clothes, but even though Prescott and Kit wear amused smiles while they watch me trip over myself, I ignore them. The sooner I'm naked, the sooner they'll be on me.

Inside me.

Against me.

I don't care.

The need I have for them when we're all together is above any other.

I finally step out of my underwear, the last item of clothing to go, but now that I'm naked and neither of them is, I realize my mistake. When I'm eager, they like to drag it out. They love a desperate

Brady, and they have the damn patience and willpower to hold off for longer than I can handle.

I try to approach Kit, but he spins and pushes me toward the bed and makes me sit on the edge.

If he's going to play games, then so will I. I reach for the bulge in his pants, but he catches my hand. Wordlessly, he signals to Prescott to get over here.

Prescott climbs on the bed and rests on his knees behind me. His big hands grip my shoulders, his thumbs kneading into my sore muscles, and I moan.

"Wow," Kit says. "We haven't even gone near your dick yet and you're making sinful noises for us."

"That will make a different moan come out of me. Why don't you try it and see?"

"Just for that …" Kit grabs hold of my knees and pushes my legs up so far I have to lean back on Prescott so I don't fall flat on my back.

My ass hangs off the end of the bed, my knees are near my ears, and my heart thrums wildly as Kit's breath ghosts along my cock, down to my balls, and then hits my hole.

But instead of kissing me in any of those good places, he turns his head and kisses my thigh.

Tingles race over my skin. My ass contracts, craving to close around something. A finger, a cock, a dildo—anything.

Kit opens his mouth and trails his tongue along my skin, skirting closer and closer to where I need him to be, but in true Kit fashion, when I think he's going to suck my balls into his mouth, he moves to my other leg and farther away.

When I whine, Prescott's body vibrates from silent laughter.

And even though I consider what they're doing pure torture, for some reason, I want to come back for more.

Every. Single. Time.

Because when they finally give in, when they finally give me what I want, it's worth it.

Kit's tongue lands on my entrance, teasing, licking … driving me so wild I can't help but call out. That earns a hand across my mouth from Prescott.

I lick his hand to try to get him to move it, but all he does is chuckle in return.

Fuck, why do I love this so much?

I'm so turned on I'm leaking like crazy, and all I want is for Kit to move his mouth to the head of my cock. Even imagining him doing it gets me closer to the edge of coming.

Instead of that though, he gives me something better. His tongue pushes inside me, and his hands that were holding my knees skate down my sides to push my ass cheeks apart.

Prescott removes his hand from my mouth and helps hold one of my legs up high. Kit eats me out like an expert, but my poor neglected cock aches.

I'm trembling, I can barely breathe, and the only thing holding me up is Prescott. That's when he whispers in my ear, "Rest on your elbows for me," and shifts right out from underneath me.

Instead of doing as he says, I fall onto my back.

"Nuh-uh," Prescott says. "Elbows. You'll want to be able to see this."

The second I raise my head, Prescott lowers his and sucks my cock into his mouth.

"Holy fuck," I hiss. My hips try to buck off the bed, but hands—I don't know whose—hold me down.

Kit buries himself deeper inside me, and with the added slurps from Prescott's mouth on my cock, they consume me. All of me. If you've never had a tongue in your ass and a mouth on your dick at the same time, you haven't lived.

I writhe but get nowhere. I beg for release, but they ignore me. As much as it should annoy me, it does the opposite.

My brain switches off, my mind fuzzes over, and I reach that euphoric state where energy buzzes under my veins and the real world disappears. And I owe it all to Prescott and Kit.

Soon, my legs start to tire, my abs ache like I've done two hundred sit-ups, and pain becomes the dominating sensation rushing through my body. I'm sweating, gritting my teeth, and trying to hold on to that euphoria. I want to go back to almost passing out from pleasure, and as if hearing my silent plea, Kit's mouth leaves my hole and is replaced by one of his fat fingers pushing inside.

"You ready to come for us?" he rasps, his voice sounding like sex. "You going to give Prescott your whole load?"

I nod, unable to speak.

Kit's finger pushes deeper and hits my prostate. I go off like the fireworks on the fourth of July, stars swarming the corners of my vision. I throw my head back, relax into it, and enjoy as muscle by muscle, my whole body goes lax, and I sink into the mattress.

Slumping backward, I'm vaguely aware of Prescott and Kit kissing, the rustling of their clothes, but I'm too busy swimming in bliss to catch their second act.

It's only when I sense them leaning over me that I open my eyes again. They're both on their knees, each straddling one of my legs, while they jerk each other off.

"We're close," Kit tells me and glances down at my stomach in silent question.

"Make like the Beatles and come together. Right now. Over me."

Kit laughs. "I don't think that's what they meant when they wrote that song."

"I don't care. Just come on me."

Mark me as yours.

Give me everything you have.

Prescott spills first, but it doesn't take long for Kit to follow. Their cum mixes on my skin, and my only regret is not telling them to come on each other so I could lick off every drop.

When they're both finished, their chests heave, and I open my arms for them to fall into them.

It's not the first time I've been in between them, but it's usually *them* cuddling *me*, not the other way around. I like the reversal. Surprisingly.

Then again, there hasn't been anything these guys have done that I haven't enjoyed. We have our recurring dynamic that we seamlessly slip into. Kit is a power top, Prescott's a switch, and I'm a total bottom, and that seems to be the way it is outside of sex too. At least when I'm with them.

But the thing I probably love most about what the three of us have is even in moments of irregularity, I've never felt out of place.

In fact, with them might be the only place I've ever been fully comfortable in my own skin.

They embrace who I am. Not who I'm supposed to be.

It's why being away from them always sucks.

I don't know if I can keep doing it before they break me.

CHAPTER SEVENTEEN

IT'S amazing how much better I sleep when Brady and Prescott are wrapped around me. Sure, it's like a furnace in here, and we're a sweaty pile of limbs, but when I think about having to get on a plane tomorrow to go back to my apartment in Virginia where the sheets are cold and the bed is empty, I try to hold on to my perfect sleep that little bit longer.

That is until voices filter up the stairwell.

"Brady?" someone calls out. "Four?"

Brady bolts upright in between Prescott and me. "Fuck, that was my brother."

"What was your brother?" Prescott sits up and yawns.

"Oh, Braaaaaaaaay." New voice. A closer voice.

Brady groans. "And my dad."

"Four, you better not still be in bed!" Different voice again.

"Shit, shit, fucking shit." Brady climbs over me and throws on the first pair of underwear he comes across. Which happen to be mine. They're way too big on him, but he's too frantic to notice, and I don't have the heart to point it out.

"My brother, my dad, and at least one uncle is here. That means more of them are going to show up any minute, and why the fuck can't anyone pick up a damn phone anymore and send a simple text: *Heads up, we're surprising you, so you might not want to have two superhot navy SEALs in your bed when we get there.* Is that so much to ask?" His jeans are on now, and then he picks up a shirt off the pile of clothes in the corner and throws it over his head. "You guys have to go."

"We can't hide out in here while you get rid of them?" Prescott asks.

Brady presses the heels of his hands against his eyes. "You don't understand. There is no getting rid of my family. Peyton was supposed to go to Chicago to see our dads after his vacation. Four's dads also live in Chicago, even though this is their house. If they're all here, it's because they've decided this one big fucked-up found family of queerdos is in need of quality time. I could tell them I had Ebola and they wouldn't leave."

My heart sinks. "So, that's it? That's all the time we get with you this weekend?" I'm not ready to say goodbye again. But to be fair, I'm never ready to say goodbye. We knew this was a possibility when showing up without warning, but when it worked out last night, I thought we'd have the whole weekend together.

"There's no other way." Brady sounds so disappointed.

"You can't just tell them that—" Prescott starts.

"That you two are some randos I let fuck me whenever we get the chance? You're twice my age, and—"

"Not twice your age," Prescott grumbles.

I nudge him because Brady seems genuinely stressed-out. While it stings that he put us in that box—some older guys he lets play with him occasionally—I'm hoping it's because it's his way of separating what we say we have and what we actually have. Something that's impossible but special.

"I can't …" Brady takes a deep breath. "I can't tell them. I'm not ready."

I get out of bed and approach him because he's on the verge of a meltdown. I cup his face, and he tries to pull out of my grip, but my fingers tighten around his chin. "Tell them what, sweetheart?"

Brady's practically hyperventilating. "I don't want them to know in case they tell me to end it. I'm not ready to end it."

"Hey, it's okay." I rub Brady's arms from his shoulder to elbow and back up again. "We'll go." I kiss the tip of his nose.

He relaxes for only a fraction of a second when footsteps sound up the stairs.

"I gave you plenty of warning, brother. Hope you have your clothes—" The door handle rattles, and I step behind it as Prescott uses SEAL stealth to roll off the bed so he can't be seen.

Brady opens his door only enough for him to slip out. "I heard you, I heard you. All of Manhattan probably heard you."

"You're grumpy today," Peyton says.

"I was woken up by some asshole who was supposed to go see Dad and Pop first."

"I did. They wanted to come here to see my wittle brother."

Their voices disappear, along with their footsteps, and I let out a breath.

"How are we supposed to get out of here without them seeing?" Prescott asks.

I go over to the window I opened in the middle of the night to let some fresh air into the sex-scented room. Outside, there's a large drop to the ground and no trellis, but there *is* a bit of a ledge, and it's only one floor.

Prescott appears beside me, fully dressed. "Think you can make the jump, old man? You've been out of the game for two years now."

"Not only will I make it, I'll make it look good."

Prescott snorts.

I move away from the window to get my clothes—minus my underwear, thanks to Brady. Once I'm dressed and we both put our shoes and socks on, we approach the window again.

"We need to be stealthy," I say.

"Did you not see that awesomely silent maneuver of getting to the floor? But, uh, what do we do about our bags?" Prescott asks.

"The ones we left in the living room yesterday? Abandon them. Say goodbye to whatever you have in there."

"Aww, man, my favorite pair of jeans are in there. I thought Brady might've taken us out New York clubbing."

"You're too old for clubbing. It's time to let go of your youth." I pat his shoulder. "I don't want to be the one to tell you this, but … you're an adult now."

"Fuck you, am not." Prescott's a bit too loud, so I have to cover his mouth.

I put my finger to my lips with my other hand. "What happened to stealth?"

Prescott murmurs something, but it's too muffled, and I refuse to let him talk until I know for sure no one downstairs heard us.

When I think it's safe, I release him. "Let's get out of here before Brady's family finds us."

Something passes over Prescott's face before he covers it and pushes me toward the window. "Age before beauty."

"Fuck off. Watch how easy I can get down."

"I know you're easy to go down. Getting down is another thing."

I put my leg out the window and sit half inside, half out. "First one to get down will go down when we find a hotel room for tonight, seeing as Brady's place is no longer an option."

"I'll take that bet. I'll even give you the head start." Prescott pushes me out the window so he can join me, and then we're both standing on the small ledge that's not even a foot wide.

"If you get caught, you're disqualified," I say.

"If we get caught, Brady won't let us live at all."

"True. Ready?"

"Whenever you are."

I take off for the side of the building. We need to be fast so we aren't seen by passersby or anyone who could call the cops on us at any minute.

Unlike me, who's going to the corner of the house to avoid being seen through the windows, Prescott is cocky enough to think he's invisible. He smirks at me as he turns and flattens himself against the brick wall, and as easy as stepping off a train platform backward, he drops and catches the ledge with his fingers. Now he hangs there, feet close to touching the window shade below, and I know I need to move even faster.

When I get to the edge of the house, I try to find somewhere to put my hands so I can lower myself down in steps, but the smooth brick is impossible to get a hold of, so I'm going to have to do the same as Prescott.

But as soon as I look over at him, his foot rests on the window shade, and I know he's going to jump down now he's close enough to the ground that he won't break anything. I have to beat him. Not because of the blowjob on the line—giving, receiving, I don't give a fuck. It's about the pride and principle of it now.

"Call me old man," I mutter and then let go. He's barely younger than me.

As if I were a parkour champion, I only need a split second to get my foot in the right spot to turn and jump, hitting the pavement in front of the house.

I stand upright as Prescott joins me on the ground, but because he's practically in front of the window, the loud thump catches the attention of someone inside. Peyton Miller. Brady's brother.

Without thinking, I charge at Prescott and tackle him to the hard ground. The window above is open a crack, so we can hear when someone speaks.

"Who's …" The voice comes from inside, so I roll off Prescott and pull him to the side of the house so we can flatten our backs against the wall.

"Who's what?" another voice says.

"I … I thought I saw someone outside." The window starts to slide upward, and I hold my breath. I can feel my heartbeat in my ears.

Prescott looks as frazzled, but we know how to remain still.

Once, we were sent on a mission where we had to lie as still as possible in a swamp in the middle of the Andes and count how many cars rolled by on their way to a coca farm. One move and we would've been dead.

That I could handle. This? There's more than my life on the line. It's everything that's good in it. Brady. Prescott.

While I wouldn't care if Brady's family found out, he has issues with it, so I can't ruin this for us. *For him.*

I'm sure we're about to be caught out when—

"You're crazy. One too many footballs to the head." The window slams shut.

I'm not sure who our savior was, only that it wasn't Brady's voice. Maybe it was Four. Though I didn't hear if he even came home last night. And as Prescott and I crouch down and head for the street, I get a single glance back and see who it was.

Peyton's partner, Levi.

We met him once when Brady was in college, and Brady assured us he wouldn't say anything. It's obvious he never has.

He gives us a mock salute, and I smile back before making our exit.

"What hotel you want to stay at?" I take out my phone from my pocket.

"Ugh. None of them?" Prescott says. "I want to stay back there. With him."

So do I.

"We have to respect Brady's wishes though."

"I know that, but it doesn't mean I have to like it."

"Not everyone was blessed with free-loving parents like yours," I say. "He needs time, and I get the impression it's not his family he's worried about but public backlash. He became a sports agent to stay out of the spotlight. Something as scandalous as being in a throuple could derail not only his own career but Peyton's as well."

Prescott stops walking. "Is that what we are? A throuple? Eww, are we falling victim to using that cutesy nickname?"

I huff. "What would you rather call us? It's not like we completely fit it anyway. Because we're not *together* together. We're just … together temporarily. When we're on leave."

"When *I'm* on leave. You're no longer one of us."

Even though it's true and I've started my new job, it still sounds weird. Like I didn't really leave. "I will always be navy. You don't need to keep bringing up the ultimate betrayal of me choosing to be discharged."

"Hooyah," Prescott deadpans.

I throw my arm around his shoulders. Prescott's only acting out because he can't have things his way. "Let's stay somewhere nice, overlooking Central Park."

"Whoa, Mr. Money Bags. How big a pay increase did you get?"

"You don't want to know."

"Any job openings for me in your department?"

My heart twinges because I know he's joking. "What happened to being an abomination for leaving the military to do it?"

"For enough money, I could sell out too."

My arm drops from his. "Do you really think that's what I did? That I sold out?"

Prescott slumps. "No. I don't. I understand the job opportunity part, but it shocked me, is all. You'd never talked about wanting a desk job before. From the second we met during BUD/s, SEALs were our only futures we'd ever mapped out. And … well, I guess I hate your job because it made you move across the country, okay? I miss you."

The words cut deep because I know it's not how I want them to mean. "As your roommate?"

Prescott licks his lips and hesitates. "As my best friend."

And as if he'd stabbed me in the heart for the millionth time, I rub my chest and try to accept that if I didn't want an honest answer, I shouldn't have asked. He already balked at the mere mention of being a throuple. Why would I expect him to call me his partner?

Nothing has changed. I'm not sure anything ever will.

brady

MY HEART IS STILL HAMMERING in my chest, even though Prescott and Kit are long gone. My brother almost saw them, and I'm thankful that Levi diverted his attention. I send him a silent thank-you across the room, and he gives me an up-nod in return, but his lips are pressed together in disapproval.

Levi thinks I should tell my family because they won't care, and I know they won't. But my family isn't exactly known for being subtle, and I want to protect them. Even if it's from themselves.

Not only them, but I also need to think of Prescott. He has just as much to lose if he's put in the public eye. With Kit's new position at the Pentagon, he's probably in the same boat.

Keeping it under wraps protects everyone involved. Including me. Because if the truth got out, I could no longer dismiss my feelings for Prescott and Kit as shallow. Not that I'm doing a good job of that at the moment. I'm one thread away from giving up the future I want, the future I've planned for years, so I could be with them. Both of them. However it could work.

Everyone in the room is staring at me like they're expecting me to lead this sudden family reunion.

"Where's Four?" Uncle Noah asks.

"He, uh, didn't come home last night, I don't think. He said something about crashing in someone's dorm."

"Whose dorm? It's summer. The dorms are empty." Uncle Noah frowns.

"Isn't there summer housing?" I'm sure the guys said Four said he wouldn't be coming home, but I didn't talk to him. The text he sent me said for me to get home and not much else.

Uncle Matt grips Noah's shoulder. "He's a fully grown boy now. He can make those decisions on his own."

Uncle Noah is rather protective of his kids—something I've grown up with, so have always known, but it still surprises me when my dads laugh at him for it because before Jackie, their eldest, was born, he was supposedly the least parental of them all. They say he was a selfish playboy and Uncle Matt somehow got him to settle down. I can't see it.

Uncle Noah turns to his husband. "He also voluntarily chose to study poli-sci and wants to be a politician. A politician, Matthew. I don't trust our son's instincts."

Four is taking one poli-sci class. *One*. But Uncle Noah isn't only dramatic when it comes to his kids. Politics is another. I smother my amusement when I get a "don't encourage him" glare from Uncle Matt.

I turn to my dads. "So, why the ambush?"

Pop shrugs. "Matt and Noah were coming to visit Four, your dad and I didn't have anything on, and these two arrived last night." He points to Peyton and Levi.

Dad sniffs. "Because unlike other children of ours, they make the time to come and see us."

I barely find the time to have sex with two navy SEALs; flying to Chicago to reassure my dads that I love them is low on my list of priorities. But I can't exactly say that. "You two are retired and have an endless supply of money. Why is it up to me to come see you?"

Dad turns to Pop. "Why doesn't our child loooove us?"

"Maybe because you turn up unannounced and interrupt se— leep." *Sleep*. Definitely sleep. Not a weekend of orgasms.

I'm so pissed, but it's not like I can tell them why I'm mad.

"He woke up on the wrong side of the bed this morning," Peyton says.

"I was woken up," I correct him.

"Someone get this boy some coffee stat," Dad says and pushes Pop toward the kitchen.

"As much as I'd love to stay, I really should go into the office this weekend. You know, law school doesn't give me much time to get all the admin stuff done that Uncle Damon expects of me."

Dad slips out his phone, hits a button, and puts it to his ear. "Hey, Brady's not coming into the office today." He hits End before Uncle Damon would even be able to reply. Thankfully. Because I'm sure his words would have been *He's not supposed to come in today.*

"Look, I love you all. You know I do. But if I'm going to be good enough to take over as Peyton's agent next year when I graduate law school, I need this experience now."

"Damon won't throw you into the deep end if you're not ready, and if you ask me, you're ready now to take over." Dad has way too much faith in me.

"I agree," Peyton says. "Plus, I'm your golden ticket. You don't really need to do anything."

The fact he thinks that makes me realize Peyton has no idea how much Uncle Damon actually does for him. It's not just contracts. It's finding endorsement deals, squashing scandals and rumors, making sure players are at the top of their game, and, if they're not, finding what we can do to fix it for them. Uncle Damon goes above and beyond for his clients when not a lot of other agents will. Personal issues, health issues … we're basically a therapist, a parent, and a babysitter all in one, and it's important that we stay behind the scenes so our precious athletes' minds aren't wrapped up in anything other than the game.

With Peyton being as high-profile as he is, I need to make sure I have enough experience before I take over. Kelley would be better experience than Torey to prepare me to take over Peyton, even if they're separate sports, but bottom line is, I'm still green, and Peyton's future isn't something I want to gamble with.

Pop brings me a coffee in one of my purple Franklin U mugs from college. It's perfect for my mood with the big golden yellow F U on the front. I make sure that's pointing outward as I drink.

I can't believe I could have two dicks inside me, and instead, I'm here with a family I love. Apparently. At the moment, I'm struggling to find that love, but I do love them.

Four arrives home, coming through the front door with his eyes closed. "You better be clothed, Brady, or I'm telling your dads that—"

"Four!" Levi yells.

Four's eyes fly open, but everyone is focused on Levi's little outburst.

That's not suspicious at all.

Levi, usually a quiet, broody artist type, tries to play it off by smiling and hugging Four. "It's been so long since I've seen you."

"You've met me, like, once."

"And it was so long ago." The enthusiasm in Levi's voice is unsettling.

I sigh into my coffee.

Today is going to be a long day.

All throughout family lunch, at some fancy restaurant Uncle Damon got us a private room at, I can feel Uncle Damon watching me from the other end of the table.

Nearly the whole extended "found family" is here. My uncles Damon, Maddox, Matt, Noah, Ollie, and Lennon, plus my dads, my brother and Levi, and Four, but Damon's focus is all on me, and I know it's because I lied to my dads and said I had to work today.

Getting away to go see Kit and Prescott is going to be impossible, but I'm still going to try. Sometime. Somehow. Even if I have to sneak out of the house in the middle of the night like I'm back in high school.

"I can't believe you called me out for that fumble on national TV," Peyton says to Uncle Lennon. "I was supposed to be your favorite nephew."

Those two have been talking football nonstop. Uncle Lennon and Uncle Ollie have their own cable sports show, and they don't hold back. Though Uncle Ollie is a retired NHL player, so a lot of the football talk goes right over his head. It makes for entertaining television when he has no idea what's going on or mixes up hockey terms with football terms. Like that one time he called a touchdown a goal, and Uncle Lennon facepalmed. I'm sure Uncle Ollie acts dumb on purpose—it's part of the show's charm.

While they talk about Peyton's embarrassment, I stab my food with my fork. I'm not all that hungry because I'm too stressed.

I excused myself to go to the bathroom earlier so I could text the guys with some privacy, but Peyton interrupted me before they could reply, and I haven't been able to check my phone since.

Levi's next to me at the head of the table, and while the others are distracted, he leans closer. "That thing from college still happening, huh? Your deal was only when they were on leave, right?"

I glance around at my family. Everyone's focus is everywhere else, except Uncle Damon's, who still glances at me every five seconds. He won't be able to hear me up this end, so I match Levi and move in closer to talk low. "Technically it's still happening, but I've only seen them a handful of times since graduating, so it's not like it's a thing. It's just a ..."

What is it?

An amazing handful of times. Moments that both filled my heart and broke it at the same time.

"A temporary thing?" Levi asks, and my chest twinges.

It feels like it's more than that, but if I look at it from a black-and-white perspective, I can't deny it. "They surprised me for the weekend, and now I can't even have that with them."

"I guarantee if you stood up in front of this entire table full of queer men and said, 'I have a three-way to get to,' not one of them would stop you."

"You know it's more than that. Peyton, for one."

"Peyton what now?" my brother cuts in.

"Is a douchenozzle," I say.

"Ah, brotherly love," Uncle Ollie says wistfully. "I should call my real brothers."

Dad overhears that and gasps. "Blood doesn't equal *real* family."

Uncle Ollie waves him off. "You know what I mean. Peyton and

Brady arguing reminded me of my overbearing family, who I haven't made the effort to go see lately."

"What are they arguing about?" Dad asks.

I throw my head back. "Why is our entire family so fucking nosey?"

"Brady had a hookup back at the house," Peyton says. "I saw him sneaking out the window."

Levi and I lock gazes. The only thing I'm gripping onto is the fact Pey said *him*. Not *them*.

Peyton smacks Levi playfully, but it makes a thwack sound. "You knew, didn't you?"

Levi puts up his hands. "I'm Switzerland."

"Who is he?" Uncle Maddox bounces in his seat.

"He's no one. Which is why I told him to take the window because no one wants to be introduced to this family until it's serious. Which this is not." No matter how much I want it to be.

Levi cuts in. "But I happen to know it's someone we went to college with, and he's only here for this weekend. We can't keep Brady from having fun."

I scowl at him. "What have you done? They're going to tell me to go to him only so they can follow and catch a glimpse and then embarrass me mercilessly."

Dad puts his hand on his heart. "Our baby knows us so well."

Under the table, someone kicks me, and when I look in front of me, Peyton winks. I don't know what he's planning until he grabs his right arm.

"Ouch, fuck." He spreads his fingers out and then makes a fist a couple of times.

Everyone goes into "Oh, shit, super-talented NFL player is injured" mode, and I seize my chance.

I could kiss my brother for redirecting the attention to him and giving me an opportunity to get away.

I'm out the door to the restaurant and ordering an Uber before they even realize I'm gone. Hopefully. I make my pickup spot around the corner, just in case.

There's a message waiting for me on my phone:

Kit: *If you can get away, we got a room at the Plaza.*

Me: *OMW. So which one of you won the lottery to afford that place?*

Prescott: *Kit is Mr. Money Bags now.*

Kit: *Ignore Pres. He's drunk.*

Prescott: *Am not!*

Me: *Are you guys literally texting right next to each other?*

Prescott: *Yep.*

Kit: *Yup.*

They never fail to make me smile. I reply: *I'll see you guys soon. Come meet me in the lobby.*

CHAPTER NINETEEN

"YOU COMING DOWN TO MEET BRADY?" Kit asks.

I want to, but the way Brady kicked us out of his place earlier has me doubting what I'm even doing here. Which is driving me crazy because I know what this is, and I know what we agreed to have.

Before arriving in New York, I would've said if his family were in town, we would make ourselves scarce. In the moment? I wanted nothing more than for him to take us downstairs and introduce us.

He did it to protect *me* and *my job*, as well as his own, yet the whole thing doesn't sit right with me.

"Are you all right to go? I have to check in with the parentals. Haven't called them since I got back."

"Give them my love."

"No way. Then they'll ask a million questions about you instead of me, and I already have to fight my millions of siblings for their attention."

Kit grins, his all-American charm shining. "You know I'm their favorite child."

He's right about that. My parents love him more than me or any of my siblings, but it's because they know Kit didn't have the same upbringing that they provided us. When they came to visit me after Kit and I moved into our apartment in Coronado, they asked if Kit's parents had come to see the new place yet because they didn't want to come second in the parent awards. When Kit scoffed and said they could never come second to people who claimed to love him but then cut him out because of his "life choices," my momma bear adopted him immediately.

I don't have secrets from my parents, and they know Kit's and my history. Once upon a time, they tried to convince me I belonged with him. And maybe, for a while, I began to believe it, but I was too busy being young, wild, carefree, and interested in protecting my career.

Plus, I was convinced that relationships never work despite my parents proving otherwise. But they're the exception, not the rule.

Even though I love the group dynamic in the bedroom, the very few relationships I tried in my twenties had been between two because, well, that's what you do according to society.

Being in Kit and Brady's orbit again, I'm convinced society is a toxic place of closed-mindedness and tradition.

Kit's my best friend, and we always had this intense connection that surpassed friendship, but Brady came along, and somehow, I fit with him as well as I do with Kit.

When Kit leaves to wait for Brady in the lobby, I take out my phone and video call my parents in Hawaii.

"Aloha, Jimmy!" Dad answers in his chipper tone. He's where I get my Polynesian genes from.

"It's afternoon in New York, Dad."

"New York? Why are you in New York? I thought this was going to be the phone call your mother and I always dread." He turns his head to call out, "Abbey! Our least favorite son is calling." He thinks he's so funny.

"I'm actually here with your favorite son," I say.

"Kit's there? Put him on." He ducks and weaves his head as if he'll be able to see Kit from a different angle. Parents and technology, I swear.

"He's not here."

"You said—"

"He's in New York. Not in the same room this very minute. Besides, *I* called to talk to you. The one who Mom actually birthed, and I need advice."

"Marry him." Mom appears next to Dad.

"Yeah, not that advice." Even if she's determined to make it happen one day. "But it is about Kit. And ... someone else."

"Uh-oh," Mom says.

"Did you go and get yourself stuck in a love triangle?" Dad asks.

"I thought it was only girls in teen movies that did that," Mom says.

"It's not a love ... triangle ... exactly." I may not keep secrets from my parents, but it's not like talking about sex with them is easy.

"Oh, is it a three-way situation? A ... What do you call it?" Mom's brow pinches while she tries to think.

"A ménage à trois," Dad says.

"I know we taught you to share as a child, but this takes it to a whole new level." My mom also thinks she's funny.

"Why did I call you guys for advice again?"

"We're listening," Mom says. "But you're not talking. You're being vague."

Sure, vague. Has nothing to do with them not letting me get a word in yet.

I let out a loud breath. "How did you two know you were with the one, and how did you know ... that there was only one for you?"

"I don't understand the question," Mom says.

"I think he's asking what made us choose to marry each other and be faithful that whole time."

"I have a boy toy on the side." Mom laughs.

Dad and I don't join her.

"Oh." Her face falls. "You're serious."

"I know you're all about love is love and you're free thinkers, but there's this guy. Brady. Both Kit and I are into him, and when we're together, it's amazing, but it's finding time to be together that's the issue, and we were at his house earlier, and he kicked us out when his family came home—"

"Family as in wife and kids?" Mom asks.

"God no. His dads and brother. And a few uncles, I think. There were a lot of people there."

"How old is he?"

"He's twenty-four, Mom. In law school. He's really smart."

"Not so smart of him to come between you and Kit though, is he?" Dad says.

"It's not like that. At all. If anything, he brings me and Kit closer in some ways. When Kit left California and then quit the navy entirely, Brady's been the one talking me through it. He's the entire reason Kit and I still see each other at all anymore."

Mom purses her lips. "It sounds like you're saying you're using this Brady kid to get to Kit?"

I grunt and run my hand through my hair. "No. I'm saying that somewhere along the way, I might have developed feelings for Brady. The same kind I have for Kit."

"You always told us you and Kit were only friends," Dad says.

"We are!" This is not coming across right. I try to find the words, the words I've probably been denying for way too long. "I didn't think I'd miss Kit as much as I have. I don't miss him in the way a best friend misses his roommate. At the same time, when I think of Kit, I think of Brady, and I … I want them both. But I can't even make a relationship work with one person. With two, I could fuck everything up. And there's also no point in even thinking about this because of the distance between us all. So why can't I let it go like I always have? Why, when Brady's family came home and he freaked out, did I feel like a dirty little secret doing something wrong instead of what we are, which is … well, I guess technically we could only be called fuck buddies, but it's so much more than that. At least it is for me."

"I'm going to maybe suggest something radical here," Dad says. "You could talk to them and see how they feel about being in a permanent thing. Hey, in that situation, who's the bun and who's the hot dog? Is there two hot dogs or two buns?"

"And I'm done talking about this with you two."

Supportive parents are great, don't get me wrong, but I'm not so sure boundary-crossing parents are the best.

"Your dad has a point though," Mom adds. "About talking to them, not the hot dog thing."

There's a nagging feeling at the back of my mind that if it's brought up, the answer will be a no and end our arrangement completely.

Which is worse: pining after them but still getting to see them once a year to explore our strong bond or not having them at all?

When I look at it like that, the answer is clear.

I can't risk blowing it all up over a relationship that would be impossible to maintain while living in three different states.

When Brady and Kit come up to the room not long later, I end the call and do what the three of us do best. We get naked and pretend we're not saying goodbye again.

Until tomorrow.

CHAPTER TWENTY

WHEN I DRAG my ass into work on Monday, I'm physically satisfied but emotionally wrecked. Because my family showed up, I only got in a couple more hours with the guys, and then I had to say goodbye.

It feels like it's all I ever do to them.

As an intern, I work in the bullpen, which is usually fun and upbeat because everyone is young and interning or is fresh out of school and working their way up, so we're all in the same boat. There's a camaraderie between us, business friendships, and these are the networking years, so it pays to be friendly to everyone. Especially me, the firm's name partner's honorary nephew.

But I can't deal today.

"Rough weekend?" Thad asks from the cubical beside me.

"Something like that," I murmur quietly.

Uncle Damon enters the bullpen area. "Brady, can I see you in my office for a second?"

Uh-oh.

"Uncle's favorite employee," Thad mocks.

"That was his 'you're in trouble' tone, so don't be too jealous."

"Are you kidding? I'd hate to be in your shoes, man. Well, no, I take that back. I'd kill to be Brady Talon, son of Marcus Talon and Shane Miller, but I digress. Your current life—where you're Damon

King's favorite bitch boy? No, thank you. I'm happy to fly under the radar."

I hold my heart. "You make my life and my choices sound so glamorous."

"You voluntarily gave up football to look after diva athletes. Your life choices are dubious at best."

"Do you even want to be an agent?" I ask. "I understand the disappointment of not making it in baseball, but are you going to be able to rep the people who did without letting your bitterness show? All you did with Kelley was roll your eyes behind his back."

"Dude, I just let baseball go. Give me at least a little time to accept it."

Fair enough.

"Besides, Kelley doesn't know how good he has it. He has my dream, but all he does is cry about it."

That's not true at all, and if Thad was in his position, with everything's that's being said online, he'd be frazzled too. But all he can see is someone with his dream job not appreciating it, when it's actually the opposite. Kelley wants it so much that any risk to it is tearing him up inside.

"Brady, now," Uncle Damon calls out loud enough for the entire bullpen to hear.

Well, fuck. I really am in trouble, but I have no idea what I've done. When I get to Uncle Damon's office, he's sitting behind his desk, resting back on his chair with his fingers steepled beneath his chin.

"What did I do wrong?" I ask, taking the chair opposite him.

Uncle Damon's green eyes narrow. "You're hiding something."

"Huh?" I squeak.

He points. "That, right there. That little high-pitched break in your voice. You did it the other day at lunch when Peyton and Levi ratted you out for having a hookup in the house."

I swallow hard and try to hide how much I hate he can read me—maybe even better than my own dads or brother can. "So because I wanted to save my hookup from the torture that would be meeting my extended family, I'm hiding something bigger?"

"Yep."

"Explain your logic."

"One: if he was truly a hookup, you wouldn't have cared about embarrassment from us because you'd never see him again. Two: Levi said it was someone from college, only adding that this might be someone special to you. And three: call it gut instinct, but the only reason you wouldn't tell us if you were in a serious relationship, aside from the embarrassment, is if there's something problematic about it. Like if they were a client, but I've already scoured our client base for anyone current who went to Franklin U, and unless you're fucking your brother—which I really hope you're not—it's something else."

"Do you swear at your other employees, Uncle Damon?"

"No. I reserve that special treatment for you."

"I'm … honored?"

"Stop deflecting."

I lean forward in my seat and run a hand through my hair.

"Oh shit," Uncle Damon says. "It's serious, isn't it. Is it …" He gasps. "Is it a woman? Are you *straight*?"

I manage a laugh. "I know you're trying to ease my nerves with humor, and I'm grateful, but—"

"Whatever it is, we'll work through it. You just need to tell me before I freak out and think of the worst thing possible, like wondering if they're even eighteen, and if you met while you were in college, then they'd be illegally young, and—"

"Not young. If anything, I joke about them being closer to your age than mine."

"Them. Nonbinary? We can work with that, no issue at all."

I suck in a sharp breath. "Not them, singular. Them … plural."

I said it. I actually fucking said it. Yet the weight on my chest hasn't lifted at all because Uncle Damon sits there silently with a real-life thinky emoji expression on his face.

"That's the issue," I say. "I'm thinking of the media fallout when Marcus Talon and Shane Miller not only raised two queer kids, but one of them is the poster boy for debauchery and sin with multiple partners. Peyton already has enough pressure piling on his career because of who our dads are. Add into the mix that he discovered he was bi while playing college football. I'm gay. It plays into the *queer is contagious* stigma when the reality is we were raised in an environment where we could be ourselves. It turns out I'm not only gay, I'm also poly. You taught me it's our job to make things easy on our players. My private life could affect Peyton. Or Kelley and Torey. And anyone else I end up repping. But mainly, I'm worried about Peyton."

Uncle Damon's still quiet, but then he stands. He rounds his desk with a stoic look on his face, and my heart rate kicks up a notch.

"I'm fired, aren't I?"

He stands above me now. "Get up."

I'm totally fired.

On shaky legs, I stand, and in the next instant, I'm being embraced like my life depended on it.

"Is this hug a way to soften the blow of being fired?"

Uncle Damon laughs. "You're not being fired, dumbass. But you do need the hug."

He pulls back, and I meet his gaze.

"Uh, why?"

"Why aren't you fired, or why do you need the hug?"

"Both."

This time, when we sit, he takes the seat next to me instead of going back behind his desk. "First of all, when you say plural, how many are we talking? A quadruple circle jerk? A—"

I hold up my hand. "There's just two of them."

"And are you all together, or are you dating two guys at once. I assume they at least know about each other if they were both there at the house."

"That's another reason I haven't said anything. We're together when we see each other, but that's hardly ever. One lives in Cali, the other in Virginia, so in between, I guess we're single, even if I haven't been interested in anyone else, and dating is a bust because … well, I'd rather be with them."

"You're not looking to add more partners or anything."

I screw up my face. "I really hope that wasn't a hint at an invitation. I don't want to know what you and Uncle Maddox get up to, and no, I don't want to share Kit and Prescott."

That earns me a love tap upside my head.

"Do you hit all your employees too?" I shriek.

"No. Still just you. But I'm trying to think of a way to spin it if needed."

My heart sinks. "So I am right. This does have the potential to hurt Peyton."

"It does, but does that mean you shouldn't follow your heart? Fuck no. You've put your brother first your entire life. You were as good at throwing a ball as your brother was. You chose to give him the quarterback position."

"No, I didn't." Did I? "I figured Pop was an offensive tackle, so I thought blocking was in my blood. Just like being the next GOAT is in Peyton's."

Uncle Damon shakes his head. "Football is so much more than DNA and natural talent. With who your parents are, you could've played any position you wanted, and they would've hired coaches to get you where you needed to be. I know you say you didn't like the pressure of football, but I always had the impression you only quit so you could be here, doing what you've always done—supporting and protecting your older brother."

"I …" I pause. "I've never thought about it like that, but maybe you're right."

"I didn't create this firm so I could make being queer in sports palatable for the straights," Uncle Damon says. "You should live your truth, no matter what that truth is. Will it be more difficult? Will you and your guys be in the spotlight for a while? Yes. But any story can be spun. Any situation can be 'fixed.' Unless you're screaming racial slurs from rooftops or they were underage or anything else truly problematic. Loving two men in the age of love is love shouldn't be as scandalous as it will be, but it will be manageable. I promise you."

While his response makes everything sit lighter on my chest, it doesn't make the worry go away completely. "Can … you not say anything to the family? You know they'll make it a huge deal when it really isn't. If there was even a possibility of a future with Kit and Prescott, I'd be more tempted, but as it stands, seeing them once a year is killing me, and I don't know how much longer I can take it. Plus, I don't even know if they'd want a relationship with me. Sometimes it feels like it's impossible for us to walk away from each other. Other times I'm convinced I'm their toy to play with as an excuse for them to cross the friendship boundary and have sex."

And now it's Uncle Damon's turn to screw up his face. "What kind of names are Prescott and Kit? And how old are they again?"

I stand. "Is that my cubicle phone ringing? Work calls."

Uncle Damon grabs my wrist and pulls me back down. "Spill."

"They're total dude bros because they're navy SEALs—well, one's still a SEAL, the other works for the Pentagon. Oh, wait … I might not be able to tell you that. They do top secret government agency type shit."

"They're … how old?" he asks again.

"They're, like, nine or ten years older. The age gap is nothing. It's the same between Uncle Jet and Uncle Soren."

Uncle Damon rubs his chin. "I know I'm not allowed to tell your parents anything, but can I please tell Maddox? You have no idea how proud he would be of you for pulling SEALs. Damn, even I'm impressed."

"Can Uncle Maddox keep a secret?" I ask.

"True story for you: Maddox knew your dads were hooking up before anyone else on this planet. He never said a word. Not even to me."

"Then yes, you can tell him. Though, it's really, really weird that you're applauding my sexploits. What kind of uncle are you? Oh, the dirty, dirty kind that—"

"Now who's being weird? Don't make it weird, Brady."

I laugh.

"Oh, and one more thing …"

"Get back to work?"

He pats my head. "I've trained you well."

CHAPTER TWENTY-ONE

WORKING at the Pentagon as a civilian isn't everything I'd hoped it would be. I have less security clearance but a lot more money. I don't think the trade-off is really worth it.

Still, every morning when I clear security and head inside, I still get that special ops zing in my veins. Which is stupid because I'm merely a pencil pusher now. "Leader of training operations" sounds like an important job, but it's not. Not really. It's a necessary job, but it mainly consists of approving training drills, equipment, and any other training resources for special ops forces in the military.

Before, I was being informed of military operations going on in the real world, and now I'm in charge of fake situations and approving training modules.

Do I regret it? Maybe a little bit. Will I admit that? Not while Jimmy Prescott is alive. I won't give him the satisfaction of being right.

I reach my office in my own little corner of the Pentagon and groan at the pile of applications on my desk. I know that having served in the navy, I might be biased, but for fuck's sake, the army is a needy little wench. If their soldiers really need that much training, maybe they should look at their training techniques. Hell, send 'em all to BUD/s training and see how long they last.

I quit my internal bitching and get to work, only to be interrupted a couple of minutes later by a knock on my open doorway.

When I glance up from my desk, the warmest set of brown eyes meets me, and I'm convinced I'm having a delusional dream. I haven't seen him or spoken to him since New York, but it's only been a month.

"Pres? What are you doing here?" I blink, thinking he'll disappear any minute.

"You don't know? You approved this stupid training swap operation."

"Training swap—oh, where you swap with SEAL Team Ten for a training op to see how the different coasts do it?"

"That's the one. I half wondered if you suggested Team Three for the swap so you'd get to see me, but you wouldn't be so cruel as to send me to the East Coast, would you?"

"Hey, if I had that kind of pull, I definitely would have. Unfortunately, I don't get much of a say anymore. Just have to file the paperwork."

He looks around my tiny office. "You really are moving backward in the world. Didn't you used to report to command central?"

"Yeah, but having that much space to think was too difficult. I like closed-in walls that try to suffocate me."

Prescott smiles. "You available to catch up for a drink when we get back? We're heading out tonight. I assume we'll only be gone a couple of days."

"I'll be here." Damn, I want to go over and kiss him, but we're both on duty, and if I did it without the pretense of it being for Brady or because of Brady, is that crossing the line?

Our relationship is so confusing when it comes to stuff like that.

"I'll see you soon," he says and walks away.

I rack my brain trying to remember what this particular training op involved, but my mind is blank. Most ops only go for a few days, but there are extreme ones that last almost a month. I hope it's only a few days because those two minutes with Prescott were nowhere near enough to get my fill.

When it comes to him, I'm not sure forever would be enough.

❦ ❦ ❦

After two weeks of no word from SEAL Team Three, I try to tell myself to not worry or be impatient because top secret training ops are top secret for a reason. I found the paperwork for the training op he's on, but it was vague with the length. It said approximately one week with subject to change. So I shouldn't be panicking yet. That doesn't stop me from making my way to command central to ask the new SEAL liaison if he's heard anything.

Even though I'm a civilian now, when I see a colonel, I salute them.

Colonel Bryan Parker cracks a smile. "You know you don't have to do that anymore, don't you?"

I shrug. "Habit."

"What can I do for you?"

"I wanted to check in on SEAL Team Three. They were running a training op I approved, but I thought they'd be back by now."

Colonel Parker hesitates to answer, and I get it. I'm not supposed to know this kind of stuff anymore. If I hadn't served under him and knew him, I wouldn't even be asking. He's the type of soldier who's usually in the liaison position. Nearing retirement, experienced, high-ranking. Prescott wasn't the only one who questioned my move to the Pentagon, but I don't regret that. Taking this civilian job is another story, but I took it because it's even less involvement with the navy than the liaison job. It's another barrier I could put between Prescott and myself. It still hasn't helped, and now, when I have this worry in my gut over him, where he is, and what's taking so long, I realize it was the wrong move.

"They, uh, they should be back any day now," Parker says, but there's something in his voice that makes me think he's lying or covering something up.

"Why don't I believe you?"

"Because you're an overprotective jerk, maybe?" He smiles, but it fades quickly. "You and Prescott are close, aren't you? Roommates?"

"Until I moved here. Obviously."

"Look, I'll see what I can find out for you."

"Translation: you'll find out what you're allowed to tell me."

Parker's eyes are sympathetic but don't give anything away.

I nod. "Anything you can tell me would be great. Thank you."

"Let me make some calls, and I'll come see you in your office later."

It's not the answer I was hoping for—nowhere near it. Because if it was a standard training op and everything was going fine, he'd simply say everything is on track. Or maybe even be able to give me a rough date of when they were scheduled to come home. Instead, he took the classified route. I know what that means in these situations.

The training op is FUBAR.

I go back to my office and try to work through my worry, but I can't concentrate. Every training op application I read, every risk assessment I do, all I can think about is how Prescott's might be going wrong.

I pick up my phone to call him, though he won't be able to answer even if he wanted to, so instead of hitting his number, I dial Brady and hope I'm not interrupting anything like work or, worse, a date.

"Kit?" Brady answers. "This is … unexpected."

"I know." It's not that I never call, but if I ever need one of them, it's usually via text. Calls have purpose, and if there's something I need to talk about—meeting up or whatever—I try to organize a time to get both of them at once. I know Pres and Brady have their phone calls, but I'm not a phone call kind of guy.

"What's up?" Brady asks.

"You're not busy, are you? If you're working or got classes, I can—"

"Just on my way home from the office. It's summer. I don't have classes."

"Right. Of course. I knew that." I'm not thinking clearly.

His tone switches. "Is everything all right?"

"I … I wanted to hear a familiar voice. That's all."

"Are you sure that's all?"

Before he's got the sentence out, I practically blurt, "Have you heard from Prescott lately?"

"No, not since he was sent on some training mission. He said he was going to meet up with you after it, and I was trying to plan to come to Virginia to be there as well, but it's been difficult without knowing exactly when he'd be back. What's happened?"

"Nothing. I'm freaking out over nothing."

"You? Mr. Guy Kitchener, the most put-together man I know, is freaking out? It has to be something."

"Nah, I'm overreacting to a gut feeling. I expected Prescott to be back already, but he even said himself he didn't know how long he'd be gone." Though he did say it was supposed to be a short one, and it's already been two weeks. Colonel Parker was being sketchy about details, and— Nope, nope, nope. *Stop reading into everything, Kit.*

"What's your gut saying? Do you think he could've been deployed instead or …"

I don't want Brady to worry, so I try to sound confident when I say, "Yeah, it's probably something like that." It can't be that, though, because back-to-back deployments don't happen unless there's some kind of all-out catastrophe. World war, global incident, alien invasion. Prescott's team won't be due to ship out again for at least eighteen months.

"How are things between you two?" Brady asks. "We haven't really had a chance to talk without him present for a while. Did moving to Virginia help you to get over him?"

"I can hear your smirk, you little shit."

"That's because I know it didn't work."

He's right. It didn't. And having shared Brady so often with Prescott, all three of us being together, Brady's in my head as much as Prescott is. I thought it might have been because without Brady, Prescott and I wouldn't have the excuse to continue hooking up now we live apart, but in this moment, the one where I was worried about Prescott, there was only one person I wanted to call.

"Are you sure you're all right?" Brady asks.

"I'm fine. Just tired from the new office job. Overthinking every-thing. But I'm good."

"Is it weird that you were a SEAL, but it's the office job that's killing you?"

"What can I say, using my brain instead of my brawn is tiring me out."

"As long as that's all it is."

I smile. "Aren't I the one who usually looks after you, not the other way around?"

"No, you're my escape from having to look after everyone else in my life, but we all need help sometimes, Kit. I'm only a phone call away if you ever need anything."

My heart fills with warmth that I'm not expecting, and my nose prickles as tears spring to my eyes.

What the fuck is wrong with me?

"I'm fine," I reassure him, even though I'm not. "But I have to go. I have a lot of work to do." And a lot of waiting around for Colonel Parker to update me.

"Talk soon?" Brady asks.

"You bet."

We end the call, and while talking to Brady helped, I'm still worried. I'm worried enough to stay at work well past my set hours, just hoping that Colonel Parker or Prescott himself will knock on my door.

When it gets to nine at night and it doesn't happen, I resign myself to the knowledge I'm not going to get answers tonight and head home. Not before checking if Colonel Parker is still on-site. Which he isn't.

No matter how many times I tell myself to shake off the unease, to not worry, that anxiety doesn't go away.

I drive home to my apartment in a blur, moving on autopilot to the point I don't remember getting here, but as I stare up at my building, I'm sure I'm seeing things.

There's no way Brady Talon could be sitting on my stoop. One, he doesn't know where I live, and two, I spoke to him only, what, two hours ago? I look at the clock on my car stereo. Oh, it was more like five hours ago now. He either drives really fast or hopped on a plane, but why?

He stands when I get out of the car. "Thought you'd never get here."

"I worked later than usual. What …" I glance around the almost full parking lot. It's a large apartment complex, with five four-story buildings. "How did you know where my apartment was?"

He starts to approach me, and I meet him on the sidewalk. "Prescott."

"You heard from him?"

He puts his hands in his pockets and looks adorably bashful. "No. When we agreed back in Florida to see each other outside of the three of us, he sent me your address and told me to come see you. I didn't want to impose until now."

"And why now?"

"Because it's obvious something's wrong." He looks up at me, his brown eyes a shade lighter than Prescott's seeing right through me. I don't think I've ever taken notice of him doing that before.

I didn't know he had the ability to reach my soul with just one look.

"You came here because of that?"

"No. I came here because I know the type of man you are, and I know that even though something's wrong, you're not going to ask for help. So I'm here offering it, because like I said on the phone, everyone needs help sometimes."

My lip trembles, so I press forward and wrap my arms around him. We sink into each other, and I lower my head to his shoulder.

I will my eyes to stay dry, but they don't listen. Neither does my nose. When I sniff, Brady pulls back.

"Well, that's the response I was hoping for. Brady Talon, bringing men to tears for being in their presence. It's a talent."

I huff a laugh, but it's weak.

"Have you eaten?" Brady asks.

"Hey, that's usually my line."

"Not tonight. I'm here now, and it's time someone looked after you for once. Lead me to your apartment."

I let it happen. Brady follows closely behind me, picking up a duffle bag on the stoop on the way.

I lead him up the stairs to my third-floor apartment, and as soon as we enter, he heads for the kitchen.

He opens the fridge and then the cupboards.

"I don't have—"

"How in the world do you live on this?"

"I haven't been to the grocery store in a while."

And he's right. My kitchen is pretty barren.

"Okay, ordering in it is. What's good around here?"

"You don't have to—"

"Stop fighting me on this. Once Prescott's back, you can go back into overprotective alpha mode. But not now. So sit down or take a shower, do whatever you need to. I'm here when you're ready to talk. Or eat. Or need a blowjob to keep your mind off everything."

My dick twitches. I'll be down for that later. But a shower sounds amazing, and it will give me time to compose myself and not break down and cry in his arms again.

Maybe.

"How long are you staying for?" I ask.

"As long as you need me. I asked my uncle for the day off tomorrow, and I don't work weekends unless I have to scout. So I'm yours."

He means temporarily—only for the weekend—but I can't help that wishful part of me that gets stuck on those two little words: *I'm yours.*

CHAPTER TWENTY-TWO

I DON'T TELL Kit that I'm also freaking the fuck out. For Kit to be this messed up, whatever's happening with Prescott must be serious. I don't let my concern about that show though.

Kit and Prescott haven't seen this side of me—the caretaker, the problem solver. It's because I've never needed to show them. They give me a break from that side of my personality, so I'm sure it's a shock to Kit that I'm actually capable of ordering food or cooking or taking care of things, but I can do this shit in my sleep.

And I don't even hate it. What I've liked about the dynamic between the three of us is that I haven't had to tap into that. While I still love the escapism of responsibilities and adulthood when I'm with them, and no way will this be a permanent switch in our … semi-regular meetup sex relationship—whatever we want to call it— I don't mind doing it for them. If Prescott needed help, I'd be the first —okay, well, no, the second—to offer behind Kit.

These men mean a lot to me, probably more than I do to them, but that's not going to stop me caring about them and doing what I can for them.

The food comes while Kit's in the shower, so instead of eating out of the Chinese takeout boxes, I dish out a bit of everything onto plates. I'll even wash the dishes afterward.

I hope my take-charge attitude and showing up unannounced allows him to open up a bit. The way he was talking … I fear

Prescott is either deployed or, worse, has been in some kind of accident, but I'm hoping Kit is overreacting.

Kit comes out dressed in sweatpants and nothing else, and I have to swallow my tongue so it's not tempted to dart out and lick every inch of this man's abs. Or attack the dick print that's showing through the tight material.

He doesn't notice me practically drooling though. He's running a towel over his hair, even though there's not much of it. He must have recently shaved the sides of his head, but leaving the military means the stuff on top is growing out. It's kind of in an in-between stage where it's too long to fit in with the short sides but not long enough to cover the shaved bits.

When he's done, he turns and throws the towel back down the hallway toward the bathroom, but it doesn't make it. He doesn't care.

Considering how uptight he is about being neat, it's another red flag. So I put on my *I'm here for you* face, take over a plate of food with the choice of using chopsticks or a fork, and then go pick up his towel and hang it on the towel rack in the bathroom.

I come back out, but Kit's frozen, sitting on the couch, plate on his lap, and his fork halfway to his mouth.

"What's wrong?"

"Who are you, and where is the Brady I know?"

I chuckle. "I'm still in here."

"No, you're not. You're messy, you're bratty, and you need us to do everything for you."

"That's one side of me. Plus, it's not like I ask you to do everything for me. You just do it, usually while Prescott is distracting me with his mouth."

"Or his dick."

"That too." I grab my plate and take the spot next to Kit on his leather couch.

"What you're telling me is you're not really a lazy slob?"

"Oh, I'm a slob by nature, but I can clean up when I need to. Or, you know, when no one's there to do it for me."

He shakes his head. "You really are a little shit."

"But you wouldn't have me any other way."

He throws a dumpling in his mouth and talks around the food. "I dunno. I think I like this side of you as well."

"As long as you don't expect put-together Brady all the time. He's exhausting."

Kit laughs, but his face slowly fades back into the worried look he arrived with.

"What's going on with Prescott?" I ask.

"I don't know. It's typical of the navy to keep everything under wraps, but … my gut … it's telling me something is wrong."

"And there's no way of contacting Prescott?"

Kit shakes his head.

"I'm sure he's fine. Maybe his training op ran long. Or he was needed somewhere important."

"You're probably right."

Yet, it's obvious he doesn't believe that as we eat our food in silence.

He doesn't finish his meal—eats barely any of it before leaning forward and putting his plate on the coffee table.

I stand and take our dirty dishes into the kitchen to rinse and put in the dishwasher.

"That's still weird," Kit says.

"I promise to never wash a dish again if it'll make you feel any better."

"Let's not go that far."

I smile over at him, and he tries to return it, but his eyes are uncharacteristically filled with worry.

"Is it too weird that I'm here?" I ask. Maybe I'm reading too much into his off mood.

His head snaps up. "What? No, not at all. I love that you came here for me."

I slowly approach him. "Are you sure?"

He watches as I continue toward him, his gray stare darkening with each step I take.

Kit nods. "I'm really glad you're here. That you care enough to be here."

I'd always be here for him.

For Prescott.

Even to the detriment of my heart.

Kit tries to get up, but I push him back onto the couch.

"What are you doing?" he rasps.

"I recall promising you a blowjob to make you forget your troubles." I sink to my knees but wait for him to give me the green light.

He stares down at me, his face stoic and so Kit-like. It's hard to get a read on him usually, but tonight, I've seen the naked vulnerability as plain as day on his face. He's worried about Prescott, I'm worried about both of them, but most of all, in this position, on my knees between Kit's legs, I realize I just miss them.

I miss them so much, and I saw them a month ago.

But I can't let myself think about that. Not while I'm here. Not while I'm trying to help Kit.

"What are you waiting for then?" he rumbles.

It's tempting—so fucking tempting—to play the brat card by saying *I'm waiting for you to make me*, but he needs me to be the Brady I am at home. The one looking after everyone else.

I need to look after *him*.

So instead of a snarky remark, I reach for his sweats and pull them down his legs. Kit stares down at me, his usual sternness unwavering in his hard features, but I see it—the thread of control that's about to snap. It's in the way he fists his hands at his sides, the slight tremor in his thighs as I lower my head and lick the tip of his cock.

I sense the need in him. The need for this to be different. For it to have meaning. Even if it's just to reassure him that he has someone other than Prescott in his corner.

I want to tell him everything. How much I love spending time with him. With Prescott. How I crave it. How being on my knees for Kit feels more selfish than selfless.

I take him into my mouth, deep, and then slowly bob my head a couple of times.

Kit lets out a shuddery breath, and my pants tighten. The smallest of sounds Kit makes has the ability to make me rock hard. But I ignore it because this is about him.

I slowly lift my head, sucking his shaft hard as I pull off and revel in the whining sound he makes. "You know what I'm thinking about?" I replace my mouth with my hand, stroking him teasingly slow.

"If it's anything other than how I taste, I'm gonna be pissed."

A bead of precum leaks from his slit, and I run my tongue over it. "You do taste amazing, but that's not it." I turn my head and kiss along his thigh, making my way up his leg to nuzzle his groin. My tongue darts out and licks his balls, then moves up, running along his cock.

"Brady," he breathes. "Tell me."

"I was thinking of those photos Pres sent me. Of the last time you two were together. They were so hot." I alternate stroking him and licking him in between sentences. "Especially the one where you were in my position, sucking Prescott's cock. I love watching you two together."

"I love watching you and Prescott too."

I glance up at him but suck him into my mouth at the same time. When I pull off again, I ask, "Do you ever get jealous?"

"Of you and Prescott? No. Of you or Prescott with anyone else? Surprisingly, yes."

Damn. I wasn't expecting such an honest answer. Or for it to be *that*.

"Do you?" he asks. "Get jealous?"

"Not in the way other people would. The only thing close to jealousy I feel is when you two are together without me, but not because I don't want you to be. I'm jealous because I don't get to be there too. All three of us can't be together all the time, and I'd rather know you two were with each other than anyone else too."

Kit's hand presses against my cheek, and I lean into it. His thumb brushes my lips. "Why are you telling me all these things?"

"Because when Prescott comes back—and he will come back—I don't want you to think that you have no one else. You have me."

Kit's eyes widen slightly.

"You will always have me," I add so my message is clear.

It doesn't matter if we're miles apart, if he's a SEAL or a measly government employee. If he or Prescott needs me, I'll be there.

Kit looks uncertain. Almost like he wants to believe me but can't.

"Let me show you," I whisper and go back to putting all my focus and attention on his cock.

I lick, I suck, worshiping every inch of velvety skin until he's gasping for air.

His entire body stiffens, the muscles in his thighs tense under my fingers, and then Kit unleashes in my mouth.

I drink him down as fast as I can until his orgasm ebbs. Everything else about him calms—his breathing, his muscles—and I swap from eager swallows to long and gentle sucks.

His body is still shaking from the high, but when I look up, I realize that's not it at all. He's not thrumming with satisfaction. He's trying not to fucking cry.

"Kit?"

In the next second, Kit leans forward, hooks his arms around me, and hauls me into his lap.

I hold him close, my arms wrapped around his upper body tightly while he buries his head in my neck.

The blowjob was supposed to make him feel better, not worse.

Great job, Brady. Way to go.

"Thank you," he murmurs.

"You never have to thank me for a blowjob."

"I meant for showing up for me. I don't ... there's not ... there aren't a lot of people in my life I can count on, even if I ask. You came here because you knew I needed someone, and ..." He pulls back and flashes me those pale gray eyes. "Just, thank you."

"Anytime." I lower my forehead to his, and we stay there like that for what would normally be an awkward eternity if it were anyone but Kit or Prescott.

We breathe each other in, Kit's hands run up and down my back, and I caress the back of his head and thread my fingers through his hair.

"You're an amazing person, Brady Talon."

It's a perfect moment.

It's everything I want to hear, especially from Kit.

If I could bottle this emotion, this content feeling, I'd do it in a heartbeat. But if there's anything I've learned in my short twenty-four years of life, it's that with the highs come the lows.

And as if on cue, Kit's phone starts ringing on the armrest of the couch.

He scrambles for it, and I go to climb off him, but he holds my hip with his free hand.

"Talk to me, Parker," he says, answering the phone. "What did you find out?"

We're so close I can hear the words coming through the other end.

"Official word is SEAL Team Three went radio silent two days ago."

"Unofficial word?" Kit asks.

There's a beat of silence before a quiet response is given. I suddenly wish I wasn't close enough to hear.

"Their Hawk went down somewhere in the Atlantic Ocean near Bermuda. They haven't been able to locate them since."

Kit and I stare at each other, both unwilling to say it out loud.

Prescott's … gone?

CHAPTER TWENTY-THREE

IF I CLOSE MY EYES, the cool breeze, the shade of some palm trees, the sound of the ocean, and the smell of salt water are almost enough to convince me I'm anywhere but here.

Wherever the fuck *here* is.

If it weren't for the raging hot fire in my leg, my clammy skin, and the chances of surviving this hell running through my mind, I could pretend I was on vacation.

I glance down at my leg again, hoping that the sight before I passed out was a dream. It was not. My left knee is twisted, and there, sticking out of my skin, is either my tibia or fibula. I can't tell which.

Other than the burning sensation, I can't feel much of anything, so that's a bonus. Or maybe it means I'm so far past gone that I'm numb to everything else.

All the possibilities I could have after something like that.

The actual moment it happened is all a blur, but there's a clear memory that's replaying in my head over and over. The alarms in the helo, the rapid descent, the moment of impact where water smashed through the cockpit windshield, and then … darkness. Painful, fiery darkness.

Don't ask me how we got to land because I don't know.

"You know," Shanahan says beside me. He's been designated my official babysitter while the others try to figure out where the fuck we are. The ones who can move, that is. Our pilot, Levenson, and copilot, Moran, lie on either side of me, and I'm too scared to ask if they're dead or alive.

"You know what?" Fuck, talking hurts. I try to shift to get comfortable, but that makes sharp pain shoot through my body.

"All those times when being asked hypothetical questions like, what would you do if you were on a deserted island, none of them ever included this part of it."

That doesn't even make sense. "What?"

"Well, to get on a deserted island, there has to be some big event before it. No one would choose to have no technology—that's not a vacation. So really, that question is asking, 'what would you do if you almost died?' It's dark if you think about it too hard."

I close my eyes. "While you think of that, I'm more asking myself how it's possible that I've been on dangerous missions, faced enemy fire, lost teammates to war, and it's a mechanical failure on a training op that takes me down." That's what they think it was, anyway.

It all happened so fast. One minute we were completing stealth exercises, the next, we were in a tailspin and hurtling toward the ocean. Most likely, it was minutes, but the crash seemed like seconds. We didn't have time to do anything to stop it or get ourselves out or anything.

I've had days of being in and out of consciousness, in agonizing pain where I've been close to asking one of the guys to end it for me, but my thoughts always venture back to that question. How is it that this is the thing that kills me?

Kit and Brady are a close second. Because while I'm here begging for death, I can't help thinking what it would do to them. How I never got the chance to tell them how I truly feel. Telling Kit I need him and miss him is one thing, telling them both that I can no longer live without them is another.

My thoughts over surviving don't even revolve around whether or not I'll still have a navy career after this. They're all about *them*.

"You'll be back on your feet in no time," Shanahan says, but we both know that's an empty promise.

Has he seen my leg?

I can't feel anything in my other one, but I'm hoping that's only because my left is giving me so much pain, even through the painkillers and trauma treatment the guys could manage to give me.

"Either we're on an island that's so deserted the guys can't find anyone for help, or we're on a party island and they forgot we're here," I say. "It's been three days. Right? I remember seeing the night sky at least that many times."

"Two," Shanahan says. "You woke up last night screaming in agony. You probably thought another day had passed. Also, they're not back yet because our indestructible locator beacon Terri grabbed from the Hawk was broken, so Woods is on that mountain trying to fix it." He points to the east. No, west? Whatever direction is to our left. "Once that's up and running, they'll be able to find us."

He's already told me that, I'm sure of it.

"Comms?" I ask.

"Fried. Whatever happened to make us fall out of the sky, it fried everything."

"How far offshore did we crash?"

"Miles."

He's told me that too. Finding us without the locator beacon or comms would be like finding a needle in a haystack.

My mind is fuzzy, and when I'm not focused on the burning sensation in my leg, I realize I have a killer headache.

"Shanahan?" I ask.

"Mm?"

"Do I have a concussion?"

"Yeah, buddy. A bad one."

"You've already told me all of this information, haven't you?"

"Yep. Numerous times."

"I'm guessing the sound of a plane is just in my head, then?" It's like an annoying buzzing in my ear that I want to swat away but can't. Not only because I can barely move my arms without wanting to throw up but because I'm sure it's not an insect.

Shanahan stands. "It's not your imagination." He waves his arms.

The relief that swamps my body also must take away some of the adrenaline keeping me alive because with relief comes pain.

I'm on my way home, but I have no idea what condition I'll be in when I get there. At the realization that Kit and Brady won't even know what happened or where I am—that they aren't my next of kin —all hope dies.

I have to make it home because there's no way I'm leaving this world without seeing them one more time.

CHAPTER TWENTY-FOUR

I PACE MY APARTMENT, waiting on a phone call, news, anything. Last night, we were both too worried to get a decent sleep, but thankfully, Brady's getting some rest now. I'm thankful for him staying. Clinging onto him was the only thing that kept me from losing it. We were maybe both in shock, too numb to do anything but hold on to each other and hope.

But when the sun came up, I couldn't lie there anymore. I needed to be doing something—even if that something is wearing a path into my bedroom carpet with my bare feet.

A helo crash is survivable, but if the navy can't even locate them two days later with all the tracking technology they have …

Every minute that goes by with no word frays the last cord of hope I have left.

Brady gasps awake and looks around the room. "Fuuuuck. I dreamed I was being trampled by elephants. Why are your footsteps louder than a marching band?"

I stop pacing. "Sorry."

As if forgetting for a second why I'm stressed, his face falls when he remembers. "Any word?"

"Not yet."

I can't lose Prescott. Granted, we haven't had much to do with each other since I moved to Virginia, but he's still always been there. I've been trying to save my heart by staying away, but knowing he was still out there didn't hurt as much as the thought that he's possibly gone forever.

"What are the chances ... I mean ... Could he ..." Brady can't finish the question neither of us wants the answer to.

Is there a chance Prescott's still alive?

I wouldn't put money on the odds. Last night, while I needed him, Brady was there for me. And now, as reality is mixing with what-ifs, he's the one who needs me. To reassure him, and maybe even myself.

"There's no way to know. My contact couldn't even tell me what took them down. They were supposed to be on a training op."

"Those things go bad sometimes, don't they? It's in the news."

"Startlingly, it's in the news less than it actually happens. We run training ops for a reason—so they're prepared for anything. That means we have to create artificial dangerous situations, but they still have an element of danger, so yeah, things go wrong. Often. Rarely does it result in casualties."

"So maybe something went really wrong, but they're all still alive."

I force a smile, but my lips barely move. "I'm sure you're right." I'm sure he's not, but I can't bring myself to say it. "Why don't you get out of bed, and I'll take you to my favorite breakfast place."

"I will never say no to food."

Now, if only I could find a way to muster up my appetite.

It occurs to me, as Brady stabs at his waffles with his fork after barely eating anything, that he might be trying to put on a brave front too.

I raise my hand for the check.

"You're not eating?" Brady asks.

"Neither are you."

"I tried." Brady hangs his head.

"I know."

"I'm too scared to eat. All I can think is—"

"Me too. Let's go back to the apartment. I shouldn't have forced us to come out."

Brady drinks down the last of his coffee, at least. "Are you going into work today?"

"I want to so I can see if I can find anything out. Are you … do you still plan to stay for the weekend?"

"I don't want to go home until I know for sure. One way or the other."

If Prescott's alive or dead.

I can't even believe we're having to think about this. Sure, being in the military, there's always that risk of never coming home. We've talked about it. We've thought about it. We've even had some close calls. But this is a whole new level. One I'm not used to and never want to get used to.

I pull Brady close when we get outside, wrapping my arm around his shoulders.

We get about halfway home before Brady stops and looks up at me. "What if he doesn't come back?"

The right answer here is to say that we grieve and move on. It's what you have to do. But the words don't leave my mouth. They can't.

Accepting it as a possibility, even if it's an almost certainty, isn't in me. Not yet. Not now. I can't break down because I don't think anything or anyone would be able to pick me back up.

I open my mouth to answer some bullshit about being positive and that he'll be okay when Brady's eyes fill with tears.

"I can't lose him," he whispers. "*We* can't lose him."

Brady's plea is the thing that breaks that last little piece of me that's holding on to control. I would give Brady anything he wanted, anything he asked for, but some things aren't in the realm of possibility.

I know Brady needs me, just as much as I need him. But where he had the strength to pull out his supportive side last night, all my effort is trying to keep myself upright.

I'm almost relieved when my phone rings in my pocket. That is, until I take it out and see who's calling.

"Who is it?" Brady asks.

"Prescott's mom," I say numbly.

This is either one of her check-in calls, which haven't stopped even after I moved across the country and away from her son, or the navy has called her with news about Prescott.

"I … I can't answer it." I'm not ready to accept whatever she has to say.

"Want me to?" Brady holds out his hand.

"I can't ask you to—"

"You're not. I need to know." He slips the phone out of my hand easily and answers. "Hi, Mrs. Prescott. Kit can't come to the phone right now."

There's a pause before Brady's lips twitch.

"My name is Brady. I'm a friend of Pr—uh, Jimmy and Kit."

She says something else.

"Am I what friend?" There's a sudden burst of laughter from him. "Uh, yeah, I guess I am *that* friend, though I'm not sure how I feel about the boy-toy label."

"For fuck's sake," I mumble and take the phone from him. "Hi, Abbey. Please tell me you've heard from Jim."

"Now, now, Guy Kitchener, I was just getting to know yours and Jimmy's boyfriend."

Hope bursts in my chest because if she was concerned, she wouldn't be so focused on torturing us with embarrassment.

"He told you about that?" I'm sure he didn't use the boyfriend label, or boy toy for that matter, but he actually told them about us?

"He did. Right before he was sent on that training op that almost killed him."

"Almost … You mean—"

"They called a while ago. Jimmy's okay. He's a little banged up, but he'll be fine. We're hopping on a plane as soon as we can to come see him. I've called Jack, Jenny, and Justin, but Jack's working on a big case, Jenny doesn't have a babysitter for the kids, and Justin isn't in the country. I was hoping—"

"Where is he?"

"VA hospital in Richmond."

"We're on our way."

"Thank you." She has that motherly tone that I'd never once experienced with my own mom. Not even before I came out and she decided she didn't want anything to do with me. "He shouldn't be alone. But before you go, put Brady back on. He sounded cute."

"Bye, Abbey." I end the call.

"He's okay?" Brady asks.

"He's in the hospital. Let's go."

brady

WHEN KIT SAID Prescott's "a little banged up," according to his mom, all I could think was how happy I am that he's alive. But seeing Prescott in a hospital bed, drugged up to the point of him being unconscious ninety percent of the time, unable to move, his leg in a full cast to above his knee, and seeing Kit's reaction to it, I realize my SEALs, my Kit and Prescott, are more human than the pedestal I've put them on for years.

I've always seen them as big, strong men who are indestructible. Here and now, when they're both in need, it's easy for me to slip into caretaker mode.

Kit's passed out in the visitor's chair next to Prescott—somewhere he refuses to move from—so I've been doing coffee runs and making sure he eats while we wait for brief moments of lucidity from Prescott. Which, there haven't really been any.

I'm pretty sure he's under the impression we're a drug-induced hallucination. It's actually kinda cute.

The hospital is quiet, considering it's midafternoon. We've been here since yesterday after his mom called, but no one has told us to leave yet. There's no point trying to convince Kit to go home to get some rest because if he said it to me, I wouldn't do it either.

This is not how I thought our next meetup would go.

The door to Prescott's room is open, nurses have been coming and going, and as irrational as it is, every time someone passes the room, I fear it's going to be Prescott's parents. His mom was lovely on the phone, her friendly and somewhat embarrassing nature reminded me of my dads, but meeting them? When they know about our … unconventional relationship which isn't really a relationship but also is? I'm nervous.

I've never cared enough for anyone to worry about this stuff. Meeting the parents. Prescott and I aren't even officially together, but that thought scares me. Probably because I want to be with Prescott —and Kit—so I can't fuck it up when I meet his parents because what if they don't like me?

My palms are sweaty at the thought.

Not as sweaty as they become when instead of Prescott's parents filling the doorway, two men built like tanks do.

They enter without knocking, pause, and one looks at me while the other sees Kit passed out in the chair.

The smaller of the two nods at me. "I'm Shanahan."

"Brady."

The other one doesn't introduce himself. He sits on Kit's lap and then laughs when Kit startles awake.

"Fuck you, Terri."

"Thanks for the offer, but I'll leave that up to Pres. You know, when his leg isn't smashed to pieces."

Kit shoves Terri off him and then stands. Just when I think they're about to hug, Kit gets him in a headlock.

"Are they always like this?" I ask Shanahan.

"I wouldn't know. I'm the guy who replaced him on their team."

Ah.

Kit finally pulls away from his friend. "What happened out there?"

"Come on, man, you know that's classified."

"You're such an asshole."

"You are."

I cut in. "And here I was thinking Prescott was the most immature SEAL."

Terri turns his smile on me. "Who's the little guy?"

I scoff because I am not little, no matter how much I love it when Prescott and Kit make me feel like I am.

"That's Brady. Duh," Shanahan says.

I decide I like him.

"Whoa, like Brady *Brady*? The Brady?" Terri asks.

"Y-you've heard of me?" I glance at Kit.

"This one"—Terri points at Prescott—"was rambling on and off something about Kit and Brady while his brain was bleeding."

"His brain was bleeding?" I ask and look at Kit. "Did we know that?"

"Eh, it was just a little one," Terri says. "No swelling. He's on blood thinners and meds to keep his blood pressure down, so he avoided surgery. All good things."

"Yeah, a brain bleed doesn't sound like a good thing. Is he going to be okay?" I ask.

"You can't get rid of me that easily," comes a weary croak.

Kit and I rush to Prescott on either side of his bed.

"You're awake again," I say.

"Again?" His brow scrunches.

"It's the concussion," Shanahan says behind us. "His short-term memory is shit."

"How are you feeling?" I ask.

"Like I was in a helicopter crash. Need. Water."

Kit's quick to grab the plastic cup with a straw next to his bed and lift it to Prescott's lips.

His hooded eyes turn to Kit and then back to me. "Wait, you're both here? Together?"

"We haven't left your side since your mom called," Kit says. "Your parents will be here soon, by the way. I also heard from your sister. She couldn't get a babysitter, so she's bringing her rug rats with her."

"They know? If the brain bleed didn't kill me, Mom will."

"It sounds like you're going to have a slew of visitors coming your way," Terri says. "We just came to check in on you."

"What's the plan?" Prescott asks. "Am I being transferred back to Coronado or what?"

"Most of us are going back," Terri says. "But you, Levenson, and Moran have earned yourselves a cushy vacation here in Virginia while they get you back to the sarcastic loudmouth you usually are."

I try not to let my excitement show, but Kit and Prescott in Virginia at the same time for an undetermined amount of time? Sure, I live in New York, but I have summer break off law school. I'm sure I could ask Uncle Damon for some personal time. The three of us could be together for longer than a week.

"I want to go home," Prescott says softly.

My hopes are dashed.

"They have a state-of-the-art rehab facility in Virginia," Terri says. "I wish I'd been here when I had that nerve damage from shrapnel in my shoulder. The nurses are hot too. I had this male nurse who was so small I could snap him like a twig, and he kept bossing me around."

I suck in my lips to stop the laugh flying out of me. If only he knew Prescott—and I—were definitely into that sort of thing.

"I'm so glad I have the hot women nurses and not the sexy twink with a control kink," Prescott deadpans.

I can't hold on to it anymore. A laugh leaves me, and then suddenly, I'm the focus of everyone's attention.

I don't like it.

Being who I am, who my dads are, my brother, I'm never the source of attention. I'm always in the background, the way I like it. When I'm with Kit and Prescott, I love being their center of attention. But *only* theirs.

Thankfully, or not so thankfully, the doorway fills with more people. Screaming toddlers and a woman wearing expensive clothes but looking disheveled with a baby in her arms. Her kids look like maybe twins and a newborn. Yikes.

"Jenny," Prescott says, and oh shit. I was worried about Prescott's parents. I didn't have time to obsess over a sibling showing up. At least, not for a while. Kit gave me the impression Prescott's parents would beat his brothers or sister.

"How broken are you?" she asks.

He waves her off. "Nothing's gonna keep me down."

"Good. Here, take your nephew." She hands him the baby.

"I can take him." Kit steps forward.

"I'm fine," Prescott says and expertly cradles the sleeping baby.

The two kids at our ankles run around, making noise and causing chaos. They kind of remind me of Peyton and me when we were younger.

"Do you want me to take those two down to the cafeteria for some Jell-O?" I ask.

"That would be great. Could you?" But then Jenny's eyes meet mine. "Wait, who are you?"

I smile while a chorus of "He's Brady" fills the room.

"Well, you're not a SEAL, I can tell that. How do you know …" Her gaze flicks between Prescott and me. "Oh. Sure." She turns to her brother. "Can I trust him?"

"I assume," Prescott says. "I don't know how good he is with kids though."

"I'm a sports agent. My clients are like children. If that helps."

Jenny relents. "Fine. I have another one if those two go missing."

Everyone stops and stares at her.

"I'm kidding."

Okay, she's not as scary as I thought she was. I kneel down to the kids' level and ask, "Who wants Jell-O?"

They scream.

"Lance. Liam! Take it down a decibel," Jenny says.

"I got this," I say confidently. Inside, I'm shitting myself.

I take their little hands and walk them out of the room, but as soon as we're out, one of them breaks loose and makes a run for it. Picking the other up and popping him on my hip, I run after the escapee, and by the time I wrangle both of them into the cafeteria, order them red Jell-O, and then have to reorder it in green instead, they're peaceful as they eat.

Kids are tiring, and I've maybe endured a whole five minutes so far. Once they're finished, I make sure to hold Runner McGhee's hand tightly while I put the containers in the trash. That's when the other one takes off.

I send up a silent apology to my dads because I'm sure this is karmic justice at work. There's a reason our uncles called us Destruction One and Two when Peyton and I were kids. We were just like Lance and Liam.

Note to self: never have kids.

When I finally manage to get both of them back to Prescott's room, I'm hoping it will be emptier than before, but no. His team-mates are gone but replaced with two new people.

People who make me even more nervous than his SEAL teammates.

"My boys," Prescott's mom cries out and takes the kids off my hands.

I've only had one conversation with Abbey, and I already know this could go one of two ways: it'll either be an embarrassing shit-show or a humiliating clusterfuck. Either way, I'm screwed.

I plaster on a smile and try to make it look natural. Kinda feels like I'm staring at them with wide eyes and gritted teeth. Not creepy at all. Nope.

Prescott's mom doesn't pay me any mind while she hugs Lance and Liam, but then she moves back to Pres. "Now, where were we? Where are you hurt? What can I do?"

"Mom," Prescott whines.

She turns to Kit. "What can I do? You look like you haven't eaten in days. I'm going to go get food." That's when she sets her attention on me. "You too, Brady. You need to eat."

"You … You know Brady?" Prescott asks.

"We had a lovely conversation on the phone, and I was right. He is cute."

And I'm bright red. Me. The guy with the most embarrassing family in the world is blushing.

Great first impression.

Awesome.

"Brady, come with me to get these men some food. They have muscles they need to fuel."

"I'll go with you, Abbey," Kit says and sends me a "you're welcome" face.

"No, no—"

"I'm not going to let you scare Brady away on the first day of meeting him." Kit winks and directs her toward the door. "Besides, he just took the kids down there." He steers her out of the room.

Prescott's dad adds, "I should go with them to prevent the inter-rogation."

"Interrogation?" I find my voice.

"About why we've only recently learned of your existence," he says and leaves to catch up.

"Me too." Jenny disappears as well, and then it's just Prescott and me.

"I'm sorry about them," he says.

"That's usually my line when people meet my family."

Prescott reaches for my hand that's resting on his bed beside him. "You're here."

"*You're* here." I reach for him and take the seat Kit was sleeping on earlier.

"Like I said, you're not getting rid of me that easily."

I squeeze his hand. "I mean, you seem more aware than you have been. You've been in and out of it since we got here."

"How long have you been here? What day is it? How did you get here?"

"It's been about eighteen hours. Kit called a couple of days ago because he was worried about you. He said he was probably overreacting, but I could tell it was more serious than that, so I hopped a plane. Lucky I did because we were together when we heard what happened. Kit has refused to leave your side ever since."

His lips quirk. "But not you?"

"Not gonna lie, I wanted a shower about six hours ago."

"Oh. That's what that smell is."

He's trying to be his usual self, and yes, he's more lucid than he has been, but his snark doesn't hit the right tone. It might be the meds, but he doesn't have the same *zing* like he usually does.

"How are you, really?" I ask.

"Confused. Tired."

"Oh good, so we're all on a level playing field, then."

"You could have gone home to shower, you know."

I shake my head. "Nah. I didn't want to leave Kit. He's been … not himself. You know it's serious when I'm the one rushing around making sure you're both okay."

That seems to confuse him more. "But … why?"

"Why was he worried, or why am I being all grown-up and shit?"

"I didn't even know you could be grown-up and shit—"

I throw up my hands. "I've never once been completely helpless. I let you guys take care of me because I love it."

"You mean to tell me you've been a multi-functioning human this whole time?"

I pinch my thumb and forefinger together. "Little bit."

"Huh. Interesting. Surprising, even. But not as much as Kit freaking out. We've been in these situations before. He knows the score."

"He also cares about you more than he cares about anyone else on this planet. You go missing, you bet your ass he's going to be worried. And he wasn't the only one. The thought of never seeing you again—"

"Hey …" Prescott's soothing voice encourages me to look him in the eye. "I'm okay. I'm here."

"You have a long recovery ahead."

"I know I do. But I'll survive it."

"Your teammates said you'll be doing rehab here."

"I guess I am."

"I was thinking … maybe I can ask for some time off work and stick around for a bit. If you and Kit will have me."

Prescott breaks into a wide smile. "You bet your cute little ass we'll have you. With how many drugs I'm on, I probably won't be able to get it up anytime soon, but I can watch you and Kit go at it."

This is where I'd usually say something sexual back—keeping my emotions tucked away. Refusing to admit that cheapening what we have and reducing it to only sex—even if that's what we agreed on—makes my chest ache. But after almost losing Prescott, I don't think I can do it.

"Actually, I wanted to stay for moral support. To be here. For both of you."

"No sex?" Prescott asks.

"Well, I want the sex too, but I want you to know I'm not only here for that. I want …" *I want more.*

Those are the words I still struggle with.

A shadowy figure fills the doorway, and when I look up, Kit steps into the room. I don't know how long he's been standing there for, if he heard my plans, or what, but he's holding three wrapped sandwiches from the hospital cafeteria and wearing a concerned look.

He's by himself.

"Where's my family?" Prescott asks the thing I'm thinking.

"I asked them to give us a minute because I want you to hear me out." He glances at me. "Both of you."

Prescott taps my hand. "This could either be a plan to seek revenge on the people who made the Hawk that crashed or asking you to stay for the summer."

"That one," Kit says. "The second."

Relief whooshes out of me. "I was just saying that myself. I don't have classes, and I should be able to get my uncle on board. I, uh …" I rub the back of my neck. "I told him about you two."

"You what?" Kit asks. "You didn't tell me."

"We were preoccupied with other things."

Prescott shifts, trying to sit up straighter, and Kit immediately goes over to his bedside to raise the adjustable mattress. Prescott meets Kit's cool gray eyes. "Please tell me one of the other things was sex."

I rub my chin. "There might have been some of that in there, but mainly we were worried about you."

"Kit is so slack," Prescott says. "If it had been the other way around, I would've made you come so much you couldn't even remember Kit was missing."

Kit rolls his eyes.

"I dunno," I say. "I think if either of you were missing, I'd be lost."

Prescott touches his heart. "Is it the concussion, or has Brady Talon learned how to be … sweet?"

"I've always been sweet, buttface."

"Just like you've always known how to look after yourself?" Prescott asks.

"Yep."

Prescott smiles, and for the first time since we've been here, he has genuine warmth behind his eyes.

"Do I need to prove that I can do it?" I ask. "I've kept Kit from breaking down for two days now. Two whole days."

They both wear amused expressions, and I'm tempted to tell them to fuck off, but then Prescott says something so much better.

"Dude, you're dropping the ball. How are we going to ensure Brady comes back to us if you're making him *adult*? You need to take him home, make him come his brains out, get the man a shower, and then spoon him to sleep like his life depends on it. Otherwise, when I'm well enough to be discharged, he'll be gone."

Sometimes Prescott has the best ideas.

"Oh! And take pictures, please."

Yep. Definitely the best ideas.

CHAPTER TWENTY-SIX

NOT ONLY DO I do what Prescott told me to do, but I make sure Brady knows just how much him stepping up means to me. He's fed with a proper meal, he's showered, and now I have him naked beneath me working on the last thing.

Knowing Prescott is going to be okay, I'm able to let go of that worry and focus entirely on Brady.

I move inside him, slowly. Too slowly. He claws at my back, but I pepper his skin with light kisses and hold firm.

He squirms under me. "Kit, please."

"Ooh, we should get that on camera."

"What?"

"You, begging. Prescott will go nuts for it. You okay with video as well as pics?" My phone lies beside us on the mattress, so I straighten and pick it up.

He nods. Brady looks so fucking gorgeous, legs parted, skin flushed, his cock hard and sticking up against his stomach. I hit Record as I pull out of him, keeping my head at his entrance, and I know Prescott will approve. It reminds me of the photos we sent Brady.

My cock is shiny with lube. Brady's hole is stretched wide as I slide back inside him.

"Fuck. More. I need more," he says and then looks right at the camera on my phone. "I need both you and Prescott inside me at the same time."

I drop the damn phone. "We'll edit that part out."

"Don't. I love how much that idea gets to you."

I manage to pick up the phone and hold it steady this time. "Let me hear you beg again."

Brady smirks. "Someday in the future, someone will ask me how I got into porn. I will say, 'My boyfriends wanted a sex tape.'" He laughs, but I don't.

Not because it wasn't funny but because I stumble over the label that hasn't passed any of our lips before.

It takes a second for him to realize what he said, and immediately, his eyes plead for me to forget. "Not boyfriends *boyfriends*. You know what I mean."

"No, I don't know what you mean."

His gaze turns downward. "Well, no, we haven't discussed what we are, so I guess—"

I grip his chin and force him to look at me. "You want more from us?"

"Yes," he whispers.

My cock inside him pulses. The idea of having more with him … it's everything my body and heart want.

"If it were up to me, we wouldn't be apart at all. I know the logistics are hard, but—"

I hit End on the recording and throw my phone somewhere on the bed. "I'm the same. If Prescott even hinted at wanting to make us, this, all three of us a permanent thing, I'd quit my boring-ass job and move back to Cali."

"You would?"

"Then we'd only have to work on getting you out of New York."

"It's doable. My uncle has offices in California, but he wanted me in New York, where he's based, to learn from him. Once I've finished with law school, I could ask for a transfer."

I pull out of him and rest back on my ankles.

He whines. "No, don't stop. We can talk about this while you fuck me."

"Priorities. We need to have this conversation, and I can't do it while I'm inside you and can't pay attention closely."

"Can't SEALs multitask?"

"I'm not a SEAL anymore, remember?"

He grunts. "Fine. Make me come first, and then we can talk about all our wants and needs because right now, everything wanty and needy is in my dick. And balls. And ass."

"Mm, talk dirty to me."

"Kiiit," he whines again. It's always the beggy tone that gets to me. That needy, obsessive, and urgent way he asks to bring him pleasure.

"Fine. Fuck now, serious talk later. Roll over for me."

Brady gets to his hands and knees, sticking his amazing ass in the air. His hole looks used and ready for more, so I don't hesitate in slamming inside him.

His moan is deep and guttural.

There's too much anticipation around having the conversation I've only dreamed of for years that I don't hold back. One of my favorite things in the world is making Brady come untouched, but this is an emergency, and I need all the backup I can get.

I push inside him over and over while jerking his cock.

He's trying to hold out. He hisses through gritted teeth, but he's no match for me. I know how to play Brady like a fiddle.

I tighten my grip on his hip, hasten my strokes on his cock, and the mere second he starts to fall apart, I join him. Coming in unison doesn't happen a lot with us because there's always someone else to play with. Plus, Brady's refractory period is a hell of a lot shorter than Prescott's or mine, so we have to draw out our orgasms so we can give him more.

This, though, coming at the same time, it's amazing. It's a new level of connecting, of combining our bodies, our souls. We experience the same pleasure at the same time, and it's the type of intimacy that happens with established partners. Reading each other, searching for that high together.

When we both eventually settle and catch our breaths, he collapses beneath me, and I follow, crushing Brady between myself and the mattress.

I know I should let the man breathe, but it's really tempting to stay like this forever.

He shifts underneath me and makes a humph noise. "You're not as light as you think, you know."

Fine. I'll move.

I roll onto my back, turning my head to face him. He's still on his stomach, his arms under his pillow, propping him up a bit.

His big brown eyes are staring intently. "Did you mean it?"

"That I want to be with you and Prescott? Yeah. Did *you* mean it?" I hold my breath, worried that now he's come, his view might be different.

"All I've ever wanted since meeting you guys was to be with you. Both of you. But I told myself that you were older, I was moving away, and that what we had was only sex. I've told myself that for so long and remind myself every time I see you that what we have couldn't be real, no matter how much I wanted it. No one outside of you two has ever made me feel the same way. When I'm with you, you're all I think about. When I'm at work, I throw myself into it hard because otherwise, my mind drifts back to you and Prescott. What you're doing. Where you are. How you're planning to turn me out the next time we manage to see each other. And every goodbye, it gets harder and harder to walk away."

My chest swells.

"I know you and Prescott have something special. Something deeper, and you're in love with him—I could tell that from the very beginning—but all I've ever hoped is that someday, you and him could see me that same way."

I swallow hard because I need the courage to say this. "What I feel for you …"

"It's not the same as what you feel for Prescott. I know that."

"It's not the same, no. Prescott and I … we've got shared experiences. We met when we were young and have grown so much together. But Brady?" I throw my arm over his waist and roll onto my side to press against him. "That doesn't mean that I don't love you. What you and I have happened naturally and fast. It comes from that primal need we all have inside us. The moment you turned up on my doorstep to take care of me for once, I could no longer deny it.

You own me. Completely and wholly. I want you to be mine. I want Prescott to be mine. I want it all."

Brady's lips turn up. "I want it all too."

"Then let's make it happen."

"Tomorrow. I need some sleep and time to recover after that pounding."

Does it send a streak of pride through me that I did that to him? Of course. "Tomorrow."

∞ ∞ ∞

As we reach the beginning of the long hospital corridor leading to Prescott's room, I pause. "On second thought, let's not make this happen."

Because making it happen would mean admitting to Prescott why I really left. How deep he's buried under my skin and how much of my heart has always belonged to him. With Brady, from the very beginning, we've always been open with each other. Honest from the very start. Ever since the moment I realized I was in love with Prescott, I built a wall between us. It's what I needed so I didn't lose him.

But I lost him anyway, and now I'm scared this will be the final nail in the coffin that holds our friendship.

"Come on," Brady says, taking my arm and dragging me. "It's about time you told Prescott how you feel about him."

"Is it though?"

"I can't believe how much of a baby you're being. If anything, I'm the one who should be nervous."

I stop walking and shrug out of his hold. "Why?"

"Because you and Pres have this connection with each other that reaches out and slaps you in the face. I felt it the night I met you guys. I'm convinced Prescott is in love with you as much as you're in love with him. Me, on the other hand … what if he says, 'Kit, I've been in love with you for years, but what do we need the kid for?'"

"I guarantee you he will not say that."

"How do you know?"

"Because you mean a lot to him as well."

"Mm. Maybe. Guess we're about to find out."

"Where'd all your courage come from suddenly? If you say you've wanted this since we met but haven't said anything because it's been geographically impossible, why the change? Why now?"

"The geography was a good excuse for the real reason."

"Which is?"

Brady pinches the bridge of his nose and then looks at me with determination in his eyes. "You know how you recently found out about my ability to actually be a grown-up and take care of people? It's all I've done my whole life. My brother might be older than me, but I've always been the one protecting him. My best friend—fuck, I really need to call Felix because we're both so busy with life we haven't been able to catch up." Brady takes out his phone and taps away on the screen.

"Focus," I say. "What was your real reason for holding back?"

"Felix was a hot mess in college. I was his shoulder to cry on because I've always been the dependable one. It's why I'm going to make a great agent. But that means that in my real life, outside of you and Prescott, I have an image I need to maintain for my clients. An athlete's agent can't be the story. They need to stay hidden."

"Which makes me ask again, what has changed?"

"I told you I came out to my uncle. This is the man in charge of my career. He said not to hold back and that while a relationship with two men will cause headaches with the media and the public, I have to live my truth. Two days ago, I thought Prescott was dead. I was all but convinced of it. It's only more reason to shoot my shot while I have the chance."

Shoot his shot.

Shoot *our* shot.

Maybe Brady's right. If I never admit aloud to Prescott how I feel about him, I may never get over him because I will never know for sure.

The only problem with that is I'm not sure I'm ready to accept rejection. I'm not ready to let him go. And I will have to if he doesn't want me. And if he says he doesn't want to be with me but wants to be with Brady, I'd have to deal with that on top of it all.

I can't see myself living without either of them. "How is it that I used to brave war zones, but walking in there and telling Pres how I feel makes my legs weak and my throat dry? I'm on the verge of a panic attack or something, and I don't get those."

"The only thing you risked in a war zone was your life. We're risking our hearts in there. That's big."

"Should we make it romantic or some shit? Buy him flowers? I don't know how to do this."

"Well, I don't think we should hijack the hospital loudspeaker and pour our hearts out or anything, but yeah, flowers might be nice. Hospitals have gift shops, don't they?"

We change direction and find the gift shop, but all the flowers are not really what we're after. I pick up one bunch that has pastel purple ribbon around them and pink roses.

"They're very flowery," I say.

"Of course they are. They're flowers."

"They don't look romantic. They look like they say, *I'm sorry you're dying.*"

"Hmm. You're right. We should find ones that at least say, *We're happy you're not dead.*"

"I can help with that," the woman at the counter says. "If you want to combine some of the bouquets, I can reorganize them for you so they blend together and give you something bigger. Special."

Brady and I look at each other and then hand over one of each bouquet she has.

She's gloaty about getting us on the upsell, but little does she know, we don't care about the money. We just want to make Prescott happy.

Fuck, I hope he's happy about this.

CHAPTER TWENTY-SEVEN

MOM HAS BEEN FUSSING over me since the minute she got here. Dad's used to her ways and has the uncanny knack for tuning her out. When I get the chance to have my sister alone, I beg her to ask Mom for help with the kids to give me a break.

They won't be gone long though, so I lie back and close my eyes, enjoying the peace.

Which lasts all of thirty seconds before I hear footsteps come back inside my room. "For fuck's sake, Mom—" My eyes fly open, and there, standing in the doorway, isn't my parents but the best sight in the world.

Kit and Brady. They wear small smiles, way too many clothes, and hold a big bouquet of flowers.

"We … uh …" Kit starts. It's so unlike him to not know what he's going to say before he says it, so the hesitance unnerves me.

"We brought you these." Brady holds out the flowers.

"Thank you." I've never been given flowers before in my life. What am I supposed to do with them?

I lower my head and sniff them because that's what I've seen in movies, but they smell like … flowers.

Still, I do the obligatory "Mmm" noise and then place them on the bed next to my cast.

"There's a card, silly," Brady says, snapping off the note on top.

"After the video you sent me last night, nothing on a piece of paper could live up to that. Sorry."

Brady leans in. "Just read it."

My gaze flicks to Kit, who's biting his bottom lip.

"Or don't," Kit says. "Up to you. It's all good. You know what, on second thought, here, I'll read it to you." Kit rounds the bed and tries to take the note off me, but I don't let him.

"Well, now I have to read it."

"Don't mind Kit," Brady says. "He's trying to chicken out."

"Chicken out of what?"

"Open it and find out." Brady points toward the note.

"Maybe we shouldn't do this to a man with a brain bleed," Kit says.

"My brain bleed is gone, according to my latest scan, thank you very much. And I'm not showing any signs of TBI, so go me!" Traumatic brain injury would be an ending to my career, and I'm not out of the woods yet, but so far, so good.

Kit is so stiff beside me, and not in the good way. He looks like he's stopped breathing altogether.

It only makes me want to read the card more. And when I open it, I realize how wrong I was about the video.

The obscenely sexy video they sent me last night was good. But this? One teeny, tiny little question beats it hands down.

Will you be our boyfriend?

I stare at it, blinking a few times to make sure I'm reading it right and it's not some painkiller-induced fantasy.

There are a million things running through my head, from it would be impossible to hell yes and everything in between.

But the number one question I have is "*Our* boyfriend?" I ask. Because that's the thing I want the most.

If I took all the logistics out and was only left with Kit and Brady, I would do everything in my power to keep what we have. To keep it going long-term but on a lot more permanent basis.

On either side of me, they both take one of my hands.

"*Our* boyfriend," Brady says. "Kit and I talked last night, and it's what we both want."

"But we totally get it if it's too much," Kit cuts in. "There's no pressure or anything. We can forget we even asked and keep things casual. Yeah, you're right, we should do that."

"See," Brady says. "He's chickening out and trying to back down. Though, he has a point about there being no pressure."

"It's not the pressure of making a decision. I only have one question." That's a lie. I have a billion, but this is the only one that matters. "How do you propose we make it work when we live scattered all over the country?"

When they stare at each other, I realize they don't have a solution for that yet.

"We have the rest of the summer to work it out," Kit says. "If you even want to."

Now Brady's biting his lip too, and I kind of want to slap both of them.

"Of course I fucking want it."

Brady's face breaks out into a huge smile, and he points at Kit. "I told you he'd feel the same way about you as you do about him."

"How he feels about me?" My best friend—or ex-best friend since he moved East—has storm clouds rolling in his gray eyes, and they're directed at Brady.

Kit pulls over the visitor's chair and sits, enclosing my hand in his two massive paws. They're hands that have been on me before. All over me. But there's something different in the way he holds me now.

"I need to be honest with you."

I'm scared of what he's going to say.

"I took the job at the Pentagon because …" He looks at Brady and then down at our hands. "Because … I needed to get away from my feelings. It was hurting too much living with you."

"Ouch." I try to slip my hand out, but he doesn't let me.

"Not because of the boundaries like I previously told you, but because I'm in love with you. I have been for so long, and I couldn't take it anymore. I wanted you in every way possible, but because of the navy, I couldn't ask you. We couldn't … All we could have was our occasional moment we'd reduce to a fun fling with others there."

My gaze darts to Brady.

I have no idea what to say.

"Brady knows how I feel about you and how I feel about him. If we're going to make this work, we all need to start being honest with ourselves and each other."

A long time ago, I would've said love was too hard. I would've said I'd never felt it. But as I take in my surroundings, the sterile hospital bed, my injured ass in a cast, the bouquet of flowers at my side, I realize this is what love is.

It's not about grand gestures or spouting bullshit sonnets of forever. It's showing up when they need you. It's taking care of each other and stepping up like Brady did for Kit when my chopper went down. It's respecting each other's careers and life goals, even if it means you have to be apart.

What Kit, Brady, and I have is love.

It's respect.

It's one hell of a relationship.

"You don't have to say it back," Kit says. "I wanted you to know."

The words are there, but the painkillers are making my head swim, and I'm not entirely sure this is actually happening. So I do what any respecting man in this situation would do.

"Yeah, I'm going to need my boyfriends to kiss me now."

Brady's grin takes my breath away, but it's Kit's look of relief that really gets me. I understand why he might think I wouldn't want a relationship, but doesn't he realize that he has always been the exception to the rule?

He has broken every damn rule I've ever made for myself: no hooking up with teammates. No crossing lines with roommates. No feelings. Only fun.

Granted, we'd been kidding ourselves for years that what we had was only fun. But right here and now, I can see how it was a lie that made breaking the rules less consequential. And Brady? He went and had to make us fall for him. He's the only one we've ever gone back to. The only one we've wanted to keep seeing even though it would be inconvenient.

Brady moves in first, leaning over me and sealing his lips over mine. His tongue pushes inside my mouth, but then Kit's there too, on the other side of me.

I grip the back of their heads to keep them where they are. Our mouths are a tangle of lips and tongues, and it's so hot. So hot that I—

I gasp, and they both pull back.

"No, don't stop. I ..." I nod toward my groin, where my hospital gown is leaving nothing to the imagination. "I thought all the drugs they're pumping through me was affecting the little guy, but you two ... Fuck, come back and give me more."

Brady dives right in while Kit moves to kissing down my neck instead. Both of their mouths on me. Both of them being here. We need to find a way to keep this going and to have us all in one place at the same time. I'm even willing to stay in shithouse Virginia to do it. I don't care if the magnificent SEAL Team Six is stationed there; Coronado is the superior base. Clearly. It's where I am.

Rivalry between bases? What rivalry?

Kit's hand travels down my chest to the bulge in my hospital gown, but I stop him.

"Dude. If you make me come, it's going to be a super awkward cleanup having to ask the nurse to clean the cum around my catheter. I can't get up."

Kit, the bastard, laughs. "That sounds like a you problem." He strokes my cock.

"I hate you," I say through gritted teeth.

"Should you come if you have a catheter?" Brady asks. "Like, could it make your dick explode?"

"It's awkward but doable," Kit says. "Trust me."

"Well, now I want to see it." Brady tries to lift my gown.

"And my hard-on is officially gone." I swat his hand away. "If merciless teasing is what having boyfriends is going to be like, I might have to change my answer."

Kit leans over me. "You love our merciless teasing."

"Yeah, when we do it to Brady, not me." I fold my arms.

"He's so cute when he's sulky," Brady says. "Am I that cute when I'm sulky?"

"Even cuter," Kit says, and I can't even argue with him.

Kit steps back and sits in the visitor's chair while Brady still hovers above me, staring at my cock.

I relent and lift my gown, only to be mortified when my mom comes through the door and announces, "We're back."

She stalls, and Dad runs into the back of her while Brady scrambles to put my dick away.

"What did you stop for?" Dad asks Mom.

"I think we interrupted them playing some kind of grown-up game of Doctor."

Brady looks as embarrassed as I feel, but I take his hand to reassure him my parents won't think he's a total perv.

"Brady had never seen a catheter before," I say.

"Whatever you boys need to tell yourselves, dear," Mom says. "Okay, so we spoke to your doctor, and here's the plan. After a few more days in here, you'll be allowed to use a wheelchair and move around. Use crutches if you can manage it. But the best part is they said you can go back to Coronado to rehab it instead of staying here like they originally said. Isn't that great?"

My face falls. "Is … is it an order that I have to go back to Cali?"

Mom's brow pinches. "I thought that's what you wanted? You spent most of this morning whining about being here."

My gaze flits between Brady and Kit. "Yeah, but then these two asked me to be their boyfriend, and, well, I said yes. I want to stay here as long as I can so I can be with them."

Mom touches her heart. "My boy's first boyfriends."

"Your parents remind me of my dads so much. It's uncanny," Brady says.

"Oh, so your parents are overbearing and intrusive too?"

"Plus sarcastic and embarrassing. I worry your parents and my parents could be soul mates."

"Your dads?" Mom asks, right on cue.

"Ah, yeah. Dads. Plural." Brady rubs the back of his neck. "They were kind of a big deal back in the day. First out NFL couple and all that jazz." He waves his hand, trying to dismiss how big a deal his family is, but there's no way he can hide it from—

"You're Marcus Talon and Shane Miller's son?" Dad asks. No, practically screams.

"But they don't know about us yet," I say for Brady's sake. "No one really knows about Brady at all because of who his brother is."

"You're Peyton Miller's brother?" Dad looks like he's about to have a heart attack.

Mom pats Dad's arm. "That's usually how family trees work, dear."

"That means you can't tell anyone," I say and glance at Brady.

"It's okay." He smiles down at me. "I'm going to tell my parents now that we're official. I just … don't know when. Or how any of us are going to handle the aftermath. Especially with you still serving in the navy and Kit's job at the Pentagon. You guys really made a poor decision picking me—someone who's been famous adjacent since I was born. I'm worried about disrupting your lives more than anything. Well, that and my brother's life, but my uncle already told me to forget that attention whore."

Mom and Dad laugh.

Kit doesn't though. He slips seamlessly into reassurance mode as he stands and rounds the bed, taking Brady into his arms and reaching for my hand. "We'll work it all out. I promise."

I have no doubts about that. If anyone can make an impossible situation work, it'll be Kit. Problem-solving is one of his many, many skills.

"You're all so cute," Mom says.

"So much like my dads," Brady murmurs.

Mom practically bounces out of her skin. "I can't wait to meet them."

"And there's your excuse to remain in the poly closet," I say. "To avoid that disaster from happening."

Brady nods. "Good plan."

My mom pretends to be offended, but she's not. I already know that she has accepted us. I can only hope Brady's right about his parents being like mine because if they are, when he does eventually come out and introduce us, they'll be as supportive as Brady needs them to be.

Real families don't turn their backs on each other. And if they do hurt Brady, I know about a hundred different ways to kill a man. Prison would be worth it.

If Brady thought Kit's and my protective streak was extreme before, it's nothing compared to what we'll be like now he's officially ours.

CHAPTER TWENTY-EIGHT

KIT SITS beside me on his couch, one arm wrapped around my shoulders, the other on my knee. "You can do this."

"Can I though? I know I said my uncle was cool with the whole poly thing, but asking for the rest of the summer off might make him have a meltdown."

"I thought you said he'd be cool?"

"Yeah, that was before I realized I'd have to actually ask for time off. And figure out a way to tell my dads. My brother. It's too over-whelming."

"Let's focus on one thing at a time. The only pressing matter is your job. Because your uncle is expecting you home, and you don't even have a flight booked."

"You're right. I can do this. The worst he'll say is no and then force me to get on a plane, even if he has to come here himself to do it." What if he forces me to come home? I can't exactly quit. He's my uncle.

I have to do this. If the three of us are going to give this relation-ship a real shot, we actually have to spend time together. Radical thought, but there it is. I hit Dial on Uncle Damon's number and hold my breath.

"Hey, what's up?" he answers.

I squeak.

"Brady? Hello?"

Kit nudges me.

"Uh, yeah, umm, hi."

"What's wrong?"

"I have … umm, so …"

"You're starting to scare me. Is something wrong with Peyton? Where is he? Where are you?"

"It's not Pey. I'm in Virginia. You know how I told you about the two guys who may or may not work for top secret government stuff?"

"Have they kidnapped you? Say the word 'bananas' if you need help."

Kit must hear everything because he wears a smile.

"They didn't kidnap me, but one of them was in a pretty serious accident. I've been at the hospital for days."

"Oh." Uncle Damon drops the act. "Is he okay?"

"He will be, but … umm, well, Kit is here too, and we've decided … We want to, umm—"

"Are you trying to tell me you're quitting and moving to Virginia? Is that what I'm hearing?"

"No! Not quitting. Just … asking for the rest of the summer off to see if the three of us can make it work. We really want to, and I know I made a commitment to you and King Sports, and asking for almost two months off is irresponsible and not—"

"You can take the time," Uncle Damon says.

"Really?"

"Do you really think if Maddox was lying in a hospital bed somewhere that I'd be coming to work? Fuck no."

"You might not be coming to work, but you'd at least have work with you at the hospital."

Uncle Damon chuckles. "Okay, that's true, but the balance between my work and my personal life has always been a struggle. Uncle Maddox has to remind me constantly to step back a bit."

"You're not … mad?"

"Maybe if you were a full agent, I'd have a different opinion—tell you to work remotely for a while. But you've got your last year of law school coming up, we have plenty of interns to pick up your slack, and I don't want to train you to be the type of partner to choose work over your relationship. I'm lucky enough I have someone who can point out to me when I'm doing it. Not everyone is as lucky as I am in that regard. You have to find the right balance that works for you and your partners. It's not going to happen if you're not even in the same state as each other."

This is why Uncle Damon is my favorite uncle. Not that I would admit that out loud to anyone.

"Thank you," I say. "It means a lot."

"But speaking of partners, plural, when do we get to meet them, and when are you telling your dads?"

"Ugh. That's on my list of things future Brady has to deal with. Maybe I'll fly to Chicago before heading back to New York."

"Though Peyton will be at training camp then. My suggestion would be to drop the bomb on a group video chat and then claim connection error and disappear while the rest of us talk about your sex life."

"There you go being the creepy uncle again."

But he has a point.

It might be the only way to rip off the Band-Aid and let the entire family know at the same time.

"However you decide to do it, please let me and Maddox be there for it."

"You're evil."

"I know. Keep me updated about your SEAL."

I love that he cares. Now to find out if the rest of the family will take it as easily as he has.

❦ ❦ ❦

As I sit by Prescott's hospital bed, laptop in hand and Kit standing beside me, I regret all my life choices up to this point.

Kit grips my shoulder. "You can do this."

"To repeat the words of one of the greatest movies of all time: Just because you can, doesn't mean you should."

Kit stumbles back and holds his heart. "It hurts so much. One, that's not the actual line from *Jurassic Park*, and two—"

I shrug. "I haven't actually seen it. Too young."

Kit grits his teeth while Prescott laughs.

"Brady, babe," Prescott says. "If you want to tell your family you have boyfriends, you might want to try to keep said boyfriends."

"Or maybe I'm trying to make you guys break up with me because then I don't have to go through with this video call." Even though I've already messaged everyone to be on at this time. I'm sure I could come up with another piece of news that would distract them. Like, I dunno, I'm flunking out of law school … Nah, they wouldn't believe that. Ooh, I'm actually bi and knocked up some girl. That's probably even more unbelievable, but at the same time, they wouldn't question it because no one wants to be that asshole who asks if someone is sure of their sexuality.

Perfect.

Kit's hard features soften. "You know you don't have to do anything, right?"

And damn his supportive tone. It cracks the wall I'm trying to build around my heart. It breaks down the survival instinct I've been fighting since I met him and Prescott. To survive in the sports industry, I have to play it straight. Well, gay. But not poly.

Letting my family know is a lot different than going public, but it's only a matter of time before it spills out into the real world. We don't even know how it will work between the three of us going forward, and maybe we're not ready for this. But Prescott's family knows, Kit doesn't have any family, and … I've been keeping this secret for far too long.

There's that little piece of doubt in the back of my mind that Prescott, Kit, and I will even be able to build a relationship after this summer is over and I go back to New York and Prescott goes back to Cali, and if that's the case, and this ends, I'm going to need my family for support.

"Think about it some more," Prescott says.

"No, I'm good to go. I've run out of excuses, and the truth is I do want to do this. But you know how Prescott's parents are a lot? I not only have embarrassing parents but about a million queer uncles and cousins who are just as bad. It's not only two people."

"A million? Really?" Kit asks.

I start to count aloud: "My dads, Uncles Damon, Maddox, Matt, Noah, Ollie, Lennon, Jet, Soren, brother Peyton, his partner Levi—though he already knows—then we have cousins Jackie, Four, and Freddie. I don't even know if it's possible to warn you enough."

"We're SEALs—"

Prescott coughs. "I'm a SEAL. You're a mere civilian. Peasant."

"So glad we've moved on to the joking portion of our bitterness over me quitting the navy. My point is we can handle anything."

"How bad can it really be?" Prescott asks.

They have no idea, but they're about to.

I hit the Call button on our family chat, and because I hesitated and am a couple of minutes late, everyone's waiting.

Some of them are using one computer, so only nine boxes come up, and everyone has made it, with the exception of Uncle Jet, but he's probably in a recording studio or has some rock star duty to attend to.

It takes less than a second for—

"Boom," Dad says. "I see a hand. Brady's got a boyfriend. I was right."

Kit's hand flies off my shoulder, but it's too late.

"Yeah, real detective work there, Dad," my brother says. "Considering we all know some dude climbed out his window in New York." He slow claps. Levi shoves him.

Uncle Lennon, the family reporter, leans in closer to the screen. "If it was only news of a boyfriend, why make this big announcement? Especially if you all saw the guy in New York."

"See, *that's* real detective work," Uncle Ollie says.

"Are we going to let me talk here?" I ask.

"Hang on a minute," Dad says. "Ever stop to think that clearly his boyfriend is there, so he wants to introduce him to us?"

"Why does that need this huge song and dance though?" Uncle Lennon says. "Unless it's that he's getting married or—"

"No—" I try to say but am immediately cut off.

"There's going to be a wedding!" Jackie cries out. "Can I plan it? I'm a woman. I know how to decorate things real pretty-like."

"That's sexist," Freddie says.

"Okay, I'll rephrase. I'm the only one here with taste."

Freddie rolls his eyes, but the rest of the family agrees with her.

Freddie is a brooding artist like his dad Uncle Jet, much to Uncle Soren's dismay because Freddie has amazing hockey talent. Could've gone all the way until he decided in high school to become this emo boy.

The whole group chat becomes a start and stop of comments, everyone trying to talk over each other, and no one actually listening when I tell them to listen to me.

"There will be no wedding!" I yell.

And when everyone is silent again, I look up at Prescott and then at Kit. "I told you both they're the worst."

I let that hang in the air.

My words slowly tick over in their brains, and the only ones who don't look confused are Levi, Four, and Uncles Damon and Maddox.

Then the explosion of chatter starts again.

"Who's the other guy?" "Where are you?" "What is happening?" "Why are you making me math?" That last one came from Peyton.

"When you're all done," I say casually. It's the only way to really deal with my family—let them have their drama, their whines, their outbursts, and then talk to them like they're children.

They settle again.

"I'm not going to do this big speech about always feeling different growing up. We all know what that feeling is like. I thought it was weird because even though I grew up in this found family my dads were a part of, I still felt different. I questioned everything—my gender, my sexuality, everything. And then a couple of years ago, I met two guys who made me realize what that part inside me was, and it's that I have so much love to give that limiting it to one person isn't enough for me."

For the first time in maybe the history of our family, everyone is quiet for longer than ten seconds. If it weren't for all the blinking and moving, I'd worry my screen was frozen. Ooh, that could be a good idea though. Be all, *Oh noooo, you're frozen. Have to end the call, byyyye.*

My brother is the first to speak. "This has been going on for *years*? How did I not know?"

"Well, one, in college whenever I stayed out all night, you assumed it was with only one person. And two, these guys ..." I glance at Kit and Prescott again. "We haven't been able to see much of each other. One lives here in Virginia, the other in California. We've only now been able to make things official. Hence, the telling you all at once and making a *big song and dance.*"

My dads aren't paying attention to me but to each other.

"Dads, I know you're worried about Peyton's career, but I already talked to Uncle Damon, and he thinks it will be fine, but if it's too much, then I won't be Peyton's agent in the future. It's not a big—"

"Screw that," Peyton says. "You're my agent, and I don't care who you're with."

"You don't, but the world might." As sad and intrusive as that is.

"Fuck the world."

I smile. "Thanks, but I've got my hands full with two partners."

"Literally," Uncle Maddox says and then does the jerking-off motion with both hands.

Beside me, Kit laughs, obviously having seen it from his angle.

"When the kids are more mature than the adults," I say.

"You told Uncle Damon before us?" Dad exclaims.

"He did the right thing," Uncle Damon says. "He didn't want to tell you first in case I told him that he had to choose between his partners or his job."

"You would never do that though," Dad says.

"Can you blame him for questioning it? Yes, times have changed since you two came out, but do you remember the huge blowout that caused? Not only in your careers but your relationship as well. You have to be ready for this kind of thing, and I, for one, am happy for Brady."

Dad's eyes widen. "Wait, of course we're happy for you."

Pop nods. "Definitely."

"But ..."

"But it's hard to turn off football brain," I say. "Which is why I took so long to take this step. Well, that, and until recently, I didn't think the three of us would become an official thing or anything."

"Can you please put them all out of their misery now?" Levi asks. "I can't wait for you all to see these guys. They're SEALs."

I slash at my throat, but again, it's too late. Look at that, Levi was able to make all of them silent as well.

"You knew?" Peyton asks.

Four holds up his hand. "So did I."

"Damon told me," Maddox says.

"I can't believe you kept a secret from me." Peyton pouts.

Levi pats his cheek. "Sweetie, I love you with all that I am, but this isn't about you. This is about your brother for once. Let him have it."

"Okay, before my news ruins any more relationships or friendships or the fucked-up brotherhood you all have, would you like to meet them?"

There's a round of "Duh" and "Of-fucking-course."

"This is Guy Kitchener, but everyone calls him Kit." Kit shuffles in, and I turn the laptop on an angle so we both fit in the screen.

A "Holy mother of fuck" falls from someone's mouth, but I have no idea who says it because the screen glitches for a second.

"And before you say it, yes, he's older. By, like, a lot," I say.

"I guarantee that's not why Freddie said that," Uncle Soren says.

Kit shakes his head. "And Brady's exaggerating anyway. It's ten years. Not even."

"Nine years and eleven months," I murmur. "It's basically ten."

"I'm younger," Prescott calls out from where he is.

"Show us the next one!" Jackie yells.

"Okay, okay, but how about we use our inside voices?" I stand and move over to Prescott's hospital bed. "This is Prescott."

And when I turn the computer around and everyone sees where Prescott's lying, gasps exit the speakers followed by a million voices.

"What happened?" "Are you at the hospital?" "Is he okay?"

And Uncle Maddox has to take it that one step further again by saying, "My bet is on sex injury."

"Wow," Prescott says. "Kit earns a whole lot of expletives for his looks, and I get sex injury and sympathy. Really?"

I pat his head. "You're gorgeous too, I promise."

"You really are," Freddie says. "Hey, if someone was looking for, say, these soldier types—"

"SEALs," both Kit and Prescott say.

"Yeaaah, navy men don't like being called soldiers. That's army," I say. "Which is kinda stupid if you think about it. You can call them seamen but not soldiers. Like seamen sounds any better. Don't get me wrong, I'll call them that all damn day, but it's a weird flex."

Prescott turns his head toward me. "You know we're *sailors*. Now who's being the immature one?"

"Uh, everyone?" I point to the screen, where everyone's snickering to themselves.

"How did you injure yourself?" Pop asks.

"Helo crash on a training exercise," Prescott says. "It's a broken leg and a concussion. No biggie. I'll be back on my feet in no time."

"And how do you think your relationship will work?" Dad asks.

"Now's not the time for that conversation, Dad."

Dad gives me his best *don't talk back to me* look. "Then when?"

Kit stands and makes his way around so he can lean over me and put his head in between Prescott and me. "We'll have to have you by one time. Brady's staying for the summer, and Prescott's rehabbing his leg here. You should come visit."

"Dude." I could slap him. "What are you doing?"

"He's being more polite than you," Dad says. "We're in. When's the soonest we can make this happen?"

Fuck.

CHAPTER TWENTY-NINE

DESPITE BRADY TRYING to put off the inevitable, he has finally run out of the million excuses he used to keep his family away for as long as he could. There was the one where he said the hospital won't take that many visitors at once, that one where he said I was too busy with rehab. He even implied I wasn't being treated as an outpatient, even though I am, thanks to staying in Kit's apartment, but that was his undoing.

Considering the military is putting me through vigorous rehab so I can make sure that the rest of my body doesn't lose its conditioning while my leg heals and that after my cast comes off, I'll have to focus on making my leg strong again, athletes, above anyone else, know rehab wouldn't keep me down or restricted.

So, it's happening. Brady's family is invading Virginia. And Brady's not handling it well.

He paces the pathway in the middle of Warburton—a large park by the naval base that's often busy with families and navy guys exercising.

But as SEAL Team Two runs a cardio session behind me, even the eye candy doesn't calm Brady's nerves.

I don't tell him I'm excited for this to happen. He'll assume I mean because I want to meet his famous dads when it's actually because of what this means to him and for us. Brady is ridiculously close to his family, and the last time we had a chance to meet, he didn't even consider letting it happen.

While he doesn't want it to happen now, it's not because of us. It's because he thinks we'll be intimidated or won't know how to take his family.

He's met my parents. He should know this is a piece of cake for me.

"It'll be fine," I say. They've set me up on a picnic bench, facing outward so I can keep my leg straight. My crutches are beside me, I have a drink in my hand, and I'm leaning back on my elbows. I'm comfortable, but it's frustrating that I can barely get around. I can't easily stand and walk over to him and take him in my arms to reassure him.

I'd get Kit to do it, but he's hauling the grill and supplies out of the car to have a cookout.

Everyone else isn't expected to arrive for another hour. We made sure to get here early to give Brady a sense of control, but I'm starting to think that was a mistake. It gives him more time to dwell on what's going to go down here today.

"We'll have some drinks, some food, we'll get to meet your family, they'll grill us with questions, embarrass you … It'll be fine. And if they don't like Kit and me—"

He finally stops pacing back and forth. "Wait, you think that's why I'm freaking out? Hell no. I'm scared you and Kit will decide to leave after everything they'll pull today. Let's just say you're lucky to have a broken leg, otherwise, they'd be challenging you to a game of football, or they'd ask to join that team of guys behind you to prove they might be old, but they're still fit. Then you two will let them win to gain brownie points, and we will never hear the end of them being as fit as navy SEALs."

I smile. "It's going to take a lot more than that to scare Kit and me off."

Kit dumps bags, camping chairs, and a whole lot of other equipment by my feet. "He's freaking out, isn't he?"

"You know what might distract him? Helping you cart all the shit from the car. I can't, obviously." I gesture to my leg. "Damn. Such a shame."

"I'm starting to suspect your leg is fine under there. You just wanted a vacation from being a grown-up," Kit grumbles and stalks back to the car.

Alone.

After hearing about how Brady took care of Kit while I was MIA and those first couple of nights at the hospital, it's like a silent agreement has happened between them. Or maybe it's not so silent, I'm not sure. But I get the sense that Kit has vowed to never make Brady lift a finger, be responsible, or be the together one. Unless I go missing again.

"He knows me too well," I say to Brady.

Brady stands in front of me. "Bullshit your leg is actually fine."

"What makes you say that?"

"As much as you're loving an excuse to have some time off to spend time with Kit and me, it's not like you're reaping any sexual benefits because you're still so hopped up on painkillers."

"I've heard sex stops once you're in a relationship anyway."

"Not true. I've overheard, walked in on, and been told way too many stories from happy couples having sex. Even when I've begged for it not to happen. The second thing that tells me there's no way you're actually faking it is you love your job. It's your priority. Kit knows it, and I know it. Hell, I even understand it because I'm the same way with mine. We're similar like that."

My lips twitch. "Maybe Kit isn't the only one who knows me too well."

Brady steps closer, making sure to avoid my stretched-out leg. His hands land on my shoulders, and he leans in close to kiss my cheek. "We wouldn't have you any other way. Well, except maybe healed enough to get in on some action. I miss your dick."

I laugh, but when he pulls back, the fire in Brady's warm brown eyes makes me want to rip my cast off myself. A few more weeks and then my leg will be free. A couple of weeks after that, after more rehab, Brady will be going back to New York.

I hope the weakness in my leg isn't going to affect any sex-acrobat maneuvers. We'll only have a short time together, and I want to make the most of it.

We might have agreed to try to make this work between us, but we haven't dared utter the question of what happens once summer is over. Once we're all back to our respective places throughout the country.

I'm used to long and lonely nights, but it might feel different now we're officially together. Before, I could lie to myself and almost be convincing that I didn't have real feelings for either of them—that it was the sex that I missed. Will the pain of longing sting even more now that I've acknowledged I want to be with them? I'm too scared to find out, but it's inevitable. I don't want that moment to come.

I can't say goodbye.

Not again.

Not now that we've chosen each other.

"Kiss me," I tell Brady because I need that connection, that reminder of why we're all here.

Together.

Brady doesn't hesitate, and his freak-out is suddenly forgotten too. He throws his leg over my waist, straddling me but still standing so there's no weight on my legs. He leans in, taking my mouth in the exact way I want it.

It's a mixture of soft but still needy. His tongue strokes mine, and I can taste the promise. Once I'm fully healed, there's going to be a marathon of nakedness—

"Brady, please. There are children present!"

Brady freezes on top of me, his lips stiff against mine until he mutters, "Fuck, they're early."

We slowly turn our heads, and I recognize Marcus Talon immediately from his good ol' days of being on my TV every week. Sure, he was in football gear, but with the number of times he won the Super Bowl, his face was everywhere in the media.

There's a whole group of them that seem like so many more people than there were on the video call.

He has his hands covering the eyes of someone who is clearly an adult, but I don't realize who it is until the guy swats Marcus Talon's hands away.

"Fuck off, Talon."

My mouth drops. "You're related to Jay Jackson from Radioactive?" He wasn't on the video call. That I know for sure.

"He's just Uncle Jet to me."

I shake my head. The lead singer of one of my favorite bands is Uncle Jet. No biggie. "Okay, *now* I'm intimidated."

Brady climbs off me. "Don't be. He's a kitten."

"Fuck you too, Baby Talon," Jay Jackson says to my boyfriend. "I'm fierce."

The group of people behind him all say, "Uh-huh" or "Sure."

Being the rock star that he is, he throws up double middle fingers to them all.

"I'm offended Jet intimidates him, but we don't." Marcus Talon turns to Shane Miller. "We're going to need to change that."

This whole moment is surreal, but nothing has changed. I knew Brady's dads were famous, and I was totally okay with letting that go because, well, I guess athlete famous is one thing. But Hollywood famous is a whole other league. I'll just have to keep reminding myself to be cool.

Brady hands me my crutches and helps me up. "Everyone, this is Prescott. Prescott … uh, everyone."

Brady's parents step forward first to shake my hand. "We're Brady's dads," Marcus says. "You can call us Mr. Talon and Mr. Miller."

"Uh—" I glance at Brady.

Shane Miller playfully backhands *Mr. Talon's* chest. "Drop the mister. Talon and Miller is fine."

Talon lowers his voice. "These guys are so much scarier than Levi ever was. We need them to respect us."

"Hey," a voice comes from behind them. "I was a Vanderbilt, and that didn't intimidate you?"

Brady's parents turn, and as they do, they part, revealing a guy I'm sure I've met before. And not via a computer screen. Brady's brother's boyfriend.

"Vanderbilt money doesn't scare us," Talon says to him.

"Good to see you again," I say to Levi.

"Don't even get us started on the fact Levi met you before we did," Talon says. "We love Levi like he's our own, but all of you lose future son-in-law points for that one."

I understand what Brady means by his parents being over-the-top, but I also know that it's done with love, so I find them funny more than anything.

Kit and two others arrive, one guy with dark hair and graying sides helping Kit carry the portable grill over even though Kit is perfectly capable of carrying it himself.

Brady immediately goes over to them, and at first, I think he's going toward Kit, but instead, he wraps his arms around the guy with dark hair.

"I see you've met Uncle Damon," he says to Kit.

So, that's Brady's boss.

"And your Uncle Maddox." Kit points to a blond guy with them.

"I helped by watching them carry that thing." Maddox points to the grill. "It was a hard job, but someone had to do it."

According to Brady, Maddox is the fun uncle, and I can see why.

"Come and meet the rest of them, and then feel free to run away." Brady pulls Kit over next to me, and Kit wraps his arm around my shoulders.

Introductions move at a blur. From uncles, cousins, and everyone in between.

But it's the person waiting at the back with Levi who I know is the most important when it comes to Brady. If Brady's dads don't like us, that would be one thing. If Brady's brother hated us? We could basically kiss goodbye any chance we have at keeping Brady forever. Or at all.

The group is already spreading out, taking over setting up the grill, putting food and drinks they've brought with them down on the picnic table, and soon enough, it's just Brady, Kit, me, Levi, and Peyton Miller.

Brady's told me how close they are. How when they were growing up, they basically only had each other at school. Friends used them because of who their dads were, and they didn't know who they could trust. It's why Brady was so reluctant to tell us who he was in the beginning.

Peyton is the current *it* boy of the NFL, the guy breaking all kinds of football records in his rookie years, but none of that scares me. Him thinking I'm not good enough for his brother? Yeah, that I'm worried about.

As Peyton steps closer, his lips turn up, and he holds out his hand. "Peyton."

I shake his hand. "Prescott."

Kit does the same. "Kit."

"I think I'm supposed to say something here like 'break his heart, I'll break your face,' but you're both tall and huge, and yeah, there's no way I'd be able to kick any of your asses. Some of my teammates might though."

"If we break his heart, I give you permission to break *his* face." I point at Kit. "I'm selfless like that."

The joke has the effect I was going for. The ice is broken as everyone laughs and settles into casual conversation.

Step one of meeting the family has been a success, but we've still got all day to survive the rest.

"Who's up for a friendly game of flag football?" Brady's dad calls out.

And yep, Brady was right about that too.

Thankfully, I don't get to play. I put my hand on Kit's shoulder. "You can't let them win."

Kit leans over and kisses my cheek. "Let? I don't think there'll be any *letting* them. They're professional football players."

"Retired," Peyton says. "I can't play. My agent will kick my ass if I risk getting injured during a game of pickup." He nods toward Damon.

"I'm out too," Levi says. "I have no sporting ability whatsoever."

"Nice try," Brady says and reaches for Levi. "You can be on my team."

I guess it's going to be me and Peyton, then. Alone.

I can do this.

I can totally do this.

"Beer?" I ask him and try to move, but he holds up his hand.

"I'll get it. You sit."

I'm thankful because it takes me longer to hobble back to the table on my crutches than it does for Peyton to pull two beers out of a cooler.

I sit sideways on the end of the bench seat so I can keep my leg out but not put my back to Peyton.

We sit in silence.

Great start, Prescott.

"Thanks." I hold up my beer and take a sip.

He only stares at me in return.

Okay, so Brady's brother has an issue with us. I'm going to find out what it is and fix it because I will do anything to hold on to this. It's only the beginning of anything official, but I'm already in deep.

I go to open my mouth to ask what I can do, say, tell him—anything that can get him on our side—but we talk at the same time. Only he gets his question out first.

"Why do you think Brady felt the need to keep you a secret from me?"

Ah. It's nothing against us. It's a brother thing.

I turn my attention to the football game. Brady and his pop are going head-to-head as centers, with Talon behind Miller and Kit behind Brady.

"Do they realize how dirty that looks?" I ask.

Peyton screws up his face. "Eww, dude. That's my family."

I don't tell him I've seen his brother in that position naked countless times. I want him to like me.

"Sorry. And, to answer your question, I think there were a few reasons he didn't tell you."

"He told Levi."

I snort. "No, he didn't. Your boyfriend was drunk one night we were over. We thought everyone was asleep, and he, uh … might have gotten a front-row seat to a pretty heavy make-out session. Be thankful it wasn't you who was awake."

Peyton lowers his head. "Still doesn't make it feel less shitty about him keeping it from me. I didn't think we had secrets. Brady and me or Levi and me."

"In the beginning, we were literally hooking up. That's all it was. We knew Brady was graduating, so it didn't mean anything. But as we got to know him better, we started putting pieces together about who Brady really is. Why he's the way he is."

"He's everyone's rock."

"Not with us. I think he kept us a secret because we were something that was just for him. Something that he didn't see a future in because he was too worried about what having a relationship with two men would do to your career."

Peyton frowns. "What?"

"Like when he said he'd step back as your agent? He's been worried about the public fallout of this. I can't say I understand what world you live in. Your fame. But I do know about needing to keep a secret to protect yourself. He kept it from everyone for *you*."

Peyton's lips purse as he takes in that little tidbit.

Our attention turns back to the game again, where Brady's team scores a touchdown thanks to Kit running it in. I don't think he knows quarterbacks aren't supposed to steal that glory.

Brady runs up and throws his arms and legs around Kit. Kit lifts him, and they kiss hard.

"Doesn't that ever make you jealous?" Peyton asks.

"Nope. They make each other happy. How could I deny two people I care about that kind of feeling?" I shrug. "One of them or both of them will show me affection later. We don't keep score."

Peyton glances at my leg. "You gonna tell us the real story of how you got broken?"

I smile and take a huge gulp of my beer.

"I'll take that as a no."

"Nah. I wish it was some amazing story about being shot down in enemy fire in some undisclosed corner of the world, but I'm sorry to say it really was a training op accident. Mechanical failure on a Hawk that's older than Brady."

"Damn."

"It sucks that it happened in an accident that could've been prevented, but we can only train with what we've got."

Turns out I got off lucky. Levenson might never walk again and is being discharged. Moran is already recovered and back in Coronado. But if you ask me, we're all lucky we escaped with our lives. Accidents like this shouldn't happen, but they do.

Peyton stares blankly at me, but it takes a second to realize he's not staring at me but behind me. "God, they're embarrassing."

I turn and see two of Brady's uncles watching the SEAL team work out. The football game is all but forgotten for most of them. Some of Brady's cousins are on the field but staring at their phones, but Brady's dads, Kit, and Brady are still taking the game so seriously.

They remind me a lot of my family in ways. Just a hell of a lot gayer.

"Your family is my kind of people," I say and drink down the rest of my beer.

Peyton glances at his brother when he says, "Yeah. They're the best."

CHAPTER THIRTY

THE GAME IS TIED, and Brady has told me that under no circumstances are we allowed to let his dads win. They may be the professionals, but we have youth on our side.

I don't point out to Brady that all the youth—mainly his cousins Freddie and Four—have no interest in football and are leaving us out to dry.

Luckily, Jackie pulls the feminine card, and the rest of the family refuses to try for her flags in case they knock her over. I guess there's one advantage to being the only girl in the family, even if it's a little misogynistic. I'm not going to point that out though. These guys have all been in the sporting industry for so long they probably don't even know when they're doing it.

The three of us huddle while Freddie and Four are off to the side, staring at their phones.

We've all agreed whoever scores next wins, and we have possession.

"Looks like it's down to us," I say.

The three of us against three ex-pro football players and two ex-hockey players. They lost some of their guys who went to man the grill and others to go watch some SEALs work out.

Brady lifts his head. "Now's your chance to switch sides to the winning team! Anyone?"

No one moves.

"Nice try," I say.

"We can do this." Jackie claps, psyching herself up. "Get the ball to me. They won't touch me."

"And remember, if we lose this, the gloating will never end." Brady grips my bicep. "Even if we break up, the story of 'Hey, remember that time Brady dated those SEALs and they couldn't even beat us in football? This proves that football players are fittest. The toughest of the tough. Tougher than *navy SEALs*.'"

"That's the worst outcome that could happen?" I'd be okay with that.

Jackie laughs. "He really is new. Competition is taken very seriously in this family."

"Got it. Let's beat them, then. Will that mean I will get gloating rights forever and ever?"

They both shake their heads.

"So new," Jackie mutters.

"No. If you do that, then you're a sore winner," Brady adds.

"So, basically, if we lose, we have to deal with the gloating, but if we win, we have to be humble. Are your dads' egos really that fragile?"

Brady stares at me sympathetically. "Oh, honey, sweetie, no. Not Pop's anyway. Dad's, definitely. And under no circumstance should you ever utter the name Tom Brady to him."

"Even though you're named after him?"

"That's a whole other story. One we don't have time for now. Let's kick their asses."

Brady takes quarterback position this time, and I face off with Brady's pop. Brady makes the call, and I snap the ball back to him. I'm fairly evenly matched with Miller, but only one-on-one. Everyone else has no one blocking them, and they're all running for Brady, who's backing up and waiting while Jackie runs to our end zone.

Brady throws the football as one of his uncles reaches him. Despite agreeing to no tackling, they fall to the ground, but the throw is glorious—something worthy of a Talon—and Jackie's underneath it at the other end.

Brady gets to his feet. "Suck it. In your face. We win."

So much for not gloating.

That's followed by a round of accusations about it being a fluke and not talent.

Is this what it's like to have a family? All snarky smack talk and games? Because I want in.

Brady bounds up to me. "We did it."

"You did it. Nice throw."

He leans in and kisses me softly. "I'm going to go gloat to Prescott."

I watch him run off.

Talon approaches me and holds out his hand to shake. "Good game."

Okay, despite Brady insisting his dad is all drama, at least he can be a good sport.

"It was fun," I say.

He claps my shoulder. "Let's get some food. I'm starving."

Brady's uncles Damon and Jet are manning the grill and refuse help when I offer. It's a team effort to get all the different foods everyone brought prepared, and then there's nowhere to sit and eat it, but apparently, that doesn't stop the ravenous appetites of athletes. Everyone starts digging in, and the food basically disappears before it hits the plates anyway.

I approach Brady and Prescott where Brady's still telling his tale of how we beat all the old guys at football.

Prescott smiles over Brady's shoulder at me. "Hey, that's a bonus about hanging out with Brady's family. We're no longer the old guys."

"Oh, you're still old. Just not as old as them." He waves a finger in the direction of his parents.

"Did I hear Brady ask for me to pass the potato salad?" his dad asks. "I can't be sure because of my old, old age and my terrible hearing."

Brady glares. "Don't you dare."

But it's too late. Talon's already dumping a huge scoop of salad on Brady's head.

Miller sighs. "This is why we always need to bring extra food."

Brady picks up the bowl of slaw and flings the contents at his dad.

"I'm guessing if I want to eat, I should've done that a few minutes ago," I say.

"Yep," nearly everyone answers at the same time.

"Can you get me out of the line of fire?" Prescott asks, and I grab his crutches. I help him hobble over to a safety zone, and I can't believe my eyes as I watch a group of grown-ass men and one woman throw food at each other. Peyton grabs the ketchup and sprays the group like it's a champagne bottle.

"They really are crazy," Prescott says.

"In Brady's defense, he did warn us."

"That's true."

∞ ∞ ∞

On the drive on the way home, I glance over at Brady. "Admit it. It wasn't so bad."

"It wasn't the complete disaster I was anticipating. And how's this for weird? I thought my brother was going to be pissed about keeping you guys from him, but all he did was hug me and tell me I deserve to be happy. What is up with that?"

My gaze finds Prescott in the rearview mirror, where his leg's stretched out across the back seat, and he's smiling. I'd bet anything that he went to bat for Brady while we were playing football. I saw Peyton and him in a deep conversation.

"It came from being your brother," I say. "Because he loves you."

"I know that. I just … I dunno. I was expecting him to be upset. We don't have secrets, and the longer I kept you guys from him, the harder it was to say anything at all."

"You had your reasons," Prescott says. "And he understands them."

Brady turns in his seat. "Did you say something to him?"

Prescott pretends to think. "I said a lot of things to him."

"Pres …" Brady warns.

"I might have pointed out what you were willing to sacrifice for his career."

"That's it? No threats?"

"Does telling him that Kit and I have been trained to kill men a hundred different ways count as a threat? I thought it was a great conversation starter."

"You didn't … did you?"

Prescott bursts into laughter. "Fuck no. I actually want your brother to like me."

Brady takes out his phone. "Well, if the family group chat has anything to say about it, everyone loves you two. A few of them think you're both hot."

"Which ones?" I ask.

"No way am I telling you. You're mine, not theirs."

A groan comes from the back.

"Can we hurry up and get home?" Prescott asks. "I have a bit of a dilemma that needs taking care of."

I don't need to look back to know what it is. "You like it when Brady's possessive, huh?"

"I love it, and I haven't been able to do anything about it since the accident. Please take me home and take advantage of me in my poor, injured state."

Brady and I glance at each other and grin.

"I have an idea," Brady says. "It involves Prescott on his back—"

"I'm in," Prescott says.

"I haven't finished. You on your back. Me on top of you—"

"Still in."

"And then Kit on top of me. Provided we can keep our weight off the top of Prescott's leg."

"Are you saying what I think you're saying?" I ask, remembering what he said while I was filming him to send to Prescott.

Both of us.

At the same time.

"At this point, I don't even care if it hurts my leg," Prescott says. "Hurry up and get home so we can make this happen."

I don't think I've ever made it to my apartment in record time before.

Getting out of the car is another story. With Prescott on crutches, it feels like it takes an eternity to get him through the door.

"Get on the bed," I order him. "I'm going to remove all the left-over food off Brady's body and start getting him ready in the shower."

Prescott salutes me. "Sure thing, boss."

"Your sarcasm is so sexy," I say.

"Hey, Brady's the one who likes taking orders, not me. I take enough orders every day."

"Can you please go and strip naked for us?" I ask nicely.

"That's better, but you know I was going to do it anyway."

I do, but I don't mind tucking away my demanding side for Pres.

I take Brady's hand and pull him toward the bathroom, but apparently, I'm moving too slow for him. He ends up dragging me in there and stripping off before I even get the water running.

When he's completely naked, he starts on my clothes while I turn on the water and reach for the lube in the top drawer.

Brady nips at my neck while undoing my pants, and I laugh. The potato salad dressing has dried in his hair.

"Why are you laughing and not prepping me like you promised Prescott?"

"Because you're a mess." I run my hand through his hair. Or try to. My fingers get stuck on the crusty bits. "And it's adorable." I slap his ass for him to get in the shower.

"Adorable or sexy?"

"Definitely adorable."

He pouts, and I laugh more.

Prescott calls out, "Stop playing and get to work. I'm getting impatient."

"It's been twenty seconds," I yell back.

"I'm needy," Prescott says.

"He's not the only one," Brady says. "Let's give him what he wants."

I join him under the water. "As impatient as he is, if we're doing this, we're going to have to go slow to get you ready properly."

I'd love to rush this because I'm just as excited to share him with Prescott in that way, but I don't want him to get hurt.

I place the lube on the windowsill and work quickly where I can, getting all the food off him and cleaning every inch of his skin. He tries to wash me too, but I'm not getting clean because he's using his tongue to do it. He sucks on my earlobe, kisses down my neck, my chest, but when I pull him up and wrap my arm around him to press him to me, he stops trying to take control.

I hold him close and slide my free hand down his back. My fingers slide into his crack, and I press against his hole, massaging and loosening up his tight ring, but I don't push inside yet.

It doesn't take long for him to become impatient, so he turns and puts his back to me, leans forward, and sticks his ass out as far as possible.

"That's not really playing fair." How am I supposed to resist that?

"Hurry up," Prescott calls out again.

"You heard the man," Brady says. "At least get me ready enough to put him out of his misery when we get back out there. You're an expert at opening me up quickly."

Not to the amount we'll need, but he's right. I can get him stretched enough for him to ride Prescott to shut up the impatient whining.

I reach for the lube and sink to my knees so I can watch my fingers work him open. He's so greedy, pushing back to make my fingers go deeper. I scissor them, stretching him, and then rub against his prostate.

He's lost, drowning in deep breaths, and I get lost right along with him.

"Kit," he breathes. "I need more."

I add a third finger, and he moans.

"You guys are killing me," Prescott says. "I can hear you."

"Please let me go ride his dick now." Brady uses his begging voice, and it's so hard to say no to that.

But he is stretched enough for one of us. I can work him open the rest of the way once Prescott gets in on the action.

I pull my fingers out of him. "Get dry and go give him what he wants."

Brady moves so fast he almost slips, and I have to catch him.

"Carefully. There's only one part of you I want wrecked tonight."

Brady shudders and moves slower.

I quickly rinse off and clean the parts Brady missed, but it's probably a waste with how sweaty and dirty we're all about to get.

I need a minute. It's overwhelming being with both of them for the first time since we became official.

Up until this point, I've been waiting for them to change their minds. To doubt what we have. I know that sex is just sex, and the three of us have had sex countless times. But I think a part of me has been saying labels don't change anything, that meeting Brady's family wasn't as big a deal as he was letting on, and that this whole thing is still shallow and new, and we don't really know how it will work between us all. After this, I won't be able to say those things. Because even if they're not all in, I will be.

Then again, when have I ever not been in when it comes to Prescott and Brady?

I want us to work so bad I'm terrified of what will happen if it doesn't.

By the time I tell myself to push down all the doubt and worries —to be in the moment and enjoy tonight as though it were any other night—I get out of the shower and grab a towel, only to stumble into the bedroom and wonder how long I stayed under the hot water.

Brady sinks down on Prescott's cock, holding on to Prescott's shoulders for leverage as he moves up and down Prescott's shaft.

I watch for a little, drying myself off at the same time. I love how they look together. The anticipation grows inside me for when I'll join them. It's been an eternity since we've all been together like this.

Naked and with all the time in the world.

Poor Pres has been so drugged up since his accident, until tonight, he hasn't been interested in sex. He's wanted it, but his body hasn't cooperated too well. He's in fine working order right now though. His head's thrown back in complete ecstasy while his hands grip Brady's hips hard. I can't tell if he's trying to speed Brady up or slow him down.

"Careful, Brady," I warn. "Get Prescott any closer to the edge and you might not be able to get what you wanted."

"Or," Prescott says, "hear me out. You could keep doing this, and we can DP you with a toy or another day." Prescott's back arches, and he lets out a long "Fuck."

It scares Brady into coming to a complete stop on top of Prescott. "No," Pres cries out.

But a quick, needy whimper from Brady has him relenting. "I need both of you. I've wanted this for so long."

There's no doubt that Brady has us both wrapped around his little finger, and neither of us cares.

I approach them and appreciate the gift left for me on the bed. More lube. A lot of lube.

I crawl onto the bed but only straddle Prescott's good leg. Brady's up high enough that he's nowhere near Prescott's cast, but it might not be possible for me as well. Which should make this whole thing interesting.

I squirt lube on my fingers and push Brady down with my free hand so he's chest to chest with Prescott.

"Can you distract him with your mouth?" I ask Pres.

"Such a hardship," he whispers.

Once they're kissing, it's as if Brady's hips have a mind of their own, and he starts moving on top of Prescott again.

This is where it gets tricky. I grip the base of Prescott's cock and hold my middle finger against his shaft. With Brady's movements, he's able to control the touch, the pressure, but more importantly, how ready he is for more.

It's slow going to begin with, but as he keeps rocking back and forth, slowly but surely, my finger joins in on the action inside him.

And then a second.

"You're doing amazingly," I murmur. "So good."

"Am I ready yet?" He sounds like he's gritting his teeth and not letting it show how much it stings.

"Nowhere near ready. You want to change your mind?" I ask.

"Fuck no." He's so determined. "Prescott, can you jerk me? I need a bigger distraction."

"Anything for you." Prescott works his hand between their bodies.

With my free hand, I lift the lube and squeeze, holding it above where we're connected. We encourage Brady to breathe and take our time. I'm pretty sure Prescott is thankful for the pace too.

Brady grunts. "I have to be getting close, right? I don't care if it hurts. I want it."

I run my hand up and down his back and let my fingers inside him sink deeper. "Soon. I want to do this right."

We keep going. Brady keeps whining. We keep reassuring him that it'll happen eventually.

And when I'm fairly confident I'll be able to fit inside him without tearing his hole apart, I pull my fingers out of him.

"Thank fuck," Brady says breathlessly.

"Keep focused on Prescott. On his lips." I throw my leg over Prescott and make sure I don't put any weight on him. "Feel his hard body underneath yours."

I use more lube—so much lube—and then press the head of my dick at his hole. Prescott's hard cock rubs the underside of mine, and as tempting as it is to slam inside Brady, to feel his hole pulse around mine and Prescott's dick at the same time, I have to ask Brady one more time. "Are you sure you want this?"

CHAPTER THIRTY-ONE

AM I sure I want this? Is he kidding me?

Sure, my ass is stinging already, and my cock is valiantly fighting from having to wave the white flag, but this? This has been on my list of ultimate fantasies, and to be doing it with Kit and Prescott adds a whole other layer.

The thought of me being that full, my hole stretched and used to get them off … I don't even care if I can't come from it. I want it.

"I've never wanted anything more." My voice is shaky, but I can't help it.

Kit shifts behind me, and the head of his cock pushes inside me. The sensation is new, and different … slightly weird and hard to get used to.

But Prescott cups my face, forcing me to look at him. "Breathe." His strong presence even in his weakened state has my body obeying before I have to consciously force myself to take in air. "You've got this."

Kit sinks deeper.

There's that high I wanted. The feeling of being so full that I doubt whether it's possible to take any more, but I have to.

Because Prescott and Kit have promised to be mine, and I'm going to show them that I'm theirs.

They own me completely.

Wholly.

I'm willing to do whatever it takes for us to be together.

"I'm good," I grit out. "Keep going. Please keep going."

Kit tests out an experimental but weak thrust, and it doesn't hurt. It stings a bit, but no more than regular one-on-one penetrative sex.

It must do something to Prescott, though, because he moans and throws his head back like he did earlier when I was riding him.

"This feels amazing," he says. "Kit moving against me while I'm inside Brady's heat."

"Do it again," I urge Kit. "I like it when Prescott makes that face."

Prescott's eyes are closed tight, his cheeks are flushed, and he bites his bottom lip as if that will help him hold back longer.

The thought of them unleashing inside me, of them taking me and worshiping my body … it drives me wilder than anything else we've done. But most of all, it's the idea of them taking care of me afterward that makes my chest yearn.

This is all my dreams come true, something that's separate from my job, my family, my real life … and I want to keep it going.

I want it to last forever.

Kit picks up the pace, and I'm able to take it easier.

Prescott starts moving too, both of them inside me at once.

It's heaven.

It's earth-shattering.

My cock has recovered from the initial sting in my ass, and the pain has given way to something so much bigger than pleasure.

Need, lust … love.

"I'm not going to be able to hold out," Prescott warns. "It's been way too long, and this is way too good."

"It's okay," I say. I've gotten what I wanted. This isn't about an orgasm for me but being owned by them.

Prescott's hips buck once. Twice.

And then I watch as his face contorts while he rides the orgasm wave. Kit behind me doesn't slow down. If anything, he speeds up.

Prescott stays inside me, even as his body slowly melts into the mattress, and his cock begins to soften. Kit keeps going, even easier now, and if he keeps this up, I could totally come like this. Eventually.

Kit can't hold out though. I can hear it in his breaths and in the tiny groans he's trying to keep in.

He's close, and when I say, "Kit, please give it to me," it's all over.

He pushes in even deeper, which I didn't even know was possible at this point, and when he finally stops and tries to pull out, I reach behind me.

"Not yet," I beg.

Kit leans over and kisses his way down my spine. "We're not going anywhere, Brady."

I close my eyes and let the words wash over me. When they hit my heart and make it go flutter, I let him go.

He pulls out of me carefully, and Prescott's cock slips out of me at the same time.

"Roll over," Kit says.

"Can't. I live here now."

Prescott shifts under me, so I don't have a choice.

I land on my side, facing Prescott. He has his head turned toward me, his deep brown eyes shining with something I would equate to pride or gratitude.

"Now to get you off," he says.

"It's okay. I got what I needed." More than what I needed.

"But we didn't get what we need," Kit says.

"You didn't?"

Prescott shakes his head. "We want you to be happy and satisfied."

"You two make me happy by being in the same room as me."

"Happy is covered," Prescott murmurs. "Let's get satisfied done too."

Kit runs his hand up the back of my leg. "How sore are you?"

I clench and, "Ouch."

"Let me know if it's too much, but I'm only going to use one finger, and I won't be moving it a whole lot."

"What are you—" I'm cut off by Kit's finger entering me and immediately finding my prostate. And he's right. He doesn't move it a whole lot, only puts pressure on it and then eases off. A little more pressure before he takes it away. "It's official. This is how I'll die." Because after being so full, to go to a single finger that's only focused on one little spot is nothing like I've ever experienced before.

Prescott joins in by wrapping his fingers around my dick. "We're going to do this until you unleash. Until you let go and give us what we want."

"You going to come for us?" Kit asks.

"Keep going." I alternate my focus between Prescott's hand working over my cock and Kit's finger pulsing inside me until they kind of blend and send warmth all over my skin.

My balls tingle. My gut burns.

And then Kit leans over me and whispers in my ear, "I can't wait to fuck you like that again."

That's it. That's what makes my body give in.

My orgasm starts as a trickle before hitting hard and long. It's hard to describe. It's nothing and everything all at once. It drains my energy, but I'm eager for more at the same time.

I don't know what's up, what's down, or where I am. All I know is I'm with who I'm supposed to be with.

Kit and Prescott.

From being my college flings to becoming my vacation hookups. I really hope this can lead to something more. Something bigger.

I want them as life partners in every sense.

Now to find a way to make it happen.

Time is blurry when there's no work, no school, nothing. It's an absolute bitch to realize weeks have gone by and that our time is running out together. At least, physically together. We're all in this relationship. We're committed. But I'm not sure what being committed will look like once I'm back in New York. Once Prescott is recovered and in California or deployed overseas.

I've been trying not to think about it. While Kit has been going to work each day, I've gone with Prescott to rehab.

Walking into the gymnasium there takes me back to my college days when I'd work out with my brother and the football team.

It's full of buff guys, smells like sweat, and provides some nice eye candy. Though, I have to say, this one also holds a tinge of sadness.

Like when Cooper Stanley, a veteran who lost his leg and is learning to walk with his prosthetic, struggles to get his body to do what his brain is telling it to do. It happens every time I'm here. He gets to a certain point where his body has had enough, yet he keeps pushing.

As I spot Prescott on the bench press, I can't help thinking how close Pres came to becoming another Cooper.

Prescott's cast comes off tomorrow, which is awesome, but it's another reminder that summer is coming to an end.

We're basically living together, and it's been easy settling into that routine. But before long, we're going to have to mix it up again and try to find another new normal.

Maybe that's what a relationship with both of them will be like. Constant change. Scheduling. Missing one or both of them.

At the beginning of summer, I was certain I could do anything to keep them, but the more time I spend with them, the more I realize being away from them again is going to hurt like a motherfucker.

"A little … help?" Prescott grunts, and I snap out of my preemptive wallowing.

"Shit, sorry." I help him get the bar back on the rack.

"You have a thing for guys who don't have use of one leg?" He waggles his eyebrows in Cooper's direction.

I know the correct answer here isn't that this whole place makes me think of our uncertain future. "Yep. It's a fetish," I say instead. "I like it when my men can't run away from me."

"That implies your guys would actually want to. And I speak for both Kit and me when I say we'd never want to leave you."

I can't help hearing what he's not saying: *even though we'll have to.*

"How much more have you got to do?" I ask. "I was thinking of taking you out for lunch."

"Please, I was done two sets ago."

Of course he was. I don't know what it is about men, athletes and military in particular, but they've always gotta push their limits.

Prescott sits up, and I hand him his crutches.

"Let's go get lunch."

CHAPTER THIRTY-TWO

THERE'S something on Brady's mind, I can tell, but maybe I shouldn't bring it up. I'm not sure I want to know the answer.

"What are you going to get?" I ask as we look at our menus.

I have my leg stretched out with my foot resting on the seat next to me while Brady sits opposite. I can't wait to get this stupid restrictive, smelly, itchy cast off tomorrow. I'll be put into a walking boot instead, but at least I can take that thing off.

"I dunno. Burger, probably. You?"

"Same. I want all the meat in my mouth."

Brady's lips twitch. "I bet you do."

We order food, but Brady's weird mood settles over both of us, and I have to ask, "Are you okay?"

He smiles, but it doesn't look genuine in the slightest. "Tired. My boyfriends kept me up way too late last night."

I laugh. "Yeah, we did, but I get the feeling that's not what's bothering you."

He glances away. "It's not. I guess I'm thinking about what happens after next week."

"Ah. The thing all three of us have been avoiding."

"Yep. I've been trying to forget about it, but everything reminds me that our time is coming to an end."

I lean forward and cover his hand with mine on top of the table. "Hey, just this visit is coming to an end. We're in this for the long haul. We want this to work, so we're going to make it work." I say the words, but I still see the doubt in Brady's eyes.

He shifts uncomfortably as he says, "I believe we all want to make it work, but wanting it and being able to do it are two different things. Kit said he'd quit his job and move back to California, but I still have a year left in New—"

I pull back. "Wait. Kit's quitting his job? He didn't tell me that."

"Oh. I assumed that's what's going to happen because he said before we were official that if you wanted him for real, he'd drop everything to be with you."

"He … did?"

Brady facepalms. "Do you two ever communicate? And have I broken some unspoken poly rule here where I've interfered in your relationship with each other? Oh no. Am I bad at having two boyfriends?" If he didn't look so genuinely worried, I'd laugh.

"You haven't done anything wrong," I say. "But it does bring up the very good point that maybe we all need to communicate a bit better."

"I've heard communication is supposedly healthy in relationships or whatever."

"Then, let's do it. Tomorrow night, after my leg is free and I should know more about how long I'll be here, the three of us will have a proper sit-down and talk about how we're going to make this relationship work going forward."

Brady looks like he wants to throw up. "Why does a root canal sound more enticing than that?"

It really does. "Because putting everything you want on the line is hard?"

"Understatement."

Our food arrives, and we go back to being silent as we eat, but my mind ticks over.

If Kit is willing to move to Coronado when I'm called back from rehab and I'm in Virginia for the next few months, the only one who will be out of reach will be Brady.

But he only has one year left of law school, and then he could ask his uncle to be transferred to the LA office. It's still not ideal, but LA to San Diego is a lot easier than New York to San Diego.

There has to be a solution I'm not seeing, but until we actually talk about what we all want, no hard plans can be made.

∞ ∞ ∞

"I'm free!" I cry as soon as that damn cast is cut off me. "Now to parkour my way to the parking lot."

I can't even try to get out of the hospital bed before Kit pushes me down.

My doctor approves of Kit pinning me. "Maybe hold off on parkour until your leg gains back some conditioning. After weeks of having all your weight on your good leg, you'll be unbalanced for a while."

"Aww, your legs match your mental state," Kit says.

The asshole.

Brady laughs. What a traitor.

"My boyfriends are mean, Doc. Are you single? I might be on the market."

Apparently, Dr. Arodel doesn't find me as amusing as Kit and Brady. Maybe I'll keep them after all.

"Don't overdo it, okay?" the doctor says. "Take your time getting back on your feet, and don't skip any of your rehab sessions. Now comes the hard part—strengthening those muscles that have suffered because of the break."

"That sounds like work," I complain.

"We'll make sure he keeps up with conditioning," Kit says, and I have to admit, that makes it sound more fun than what it actually is because in my mind, they'll be working my leg real good. In bed. While I'm fucking and being fucked.

Sex acrobatics, here we come.

But no, I've known Kit long enough to know he means business. Brady, on the other hand …

I glance over at him, and the smirk on his face lets me know that he's probably thinking the same way I am. Hey, if having him beneath me while I thrust inside him over and over until I get strength back in my leg is what I have to do, then I'll do it.

It's for my health.

I've only been free of this thing for ten minutes, and I already feel like I'm getting back to my usual self. A few weeks of having confined movement, no team camaraderie … I'm already going crazy.

The only bright spark in it all is I've been able to spend extra time with Kit and Brady.

"Let's go celebrate," I say. "Dinner's on Kit."

This time when I go to stand, they let me, and motherfucker, as soon as I put any weight down on my leg, my knee wants to give out.

"Let's get this boot on you," Dr. Arodel says, and I want to cry. My face must say so because he adds, "You don't need to wear it all the time. Just when you're mobile."

I sigh. "So, all the time?"

"You don't have to wear it when you're in bed … Wait …" My doctor glances at my two partners. "You don't have to wear it while you're *sleeping*. How's that?"

"I hate it."

"It's only a few more weeks," the doc says. "Then you'll be almost as good as new."

In a few more weeks, Brady will be back in New York. I want time to hurry up so I can be healed already, but not at the expense of it meaning that Brady has to leave.

We've decided to put an actual plan in place for when that happens, but I'm scared the logistics and reality of it all will make one of us or all of us change our minds. What if long-distance is too hard? What if Brady was wrong and Kit doesn't want to move back home?

Now that I have them, how can I possibly walk away if they ask me to?

I can't.

Once the doc sends in a nurse to fit me with the walking boot, we're given the all clear to leave, but I'm still on damn crutches, which makes my mood sour. And because Brady knows what conversation is coming, he's subdued and withdrawn too.

I have the need to console him, so I wrap my arm around him while trying to juggle my crutches.

"Where do you want to eat?" Kit asks.

"Let's get takeout and eat at home," I say. "Brady and I have things we wanna say."

"You can't drop that and then expect me not to freak out about what it is."

I chuckle. "It's about your breath, man. It's so bad."

Brady shoves me, and then his eyes widen when I almost lose my balance, and he holds me so I can right it.

"Baby, I'm *injured*."

"I'm sorry. I didn't mean to shove you that hard, but you deserved it. A little."

I focus on Kit. "We want to make an actual plan. Figure out when we can all see each other again and think of ideas on how to make this long-distance thing work. I don't know about you guys, but I can't go months without seeing one or both of you anymore."

"Me neither," Brady agrees.

Kit nods. "I've had some thoughts on that, actually."

We reach Kit's car, and I lean against it to get a break from hobbling.

"Is it weird I want to have this conversation, but at the same time, the thought of being a fully functioning and communicative adult sounds like the worst possible hell I could go through? And that's saying something from a guy who was in a helicopter crash recently."

"It's not weird," Kit says but then lowers his voice. "For you."

I shrug. "I'd be offended, but hey, you knew this about me from the moment we met. Action and adrenaline, good. Being responsible, bad."

"Mm, talk caveman to me," Brady purrs.

"After food," Kit says. "And decisions."

Right. Decisions.

We can do this.

We can be adults.

CHAPTER THIRTY-THREE

I SWEAR these two can't be adults.

This was their idea, but so far, all the solutions they've come up with are winning the lottery so money isn't an issue, quitting our jobs, and living happily ever after in postorgasm bliss twenty-four hours a day.

Maybe the bottle of scotch to share with dinner wasn't a good idea. I should probably remove it from the dining table.

"Then it's settled," Prescott says around a mouthful of rice. "Lottery winning for the … well, win. Happy ever after and all that crap."

"So glad we're getting the serious suggestions out of the way first," I say.

I don't blame them for fantasizing. I get it. They're worried about the reality, which is going to include separation. There's no way around that.

I take a bite of food and swallow. "I have an actual idea, if you two are done living in an alternate reality."

"You don't like our lottery idea?" Prescott asks.

"Let's call that plan B."

"What's your boring idea, then?" Prescott sips more scotch, and if I didn't know him as well as I do, I'd mistake his attitude for his bratty side he sometimes lets out to play. But I do know him, and the way his lips press together and his brow scrunches, I can tell he's scared of what my answer is going to be.

"I hate my job," I admit.

"You what?" Prescott exclaims. "I thought you looooved it. You were doing so much goooood."

"I was in my last post, but …" I take a deep breath and mutter, "You were right about leaving the navy. I hate my new position, and I've only been doing it a couple of months. I want to quit."

"Do it," Prescott says. "Re-up. Come back—"

I hold up my hand. "But I don't want to rejoin the navy either."

"Then what are you going to do with your life?"

Brady shudders at Prescott's words. "Wow, way to sound like my dads when I told them I was giving up football."

"Eww, you're right. That sounded way too responsible of me. Kit should quit and become my housewife. Make me dinner. Clean my underwear."

Yep. It really is impossible for them to behave like adults for longer than a couple of minutes at a time.

"I was thinking of setting up my own company."

"Doing what?" Brady asks.

This is the part I'm kinda nervous about because I'm worried people will think it's a dumb idea, and I haven't even started looking into it. It's a random thought that popped into my head and I've been mulling over. "With my experience at the Pentagon approving training exercises for the military, and having gone through BUD/s, I know what level of fitness the military expects, so I was thinking I could train people before they enlist so that when they're tested and pushed to their limits, they're ready for it."

"You want to become a personal trainer?" Prescott asks.

"No. Well, yes, technically, but it'll be so much more involved than gym work, and the best part about it is I could do it anywhere."

"I approve," Brady says. "Mainly because of the doing it anywhere part."

I deflate. "You think it's a dumb idea."

Brady shakes his head. "Not at all. I'm just wondering if there's a market for that sort of thing. Like, don't people who want to enlist do it and then are put through military training to get to that level?"

"Basic training is just that: basic," I say. "This would give anyone a leg up. But maybe you're right. I might not get many clients if I limit myself to training special forces type stuff exclusively. What do you think?" I ask Prescott.

"Branching out would probably be smart. Could you imagine how many women would sign up to be trained by former navy SEALs?"

"SEALs? Plural?" I don't let my hope grow too big.

"I still have one year left on my contract, and maybe I'm not ready to leave, but … if it means the difference between all of us being together or being alone in Coronado, I'd choose us. Plus, I'd still be able to be physically active. Sure, less adrenaline, but that also means fewer helicopter crashes I'd have to survive."

Prescott offering to leave the navy is the last thing I was expecting.

"You wouldn't re-up? For us?" My heart beats wildly because, yes, we're "together" now, and we're exclusive and official, but … this is huge.

So huge I don't think it could actually get any bigger, but then he opens his mouth and proves me wrong.

"Love is about sacrifices and compromises, right?"

I try to repeat the L word, but my mouth gets tripped up by my tongue, and all that comes out is. "La-uh."

Brady laughs. "I think you broke Kit."

Prescott gets serious for a second. "Not possible. Kit's unbreakable. Are you okay? Are you stroking out on us?"

"N-not stroking out. That's the first time *you've* mentioned the L word, and … I mean, it wasn't even in relation to me, or us. Just in general. Of what our future could—"

"Kit, I've always loved you," Prescott says, and my breath catches. "Sure, in the beginning, it was a friendship kind of love and then a physical thing. I've loved you as a best friend, a roommate, a lover, and now as my boyfriend. My partner." He reaches across the table and holds my hand but turns to Brady. "And that goes for you too. You and I started out differently than Kit and me, but from the moment the three of us met, that one night together, Kit and I knew you were different than anyone else."

I reach for Brady's hand so we're all connected. "It's as if the universe made you specifically to fit with us. We couldn't have asked for a more perfect partner."

"It's like we're a jigsaw, and you were our missing piece," Prescott says.

A tear slips from Brady's eye, and I take it back. Both of them can be grown-up when they need to be, and that's what matters.

I reach for Brady and drag my thumb over his single tear. "What's wrong?"

He brushes me off and lifts his arm, wiping his eyes with his sleeve. "I … I didn't think this moment would ever be possible. There was too much standing in our way. And even though we made things official, I've still had my doubts. Like, where we'll be next year, how often will we really be able to see each other if we're all in different parts of the country. But you two really want to make us work, and you're willing to go to lengths I didn't think anyone would take for me. It's overwhelming, but fuck, it makes me feel good. It's actually surreal."

"How so?" I ask.

"My dads had this epic love story. They publicly came out for each other, they paved the way for queer football players, and all the stories of them in the media, everything they showed me about relationships growing up, it almost seemed too good to be true. And every time I tried to have a real relationship in college with someone, I always felt like something was missing. I'd never experienced the thing that I'd been raised to believe was true love. I started to think it was all exaggerated in my head. That my expectations were too high. I thought true love meant having to settle for close enough." Brady sniffs. "And then I met you two, and even though I've told myself for years that it was because of realizing I'm poly that made me feel that way about you and trying to convince myself not to fall because of insecurities about you two only using me to get to each other—"

"That's not—" I try, but Brady keeps going.

"I know that now, but for the last couple of years, we haven't exactly been pillars of communication."

"True," I relent. "But I need you to know that everything we feel for you is real, and it has nothing to do with how Prescott and I feel about each other."

"I'm realizing that … that maybe you two are to me what my dads are to each other. We're each other's perfect matches, and together, we just fit."

"Agreed," Prescott says.

It's a beautiful moment, one I'm going to cherish for a long time, but instead of being happy like I am, Brady breaks down and cries even more.

"I didn't think I'd ever find it, and now that I have, I'm terrified of it all going away." He wipes his face with his shirt again, but Prescott and I are out of our seats and pulling him up before he's even finished.

Our arms close around him, and we hold him silently, letting him know with our bodies that we're not going anywhere.

"The last thing we want to do is hurt you," I murmur.

"Sometimes that can't be helped though," Brady says. "Having thousands of miles between us isn't our choice, but there's no way around it. Unless I transfer my last year of law school to somewhere else, or—"

"You're not doing that," Prescott says. "You only have a year left. I have a year and a bit on my contract—"

"I can't do the distance anymore," Brady whines.

"We've done it before, and we can do it again." Prescott kisses the top of Brady's head. "It's only twelve months."

Brady buries his head on my shoulder. "I don't want to go to that airport in a week and have to say goodbye again. It hurts too much. I can't say goodbye."

I hold him tighter. "It won't be goodbye. It will be *see you later*."

"It'll be *see you in a year*." His tone is so petulant I have the urge to call him a brat, but this isn't a game. This is him pouring his heart out.

"What if after Prescott goes back to California and I give my notice, I come and stay in New York with you while I work out a business plan?"

Brady's head snaps up. "You'd do that?"

"Of course I would."

"What about Pres?"

"We can visit him on weekends," I say. "Or I can split my time—"

Prescott smiles. "Kit planning to fly back and forth between coasts to keep us in line sounds like such a Kit thing to do."

Brady laughs. "It really does."

"It's only twelve months," I point out again.

"It's going to be twelve months of suckage."

Yeah, Brady's right about that.

But we're going to make it work because I'm not going to let my guys slip away that easily.

brady

ONE WEEK FLIES by too fast, and even though a year is only fifty-two of them, my stupid brain likes to focus on the difference between the next twelve months and this past week: I won't have Kit and Prescott with me.

Prescott's got a few more weeks before he'll get sent back to California. Kit is trying to plan his exit from the Pentagon. And I'm on my way to New York.

Alone.

"This isn't goodbye," Kit reminds me on the drive to the airport, and for the past seven days, I've tried not to think about it. Distraction is really easy when you have two men to preoccupy your thoughts, but now what will I have?

Catching up on work and studying for my final year of law school.

I never thought I'd regret getting my law degree. I knew from the beginning it wasn't technically needed to become a sports agent, but Uncle Damon is so knowledgeable, and he's created this huge empire, that I wanted to go the same route he did. If I hadn't gone to law school, I'd already be a junior associate at King Sports instead of a lowly intern who still needs to pay his dues.

I'd have my pick of location, a decent roster of clients, and I'd have my dream job, my dream guys, and I wouldn't be here, saying goodbye. Again.

Because no matter how many times they say that's not what this is, the truth is this isn't *see you tonight at dinner*. It's not *let's plan something for the weekend* or *go see this concert next month*.

It's *see you when I see you*, and as much as I appreciate them encouraging me to finish what I started, part of me wishes they'd tell me to quit and that they need me. Want me in their lives permanently instead of sporadically.

Instead, they have to be all supportive and shit.

How dare they, honestly.

"You done sulking yet?" Prescott asks from the back seat.

"You done being an assface?" My retort only makes Prescott laugh.

"He forgets we find him adorable when he's petulant," he says.

Kit's in serious mode though. "In twelve months—"

I hold up my hand. "I don't need another it's *only twelve months* speech."

"When you think about it, it won't even be that long," Kit says. "I'll be coming to New York as soon as I can. You graduate in May. That's nine months. How soon can you move out to California?"

I stare out the window because that's another issue. Uncle Damon was amazing when I asked for this summer off. He's my mentor, my favorite honorary uncle, and he's the best boss. I'm in New York to learn from him specifically, and if I'm not even doing that, why shouldn't I switch schools to move to Cali sooner? I could go back to my alma mater and finish at Franklin U.

"He's thinking about quitting again," Prescott says.

"You a mind reader now?"

"It's the injured leg. It heightens all my other senses."

"At least you didn't lose your horrible sense of humor while your brain was bleeding."

"I'm only going to let that slide because I know you're acting out."

He's right, and I slump.

"I'm sorry," I say. "I just … hate this."

"We know." Prescott leans forward and clasps my shoulder.

"And you're not quitting," Kit adds. "You should look at this time apart to learn everything you possibly can from your uncle so that when you move, you're prepared."

"How can I do that if I still have to finish my law degree?"

"Well, when you don't have two boyfriends taking up all your time, you should be free to work all day and study all night."

I can hear the smile in Prescott's voice.

"Fine. I'll suck it up, finish my degree, and become a boss at work."

"Doesn't at all sound too ambitious," Prescott says.

"You definitely won't burn out," Kit adds.

I throw up my hands in defeat. "I don't understand what you both want me to do."

"We want you to realize that it's not all or nothing with us." Kit's using his soothing tone, but it's not working.

I'm still uptight, and I can't help thinking that I'm about to walk away from the best thing to ever happen to me. Is it so wrong of me to want to hold on to it?

"We'll be here for you no matter what. The distance will suck, but so will throwing away your plans for your career when we have forever ahead of us to work with."

Theoretically, I know all this. If Peyton had contemplated giving up his NFL dream for Levi, I would've smacked him upside the head. Our dads would've put a hit out on Levi. But Peyton never once thought of risking his career like I am.

If I don't graduate law school, I'll look like a quitter. Just because my uncle owns the firm I work for, that doesn't mean he won't be hard on me when I make mistakes. If anything, he'll go harder because he can't show any nepotism. I need my last year of law school so I can understand my job better.

Kit takes the exit toward the airport, but when we reach the short-term parking lot, I tell him to keep driving.

"Go to the drop-off zone."

"We won't be able to get out and—"

"I know. I think it'll be better that way." It won't be better this way, but maybe I won't have a complete breakdown if it's quick.

Kit pulls in behind another car unloading people and bags, but I don't open my door. Shit, maybe I should've made Kit go to the parking lot.

He reaches over the center console and takes hold of my forearm. "I will see you in a few weeks."

Prescott's hand lands on my shoulder. "And I'll see you on video calls and whenever you get a break in school."

"We're still going to be there for you," Kit says, and I know they will.

I've done this before, and I can do it again. I just don't want to.

"I love you," Kit says. Fuck, that doesn't help. Why did he have to say it now?

Prescott leans forward and puts a hand on my shoulder. "I feel the same way. I'm in love with you. Both of you. We're going to make this work."

That doesn't help either.

I take a deep breath and try to hold back from whimpering. "I love you guys too."

Kit smiles. "Then we're already halfway there."

"You better not have just referenced a Bon Jovi song," Prescott says.

I need to get out of this car. "Okay, I'm going." Yet, I don't move.

Prescott snorts. "Yeah, looks like it."

Why is this so hard?

"Want me to go find a parking space after all? Because you're going to have to decide. Security is heading this way."

Get it over with, I tell myself.

I open the car door and get out. Prescott shoves my duffle bag through to the front seat so I can grab it, and then I'm ready. All I have to do is close the door.

Rip it off like a Band-Aid.

I do it and walk away, but as I do, I realize why I hate Band-Aids. They sting like a bitch.

❦ ❦ ❦

I put off coming back to New York and left it so late that by the time I flew in last night, I crashed as soon as I got home and had to head to my first lecture this morning.

Uncle Damon told me to check in with him when I'm back, so instead of answering his rhetorical *I guess you're not going back to school this week? Are you still alive?* texts, I go into the office after my last lecture of the day. I only had the two, so it's just after lunch that I get there.

When I knock on his office door, there's a man standing next to him. He's younger than Uncle Damon, probably around Kit and Prescott's age, and he's damn attractive. Caramelly colored hair, amazing jawline, but he's still nothing compared to my guys. Who I apparently can't get out of my head even when I'm innocently checking out another man.

I'm in so deep with them. And I already miss them. I was tempted to text that to them in between classes, but I don't want them to think I'm still being whiney and annoying about the time apart. I am, but I don't want them to know that.

"Brady, have you met Camden Wheeler from our LA office?" Uncle Damon asks.

"Not in person, but I recognize the name from email chains and calls." I hold out my hand for him to shake.

"Great to meet you in person." Camden smiles at me, and I get the impression I'm missing something. Like he knows something I don't. "I'll let you two talk. I should call Xavier and make sure he's not getting into trouble back home while I'm not there."

"You can't let him take control of anything, can you?"

"Lies. He controls everything in our relationship. I just can't let him know that I'm aware of it."

Uncle Damon shakes his head. "I'm not going to comment. I'm sure there's a line between boss and employee where if I ask for more clarification, it might become a sexual harassment lawsuit."

Camden makes a "Pfft" noise. "Considering it was your fault we even found each other, you should be honored to know that when it comes to sex—"

"Do not finish that sentence. Go phone your boyfriend."

Camden leaves the office, and Uncle Damon gestures for me to take a seat.

"You set him up with another agent? I thought those kinds of relationships were frowned upon."

Uncle Damon points to where Camden disappeared. "They're the reason it's frowned upon. They hooked up at the first-ever corporate retreat and blame me for them falling in love."

"Blame?"

"It's a whole competitive rivalry thing. But anyway, seems you're alive and well. Thanks for the text."

I shrug. "I was coming by the office today anyway. I figured I could tell you in person how miserable I am. I can sell it better when you look into my sad puppy dog eyes." I lower my head and pout but don't take my eyes off his.

"That's why I asked Camden to come to New York."

I'm confused. "Huh?"

"Well, if you're going to be moving out West, you're going to need a new mentor. Someone I trust to get the best out of you."

"Again … huh?"

"Didn't your dads and I teach you better manners than to say 'huh'?"

"I'm not moving out West. As much as I want to."

"Why not?"

"Because Kit and Prescott won't let me quit law school. Or transfer … for some reason. They don't want me to rearrange my life for them."

"That's sweet, and the move would be a pain in the ass, but anything is doable. You already prioritized them once. I figured I'd help."

And as Uncle Damon gives me permission to do the one thing I've been fighting for, the momentary excitement is dimmed by the crushing weight of realization. Moving to California would be giving up an opportunity others in this industry would kill for.

Damn it. Damn Kit and damn Prescott. They're not allowed to be right. They're not allowed to know me better than I know myself.

"What's wrong?" Uncle Damon asks.

"I've been arguing with the guys because I keep mentioning

moving back to Cali as soon as possible, but now that you're giving me the option … I can't imagine not learning from you. I don't want to learn from Camden. I don't want to move back to California. At least, not yet. I have until graduation to learn everything I can from you, and then I'll move. That's what the guys want for me, and as much as I thought I didn't want to postpone moving, I can acknowledge it is what's best for me."

Even if I'll miss the guys like crazy. Even if I'll be miserable for most of the year. Or until at least Kit comes to stay.

It will be difficult. It will suck. But if I don't milk Uncle Damon for all his worth, that will be a wasted opportunity.

"I'm sure Camden's great, but he's not you," I say.

Uncle Damon puts his hand on his heart. "If I didn't know you any better, I'd say you were sucking up to me to ask for something outlandish."

I laugh. "Nope. Just asking for all your knowledge and wisdom so one day I can shove you off a cliff and take over this place for you."

"There it is." He wipes away a fake tear. "But if we've only got one more year to teach you everything I know, we need to knuckle down and get to work."

"I'm ready for it. If for no other reason than to let the full workload distract me from missing Prescott and Kit."

"Normally, I'd frown upon unhealthy work habits like that, but who am I kidding. I would do the same."

CHAPTER THIRTY-FIVE

EVEN THOUGH WE talk to Brady every night, we can tell the distance is already getting to him. So much so that Prescott insists I leave him in Virginia and go to Brady. We're having dinner at my place, and he's still in that stupid walking boot, but he's gotten word from Coronado that they'll be calling him back soon.

"He needs you more than I do," he says, shoving the pasta I made him into his mouth.

"That's not the romantic flex you think it is." I like feeling needed. By both of them.

"Don't misunderstand me. I want you to stay, but I don't *need* you to. Brady's struggling, and with you giving your notice already, there's nothing really holding you here other than me."

That brings a smile to my lips because I can see what he's doing. "You're downplaying how much you want to be there for Brady, aren't you?"

Prescott points his fork at me. "Don't tell him I have a heart."

I reach across the table for his hand. "Oh, Pres. Silly, Pres. We both know how big your heart is. You're just as worried about Brady as I am."

"True, but there's a difference between you and me."

"What's that?"

"You have the time and availability to go to him. I don't."

"What about—"

He stops me before I can even ask about my furniture, clothes, and everything else I need to organize before moving back to the West Coast. "You can hire people to clean up this mess of an apartment."

My apartment is far from messy. "Excuse me, I'm the neat one of us three."

"Yeah, but you had Brady here for close to two months. I'm surprised you haven't done a deep clean already."

"Mm, true. I've been preoccupied with some other whiney guy who's only whinier when he's injured."

"I'm not whining about being injured. I'm whining because I'm so damn constricted. I need to run and be free! I need to blow shit up."

"Of course you do. Are you sure you're going to be ready to leave the navy?"

Prescott puts down his fork. "Honestly, I'm not sure I'll ever truly be ready, but I'm making the choice to have a more stable home life. No disappearing for six months at a time. No more training accidents that almost kill me." His brown eyes peer deep inside me. "No more running from love because I'm scared of screwing it up."

I stand from my seat and round the table so I can take Prescott in my arms. He remains seated but wraps his arms around my waist.

I lower my head and murmur into his hair, "Even if you fuck it up, you know Brady and I will still love you."

"Do I? I see how my parents are with each other, and I've always thought it would be exhausting keeping up that level of affection and devotion. With you, it's easy, but … what if one day it's no longer second nature?"

I pull back and mock gasp. "Having to work hard for something? No way."

"You know what I mean."

"I do, and there are no guarantees in relationships, but we're willing to put in the work if you are."

He nods. "I am. I just worry about a time in the future where maybe one of us won't be."

"We'll cross that bridge if we come to it." Though, I have faith we won't reach that point. Not if we all keep our word and promise to communicate any issues. Even if it's not with words.

Brady doesn't need to tell us he's hating the distance. It's obvious when we see him on a video call. He claims exhaustion, which I'm sure is part of it, but Brady has a way of expressing himself in other ways that let me know he's not doing the best.

Like when he changes the subject off himself to ask how Prescott's leg is doing or giving me sympathy for having to put up with Prescott's whining. He makes sure that our focus isn't on him, and that's not the Brady we fell for. It's the Brady he is when he's not with us—the one who looks after everyone else and ignores his own needs.

"Go to Brady," Prescott says. "I'd rather know he's being taken care of than selfishly have you here with me when I don't need you, knowing he's hurting."

"I will. Do you think we should call him and let him know?"

"Where's the fun in that?"

I should've known that would be Prescott's answer.

∞ ∞ ∞

My flight to New York is delayed, but that's not a major problem because Brady probably wouldn't have been home from work when I was supposed to land anyway. But as I arrive on his stoop and ring the doorbell, Four answers the door.

"He's not home yet."

I glance at my phone. "Still?" It's going on 9:00 p.m. now, thanks to a three-hour delay.

"He's been working all kinds of insane hours lately."

That makes me wonder if he'd been calling us from the office instead of home like he'd led us to believe. That sneaky little shithead. Which I mean in the most affectionate way possible.

"You're welcome to come in and wait for him." Four steps aside.

"Is it possible to go to his office? Do I need a key card to get into the building or anything?"

"If you call him, he can leave your name downstairs at security in the building."

"He, uh, kinda doesn't know I'm here?"

"Surprising your partner. Because that never goes wrong or anything."

I must make a face because he smiles.

"Not that you'd have to worry with Brady. All he's been doing since he got home is going to school and work." He doesn't let me ask if Brady's doing okay before he takes out his phone and presses someone's number on his contacts. "Hey, Uncle Damon. One of Brady's boyfriends is here, but he's still in the off— Oh, you're still there too?" Four side glances at me and then ends the call. "Damon will put your name at security."

"Thanks! Uh, can I also—"

He rattles off an address in Hell's Kitchen, and I order a ride share after dumping my bag in Brady's room, and in only a couple of minutes, I'm on my way.

I'm eager to see Brady, to hold him, to reassure him.

When I get to his office, I'm let straight up after giving my name. The elevators open to King Sports, and I'm taken aback by the reception area.

Everyone is gone for the day, so the lights above the reception desk are dim, but the walls to the left and right of me are filled with banners of famous athletes. I notice Brady's dads immediately, his uncles, and some other players—all legends who are retired now.

"Who's here?" Brady's voice drifts down the hall to my left. "Is that Uncle Maddox coming to drag you back home because you've been working late again?"

"Why don't you go see who it is?" Damon says.

I don't move from where I stand in the reception area, waiting for Brady's face to appear, but I do take out my phone and hit Record for Prescott.

Brady turns the corner and stops in his tracks.

"Surprise."

"I hate you. I hate you both." Yet the way he runs toward me and jumps into my arms says otherwise.

He kisses me, and I have no idea which direction the camera is facing, so I pull back.

"Tell Prescott you miss him."

Brady looks at the camera and says, "Miss you, love you, okay, byyyye."

I stop recording, quickly forward it to Prescott, and then pocket the phone so I can go back to kissing. I dominate his tongue with mine until he becomes pliant in my hands. He molds to me, sinks into my hold, and moans into my mouth.

When he breaks free to catch his breath, he rests his forehead on mine. "What are you doing here?"

"Pres and I agreed I'm needed here more than with him right now."

"But he's—"

"Going back to Cali soon. He's fine."

Brady slowly lowers his legs and stands. "I thought I was hiding how much I'm hating being away from you."

I laugh. "Not even close, sweetheart. But I'm here now for as long as you need me."

"So you're never leaving? Yay. No backsies. You're here forever and ever. Or until I graduate."

Hey, there's no arguments from me. "Guess I'll need to get a job, then."

Brady smiles up at me. "About that …"

CHAPTER THIRTY-SIX

brady

I TAKE Kit's hand and lead him to the conference room, where Uncle Damon and I have been brainstorming every night.

It's like he's put me on some intense training regime to get me ready to become a fully fledged agent by the time I graduate law school in the spring instead of our original plan of letting me grow into the position.

Uncle Damon's pushing me to think outside the box, to come up with innovative ideas, and look toward the future of this industry. I've actually come up with some great ideas that have impressed him. And myself, actually.

Uncle Damon and Kit shake hands when they see each other.

"Good to see you again," Uncle Damon says.

"Thanks for keeping Brady preoccupied since he's been back."

I jump up and down, unable to hold in how eager I am to tell Kit what I've come up with. "Can I ask him now? Can I?"

"Ask me what?" Kit asks with an adorable scrunch in his brow. His hard features and five-o'clock shadow are so sexy, and if I weren't so excited about this idea, I'd leave it for another day and take Kit home to do wicked things with him.

"You know how you're thinking of setting up a personal-training business aimed toward people who want to up their fitness to SEAL level? How do you feel about training up-and-coming athletes who need to be at pro level? It would be a similar regime, more clientele, and you'd already have contacts in the industry who could recommend you to players who have potential to be stars." It's so perfect for Kit and Prescott.

"As in, work for King Sports?" Kit asks.

"Not exactly," Uncle Damon says. "At least, not at first. You would be contracted by the athletes, not by us. We were thinking if we saw potential in someone but they needed more conditioning that we could recommend they contact you, and for each referral you get, you give us a cut. You have no idea how much some of these athletes throw at their sports to become the best."

Kit's thinking about it, I can practically see the thoughts ticking over in his head, but he's hesitant too.

"Down the line," Uncle Damon continues, "if it's successful, we might be able to add you to the King Sports family and work out a program where our clients can pay us a higher percentage in the contract for your services to keep them at their physical peak."

The longer Kit doesn't reply, the more I begin to think my genius idea is maybe not so genius. He's giving me nothing on his stoic face.

"You're not sure?" I ask.

Kit shakes his head. "I think it's a *brilliant* idea, but working with athletes would be different. I know how to train future SEALs because I've been through the process. I might not be qualified to take on athletes. What if I break them? How do I even care for an athlete? Do they need watering? How often do I walk them?"

"You can get accredited," I say. "I already looked, and you can do courses online to get it."

Kit smiles at me. "You've really thought about this."

"I have. We've been researching and trying to iron out the details before I brought it to you, but you're here, and I think it will be perfect to add to your business plan."

Kit pulls me to him. "I think so too."

"What about Prescott? Do you think he'd be interested?"

Maybe I'm getting too ahead of myself because with the way Kit licks his lips and averts his gaze, I get the dreaded feeling in the pit of my stomach that he's about to say something I don't want to hear.

"I'm not sure if he's ready to leave the navy."

Damn it.

"Actually, his words were that he doesn't know if he'll *ever* be ready."

"Ever?" I croak.

Uncle Damon cuts in. "And this conversation just became a throuple thing, and I don't want to get in the way. I'm going to grab my stuff and go home to my man." On the way out, he pauses next to me. "You've done amazing work on this idea. Don't let distractions stop you from excelling."

I don't plan on it. Kit being here will make it so much easier for me to relax when I'm not at work instead of constantly forcing myself to focus on anything but him and Prescott. I can come to work refreshed instead of burned out. I can come up with a million other ideas and get ready to be the best damn agent there is. Well, next to Uncle Damon.

He found a niche in the market and has made a killing. Not only that, but he's one of the most reputable and respected agents in the business.

If Kit and Prescott can be involved with that, it'll only make it that much more amazing, but I'm not going to hold Prescott back if being a SEAL is all he'll ever want to be.

When Uncle Damon leaves, Kit tells me to sit.

We take seats side by side at the large conference table that is covered in notes, papers, and scribbles of ideas, tips Uncle Damon's been randomly writing down for me, and a rough ten-year plan Damon wants me to follow.

Kit takes both my hands in his. "What do you think about Prescott staying with his job?"

"I'm not going to lie, I wouldn't like it," I say. "But that's not really fair to him. You two didn't let me give up my dream job or postpone it or any of that, so I can't ask him to do the same. Even if it means living in LA and San Diego and only seeing each other every other weekend. Or you and I sitting at home worried about him coming home if he's deployed or on a training mission. We don't have the right to ask him to give it up."

Kit leans forward and places a kiss on my forehead. "I thought I was going to have to spell all that out for you."

I cock my head. "Maybe I should stop acting like a brat all the time around you. You seem to have no faith in me as a responsible and rational adult."

"Mm, it's easy to forget sometimes, but you always find a way to remind me." Kit kisses my cheek and then moves his lips down to my neck.

"As much as I'm enjoying this," I say while practically moaning, "do you think we should call Prescott and ask what it is that he wants?"

"There you go being all rational again. I don't know which I like more, your attention-seeking side or the efficient grown-up."

I get out of my seat and throw my leg over Kit to straddle him, though the table gets in the way, so I end up with my butt on the edge and my dick in Kit's face. "Don't get used to the efficient grown-up because when it comes to you and Prescott, he rarely makes an appearance."

"As evidenced by you spreading out for me on the conference table at your workplace."

"Damn straight."

"And as much as I want to take advantage of you in this moment, I can feel my phone vibrating. Ten bucks says it's either Prescott being in sync with us and knowing we were going to call him, or he's watched the video of our greeting and is pissed at where the video cut off."

"Only one way to find out."

Kit takes his phone out and answers the video call, holding it up so we can both be in view.

"You're not even naked yet? Have you two learned nothing from me?"

I snort. "Please, I am a professional, and this is my place of work."

Prescott frowns. "Blink twice if you've been kidnapped. Where's the real Brady?"

"He's here," Kit says. "He's currently sitting on the conference desk and putting his groin right in my face like the professional he is."

"Way to rat me out," I say.

At the same time, Prescott says, "Good boy."

"So, we have something we want to say," Kit tells him.

"Oh? What's that? You miss me already? Look, I know you're both obsessed with me, but you're going to have to live without me for a few months, okay?"

"I've been thinking about that," I say. "How would the navy feel if you faked your own death? Then you could be with us sooner."

Prescott rubs his stubbly chin. He has more growth than Kit at the moment, but that'll be gone again once he has to report back to California. "That's a bit dramatic, but I'll think about it."

"If you're both done," Kit says, regaining control of the conversation. "Brady and I had a talk, and we've agreed that if you want to stay a SEAL, then we'll support you if you want to re-up at the end of your contract."

"Wait, you don't want me to quit now?"

"I still do," I sing. Kit nudges me. "But just like you not wanting me to give up my dream, I can't ask you to give up yours. Next year, the farthest we'll be away from each other is LA to San Diego. That's nothing. We can do it. And hey, maybe I'll tell Uncle Damon to move his LA office down south. I'm sure he'll move an entire firm with hundreds of employees for us." That will never happen, but I am hoping I could persuade Uncle Damon to let me work remotely.

"You said you don't know if you'll ever be ready to leave the navy," Kit says. "But we want you to know that you don't have to. We'll support you in whatever you decide to do."

Instead of happiness and warmth radiating from Prescott, all I see is confusion. I have no idea if it's because he doesn't know what he wants or if it's because he thinks we're pushing him away or what, so I tell him what I think he needs to hear.

"If you do decide to leave, my uncle and I are coming up with an amazing business idea you could get in on, but if you want to stay, we're letting you know that no matter what, we love you, we'll be there for you, and we're willing to put in the work to make sure that we're all happy."

"Okay, seriously, where is the real Brady?" Prescott snarks.

"That's it. No more being mature ever again. I'm done."

"What's the idea?" Prescott asks, so we fill him in.

It really would be perfect. We could all live together, wherever we wanted. There'd be some travel because clients would be from all over, but they could maybe set up a gym if the idea takes off, and then the athletes will come to them. I'll still need to travel around a lot, but Uncle Damon and Uncle Maddox make it work, even if Uncle Damon has to grovel sometimes for being away so much.

I'm willing to do all the groveling needed to keep my men happy with me. Naked groveling, tied-up groveling. Begging them on my knees for forgiveness. Anything.

When we're finished explaining the idea, Prescott bites his bottom lip, and not in the sexy way. In the *"How do I say that's the dumbest idea I've ever heard?"* kind of way.

It's unfair of me to wish that he would be okay with the idea immediately. If they asked me to step back from my goal of being an agent to become a scout or a recruiter or even an admin assistant for King Sports so I don't have to travel and be away from them, I wouldn't be enthusiastic about it either. I'd consider it, for sure, because like Uncle Damon says, finding the right balance between work and personal life is important, but it might leave a bitter taste in my mouth.

It's why I respected and hated that Prescott and Kit were so supportive of me. Because I wanted the excuse to be with them, but at the same time, they knew I didn't want to leave New York yet.

"Also remember that if you remain a SEAL, that's okay with us too," I say. "Relationships need compromise, but it shouldn't be about holding each other back from what we truly want."

"We know you love your position," Kit adds. "Don't give it up for us because we're not asking you to."

"Can I take some time to think about it?"

"No, you must make the decision right here and now," I deadpan.

"You've got an entire year to think about it," Kit says.

I pat Kit's chest. "Oh, that answer is more supportive. Let's go with that one."

"I love you both so much," Prescott says.

Kit and I look at each other and then back at Prescott, saying in perfect unison, "We love you too."

With Kit showing up in New York early for me, all of us rearranging our futures to fit each other in, I'm confident enough in us to know that no matter what Prescott decides, no matter where we end up, we're in this together.

And while forever might look different in poly relationships—no marriage, no outdated heteronormative traditions to hold us back—I wasn't raised to miss that kind of thing. My honorary family that my fathers built is proof that you don't need to be traditional to be loved the way you deserve.

Marriage might not be in Prescott, Kit's, and my future, but in this moment, even while apart, I have no doubt that we can love each other. Until death do us part.

CHAPTER THIRTY-SEVEN

THE FUN PART about the military is that even though they give you plenty of time to recover, they never pressure you into going back too early. And by fun, I mean horrible. And by plenty of time, I mean the bare minimum. And by no pressure, I really mean guilting you into deploying with your team last-minute or face reassignment.

Fun, fun, fun.

After weeks of recovery and rehab, I got the call to get back to Coronado so fast I barely had time to send off a text to my parents and Kit and Brady to let them know I was shipping out.

It's not even our turn on rotation, but because of heightened political issues, we were redeployed earlier than expected.

All I can say is I'm thankful I forced Kit into going to New York earlier than planned because at least now they're together while I'm here, on a high alert, what-if kind of situation in the middle of the Pacific Ocean, closer to the East China Sea on the map. We're on standby, waiting on this assault ship in case the US needs to make a move. Tensions are high between governments, and on the surface, you wouldn't think that directly below us, there are subs basically playing a game of chicken.

Foreign warcraft encroaching on US waters moved the Pentagon to DEFCON 4 and put all inactive SEAL teams on notice.

If this all blows up, we won't be in on the action though. No, we'll be sent to infiltrate land, render their forces useless, all under the cloak of darkness and camouflage.

It's the first time in my entire naval career that I've had reservations about going into a mission and praying it doesn't escalate.

The adrenaline junkie in me is always ready for a fight, but I'm barely healed from the helo crash—enough to get passed in a medical assessment but still not back to where I was before it—and I can't help thinking about the panicked text I got from Brady before I left. All of my reassurances that I'll be fine weren't enough to make him not worry.

Having someone relying on you to come home is new to me. Before, with Kit, he'd be right beside me out here. I don't know how the married guys do it. My mind is on my boyfriends when it should be on the mission.

When we get word that things are heating up and we might be moving to DEFCON 3, my team makes their move.

We load up our CCM Mk1 stealth boat. Our commander gives us the go-ahead to start for land, and the second the order is made, Brady and Kit are pushed to the far corners of my mind so I can't reach them when I need to be focused.

And still, even though I'm not thinking about them, I am still thinking about coming home.

The doubt counteracts the adrenaline pumping through me. I'm not at the top of my game physically or mentally, and I can't pinpoint why. The only thing I can think is that Kit and Brady have shown me loyalty goes both ways, and if I'm honest with myself, loyalty to the navy is a one-way street.

When the guys gave me the option to stay a SEAL, I thought I'd be relieved. That I'd take it, no questions asked. But from the minute the words fell from their lips, something didn't feel right.

At first, I thought it was because if I stayed in the military, I would feel guilty for choosing the navy over them. They don't want me to re-up, but they'll support me if I do.

The more I think about it though, the more I realize my unease doesn't come from them. It comes from something bigger.

A sense of the end.

And maybe that's why I'm freaking out now.

Terri taps my shoulder. "You all good to do this?"

"They cleared me, didn't they?"

"Not with your leg. With whatever's going on up here." He taps my helmet with his gloved finger.

"I'll be fine once we're in there."

We skim across the water at lightning speed while the real action goes on behind and below us.

"Is it the crash?" Terri asks. "You've got the fear of death all over your face, man."

Is that what my issue is?

I have something to live for now. Not that I didn't before—I have loved every moment of my life—but I was lucky enough to be able to be selfish because the only connections I had were familial.

Does having Brady and Kit make the risk of putting my life on the line for my country too much? Death is part of this game, and over the course of my career, I've become desensitized to it. The image of Kit and Brady standing at my military funeral shakes me to my core. My parents being handed the American flag that's draped over my coffin fills me with dread.

I'm glad Kit and Brady gave me the option to keep this job if I wanted it because it has made me realize it's not what I want at all.

"I'm not re-upping," I say out of nowhere.

"What?" Terri asks.

"Unless this shitshow blows up into World War III, this will be my last deployment."

"Better make it a memorable one, then. Let's go in there and fuck shit up."

And as if the universe has been testing me this whole time, Commander Williams puts his finger to his ear and says, "Abort."

Thank fuck. My chest heaves with the weight being lifted.

The boat turns around.

Williams turns to us all. "Situation neutralized."

Terri slumps beside me. "Well, that was anticlimactic."

"Yeah," I say, even though I'm more relieved than disappointed.

It might have been anticlimactic to the rest of the guys, but for me, it's been life-changing.

The minute I get back and we have access to communicate with the outside world, I message the two men who have become the most important people to me. What we have is something I need to cherish every day.

I'm coming home. For good.

CHAPTER THIRTY-EIGHT

EPILOGUE

NO MATTER how many times you say in a relationship, "We'll make it work. We'll make it work," it's not that simple.

Time, distance, random weekend visits … it's really not the most fun way to spend the first year of our relationship.

I wish I could say it was all sunshine and rainbows, but it wasn't. Kit would split his time between Prescott and me while he was doing his online courses, and when he was in New York, I'd feel guilty for being at work all the time, and when he was in California, I'd miss them both and throw temper tantrums because they got to be together and I was stuck in New York.

I don't need to live in Kit and Prescott's pockets, but I never want to live in different states again.

Which is why when Kit tries to leave our new bed in our new apartment in Marina Del Rey, I hold him closer and mumble, "Prescott, get him. He's trying to escape."

"Don't come between Kit and his morning workout," Prescott murmurs sleepily and rolls over to face the other way.

We've only been here together for two days, though Kit moved in ahead of time and has already put everything Prescott and I own away.

It's a three-bedroom, two-bath place that has a balcony over-looking the building's pool, and if I had to guess, Kit's either trying to sneak out to go do a hundred laps, or he's going to run to Venice Beach and back.

With its location and both Kit and Prescott starting up their new personal-training company, we couldn't really afford this place, but now that I'm a law school graduate and a full agent at King Sports, I can pay the mortgage repayments … thanks to my dads providing the down payment for us.

The guys are adamant we'll pay them back, no matter how many times I tell them that helping us buy the place is cheaper than the therapy I would need if I opened the locked box in my head labeled *childhood.* In my eyes, it's a win-win.

So after months of pining, of missing Prescott, of having doubts about moving back to California, and even briefly discussing having Kit and Prescott move to New York instead so I could continue to learn from Uncle Damon, we're finally here.

Together.

Ready to start the rest of our lives.

And someone is trying to ruin it already by sneaking out.

"No. Bad Kit," I say.

"Go back to sleep, and I'll be home before you know it."

"But my family will be here soon, and I haven't come today. It's amazing my dads and brother gave me two days to settle in before coming to annoy us. We need to take advantage of what little time they're giving us."

"They won't be here until lunch. You're being dramatic. I've lost count how many times you've come over the last forty-eight hours."

I huff. "We were apart for so long. We have to make up for every orgasm we didn't share over the last twelve months."

Kit manages to pull out of my hold. "Prescott, you're up."

"Sleep," Prescott grunts. "You can come later."

Kit leans over and kisses the top of my head. "It wouldn't kill you to learn some patience anyway."

"Why did I move in with you two again?" I complain.

"Because you love us," Prescott says.

"Apparently."

Prescott rolls over. "Fine. Come here. I'm in the mood for some bondage." His arms and one leg wrap around me, and he pins me to the bed. Then proceeds to fall back asleep.

"This isn't the kind of bondage I like."

"You can't move, can you?"

"Prescott," I whine.

"Good luck," Kit sings on the way out.

"I want sex," I demand.

He covers my mouth with his hand. "Ooh, look, more kink. I like you bound and gagged."

I wriggle my way out of his hold. "Cuddling is not bondage, and your hand is no ball gag."

Prescott laughs. "You sound so offended."

"I am. If I'm not going to come, I may as well get some caffeine." I climb out of bed.

"Yes, please."

"No, no, you're sleepy. You sleep now." I throw a pillow at him.

He pushes the pillow off him. "You're asking for it."

"Duh. I've been asking for it all morning."

I walk into the kitchen to find Kit at least put the espresso machine on for me before he left. I'm grateful, but now I can't pretend to be mad at him anymore.

Same goes for Prescott when he ambles out of the bedroom in his boxer briefs and closes in behind me. "If you give me caffeine, I'll give you what you want." He stays pressed against me while I make us lattes, and his cock against my ass gets harder and harder as he follows me around the small kitchen.

"Can you give me what I want first?" I ask.

Prescott pushes me against the counter, but instead of giving me what I asked for, he reaches around me and takes his coffee. "Later. Kit wants to teach you patience."

"Since when do you listen to Kit?"

He pulls away. "Whenever I feel like it, and right now, I feel like it."

"Is this what our relationship is going to be like? You were so nice when there were thousands of miles between us."

"Are you saying you prefer the distance?"

"You woke up and chose violence today."

"I did, but just think how hot it'll be if we can time it for when Kit gets home. I'm thinking we could prep each other, so that when he walks through those doors, I'll have you on your hands and knees on the rug, taking you from behind, and then Kit can drop his cute little shorts and sink inside me with no prep time."

Fucking hell. "Kit better make it a quick workout."

"Come out onto the balcony with me."

Outside, Prescott leans against the railing, putting his amazing ass and back muscles on display. I almost don't want to join him just so I can enjoy the view, but he glances over his shoulder at me and smiles. There's no way I can hold myself back from that.

As I approach, he pulls me close and wraps his arm around me, gripping my hip.

"It feels so good to have you back in my arms," he says and then sips his coffee.

"This past year has sucked balls, and not in the fun way."

With Kit flitting between the two of us, Prescott and I haven't been alone for that whole time. We had occasional weekends where Kit and I could fly out to see Pres, but it was always the three of us then.

"I missed you." I lean in and kiss his cheek.

"I missed you too. So much. And I want you to know that even though we haven't had as much time together as Kit and either of us, my feelings for you are still the same. I still want the future we've mapped out. There's no going back for me."

I didn't realize how much I needed to hear those words until this second. I close my eyes and soak it in. On a wistful sigh, I let out, "I love you, Jimmy Prescott."

"I love you too." He lifts his coffee mug, directing my attention to the pool below us where Kit's doing laps. "So does he. We're his world, and he deserves the same from us."

"I wish we'd kind of worked it out earlier that we had something real. The last three years could've been spent together," I say.

"And then where would we be? Would you have gone to Franklin U for law school instead? What about Kit in Virginia?"

"If you had realized how much you loved him sooner, he never would've left."

Prescott shakes his head. "Let's not think about that."

"Because you'll want to kick yourself?"

"Exactly. The important thing is we're all here now. We have an amazing future ahead of us, and we'll never be apart again."

"You know, unless I'm out scouting new talent or tending to an athlete's PR problem."

"Or Kit and I need to train one of said athletes and they live out of state."

"Or if my family call me back to Chicago or New York with some kind of emergency, only for it to be that one of my cousins has come out as straight, and they all think it's the end of the world."

Prescott laughs. "Hey, I want to go with you for *that* intervention. But no matter what, the lives we've chosen have given us the freedom to be there for each other when we really need it."

I lay my head on his shoulder. "I will always need you two."

"Good. Because we both plan to stick around."

Below us, Kit gets out of the pool and towels off.

I nudge Prescott. "Quick, he's getting out already, let's go prep—"

The apartment buzzer sounds, letting us know someone's wanting to be let up.

"Motherfuckers," I hiss. "My family is here early."

Prescott chuckles. "Of course they are. They're so much like my parents. Let's make a pact. We hold off letting your parents and my parents meet for as long as we possibly can."

"Deal. And when that day finally happens, you and I can disappear and leave the parentals with Kit. He had terrible parents, so he can have ours to make up for it seeing as he had a traumatic childhood and ours were full of unconditional love and support by overbearing parents."

"It really was the worst," he says.

The buzzer sounds again.

"They're so impatient." I quickly dress so I can go let them in.

⊗ ⊗ ⊗

"It was the closest Super Bowl in history," I argue. I might hit the dining table a little too hard because the cutlery next to my plate clatters. "That's what makes it the best."

"No way," my brother exclaims. "New England versus Seattle, 2015."

"How dare you take Tom Brady's side," Dad sneers at Pey.

Pop turns to Kit and Prescott. "The boys learned early that whenever debating the best football stats in history, they can't include any games their dad played. It's like those ones never existed."

"Help us settle this," Peyton says. "Let's vote."

Pop leans in closer to my boyfriends. "We also learned to never take sides."

"We're out," Dad says.

I glance at Prescott and Kit with pleading eyes.

"We agree with Brady," Kit says for the both of them.

My brother's face falls. "Hey, wait, that's not fair. He gets two obligatory votes to my one." He turns to his partner. "What if—"

Levi cuts him off. "You're not allowed to invite a third into our relationship just to even out the numbers for when you and Brady have a disagreement."

"But—"

"Not going to happen," Levi says and shoves a fork full of food in his mouth.

"Can Prescott and Kit only get one vote between them?"

I grin at my brother. "If we do that, then it's still a tie. This way, I win. Always. So no."

"I was fully supportive of this relationship until now." Peyton folds his arms.

"If you can't tell, Peyton is a really sore loser," I say.

"He gets it from his dad." Pop points to Dad. "Uh, that one. Not me."

"Speaking of losers," Dad says to Peyton, "how do you think your team will hold up this year?"

Peyton was so close to being a starting quarterback in a Super Bowl game last season. They were one playoff game from making it to the big show, but in an upset, Carolina scored a touchdown in the last few minutes of the game, putting them in the lead and stopping Arizona in their tracks.

"Ouch," Peyton says.

"Don't worry, Pey. You still smashed all of Dad's rookie records." I smirk, and Peyton fist-bumps me.

"That's why Brady's going to be my agent," Peyton says. "Always has my back."

"I have *always* had your back." Dad's offended tone is one of those things where if you know him, you know he's only pretend offended, but to outsiders, it might sound sincere.

Out of the corner of my eye, I see Prescott eating casually, probably used to the chaos that is families, but Kit's head is ping-ponging back and forth like he's watching a tennis match.

He'll get used to them. Eventually.

"How about a subject change," Pop says, his voice over-the-top upbeat. "What are your plans now that you're all in LA?"

I fill them in on Prescott and Kit's business model, something Kit's been working on while in New York. Uncle Damon threw him a few clients, but knowing he was relocating, Kit hasn't taken on anyone permanently or anything.

Luckily, one of my guys is good at saving what he earns. Unlike the other who spends money as it comes in.

Which, right now, is not at all.

"We hope to be up and running by the end of the month," Kit says. "We got permission from the HOA to use the building's gym and pool until we have enough equity in the business to set up our own training facility."

"It's such a smart idea," Dad says. "Miller could've used you back in the day after he injured himself. I had to come to him in the off-season and train him back to health, or he was going to eat his momma's cooking all day and get lazy. Then he never would've been back on the field."

"I'd say I regret letting him train me, but it's how we fell in love, so I guess I can't complain."

I wave my finger at Prescott and Kit. "Don't you go getting ideas. No falling for clients."

"Never going to happen," Kit says.

Prescott nods. "We have our hands full enough as it is with you."

"I swear they love me," I say to everyone else.

"Would we call it love?" Prescott asks.

Kit elbows him, but I laugh. And yeah, maybe if we hadn't had our conversation this morning where he reassured me his feelings haven't changed, I might have read into the joke, but I know without a doubt that they both love me as much as I love them.

Dad wipes his face with a napkin. "After this, we were going to go check out the beach before heading back to the hotel. Though, I really don't understand why we couldn't stay here—"

"They've been apart for a year. Let them have their space," Pop says.

"They've had two days of space. How much do they need?"

"How much did you need after you had to finish out the season by yourself when I was injured?"

Dad's mouth shuts. "I take it back. And also, you don't have to come with us to the beach."

I swear Pop is the only person on this planet who can get Marcus Talon to back down, and as I glance at Prescott and Kit, I realize they might be the same for me. I'd do anything they ever asked me to.

"We're so not going to the beach," I say because I was promised quality fucking, and I'm ready to cash in.

Peyton whispers loudly, "That means they're going to have sex."

Levi pats Pey's head while Dad says, "No shit."

But even though Peyton's absolutely right, it's not just the sex I want. Two days hasn't been enough to just *be* together.

Talking.

Hanging out.

Being lectured about picking up my towel in the bathroom and putting my worn clothes in the hamper.

All those normal relationship things that we've had very little chance to experience with all three of us.

I want mundane and normal with them, and I'm excited to learn and grow as it happens. After doing long-distance, I'm sure regular relationship crap will be a breeze.

Since my family have gotten the hint, they finish up lunch in record time and hug us goodbye but also warn that they're in town for a couple of days and expect us to show up for family events.

Especially since Uncle Damon and Uncle Maddox are coming tomorrow for the official handoff between Uncle Damon and me in terms of Peyton's representation.

I've absorbed as much information as I can in the last twelve months, but I still don't think I'm ready. Not for someone as high-profile as Peyton.

Uncle Damon and Peyton think otherwise, so I'm going to try to have faith. Well, that and relying on Uncle Damon being only a phone call away.

As soon as my family is out the door and I close it behind them, I lean against it and throw my head back. "I thought they'd never leave."

"They're not so bad," Kit says.

"I know that, but I want to spend as much time with you two as possible." I push off the door and stalk toward Prescott because he's closer.

"How'd I know you'd slip right into horny mode as soon as they were gone?" Prescott pulls me against his hard chest, our stomachs pressed together.

"Because I'm me."

"True."

Kit joins us, boxing me in between them. It's my favorite place to be.

"You're forgetting one thing," Kit says.

I turn my head so I can see him. "What's that?"

"We have the rest of our lives to be together."

And because I'm me, I can't help myself. I smile. "The rest of your lives, maybe. I'm ten years younger. I'm so going to outlive you both."

"Not with that attitude, you won't," Kit grumbles.

"Ooh, is that a threat of violence, I hear? Prescott, hurt Kit for me."

"Do you really think pitting us against each other will work in your favor?" Prescott asks.

"Nope. But that's what I'm counting on."

"You're asking for a spanking," Kit says.

"Don't threaten me with a good time," I quip.

Kit laughs. "What are we going to do with him, Pres?"

I blink innocently up at Prescott. "Yeah, Pres, what are you going to do with me?"

"Give you whatever you want and make you the happiest man in the world?"

My chest warms, and a sense of fulfillment spreads through my veins. "You already do that."

"Give you whatever you want?" Kit asks. "We know. It's a bad habit, really, but it's so hard saying no to you."

I turn in Prescott's arms and playfully slap Kit's chest. "I meant you already make me happy."

Kit leans in and kisses me softly. "Good. Because we plan to do it for a long time."

Prescott lowers his head, skimming his lips over my neck. "What he said. We're in this. All three of us."

Accepting that I'm poly took longer than it probably needed to because in a found family with a lot of queer men, I still managed to be different than the norm. As if being gay wasn't enough. I only ever thought of the repercussions of having more than one partner when it came to my professional life.

I never considered what it would be like to let go and have the one thing that confused me but filled me with fire.

I'm not only happy, but I've reached true acceptance. Because this is where I'm supposed to be. With them.

thank you

Thanks so much for reading *Can't Say Goodbye*.
Brady was adamant from the moment I decided to write about Talon and Miller's kids that one soul mate wasn't going to be enough for him. I let him lead his story, and while it was a bumpy road for him to get his men, I loved going on the journey with them all.

Didn't read Peyton and Levi's love story?
Football Royalty is book eight of the Franklin U shared world series, but just like Can't Say Goodbye, it can be read as a standalone. You can find it here: https://geni.us/royalty

Also from this universe:
Brady's dads and his uncles first appeared in the *Fake Boyfriend* universe.
Start with Damon and Maddox's story here:
https://geni.us/fakeoutFB
Or, if you want to jump into Peyton's dads' origin story, you can read that here: https://geni.us/EFBLFBBK4

BOOKS COWRITTEN WITH SAXON JAMES

Power Plays & Straight A's

Face Offs & Cheap Shots

Goal Lines & First Times

Line Mates & Study Dates

Puck Drills & Quick Thrills

Egotistical Puckboy

Irresponsible Puckboy

Shameless Puckboy

Foolish Puckboy

Clueless Puckboy

VINO & VERITAS *Sarina Bowen's True North Series*

Headstrong

STEELE BROTHERS

Unwritten Law

Unspoken Vow

ROYAL OBLIGATION

Unprincely (M/M/F)

www.ingramcontent.com/pod-product-compliance
Lightning Source LLC
Chambersburg PA
CBHW061526210726
48287CB00006B/1844